Oh Father

ALSO BY CHARLIE CASSO

Going Down and Moving On

Oh Father

CHARLIE CASSO

A Starr Books Original
Starr Books
New York

DEDICATION

This book is dedicated to Mike Hunt.

Oh Father

1 BLACKOUT

Sister Petunia grabs and balls the collar of Johnny's shirt at the nape of his neck, and repeats, "We are all made in God's image and at God we do not laugh." As she seethes, drops of spittle propel, two of which find a resting place on Johnny's bottom lip. His eyes cross, his head spins, and his feet lift off the ground. Sister Petunia's grip remains on Johnny's shirt and, when the right side of his body slams against the chalkboard, a crunch emanates from his hip as it crashes into the ledge where the chalk rests. This is where it all goes black.

"Oh, dear, look at the poor thing," emotes the female voice of the cloaked figure that stands over Jonathan.

"Tsk, tsk. Well, we can't blame Sister Petunia. It's not like the big G can defend Himself," replies her male companion, also cloaked.

A thunderclap resounds and the room darkens.

"I mean, of course He can defend Himself. I just mean she's doing her duty."

The room returns to its previous state.

"Of course, yes. But what are we to do with this little lamb of God here?" She bends down toward the youth and shakes him. She prompts, "Little Lamb?" She prompts once more, raising him from unconsciousness, "I say, Little Lamb?"

Johnny's pre-teen body slumps against the wall, his eyes flutter open, and through a blurry haze he makes out a strikingly bright apparition. He blinks a few times in succession to make the haze go away. It remains. Everything else is in focus, however, the apparition remains cloudy.

"There you are, Little Lamb! You had us worried there for a second," the female apparition speaks.

"Who are you? And why are you so fuzzy?" Johnny asks.

"Catholic schools really are a let down now, aren't they? I mean, really, how this little one doesn't recognize us after, what, eight years of parochial training? My, oh, my, oh, me," she dejects. "Well, to answer your question, I'm Barbara, technically 'Saint' Barbara but I don't want to gloat or anything, what with pride being one of the deadly sins and all. Pleased to meet you. And this here is Saint John."

"Hi there," John waves a friendly hello.

"Umm, hi," Johnny replies and waves back noncommittally. "You're really pretty for a saint. No offense, it's just, well, you all look so homely in pictures and stuff. And I thought you," he directs to Saint John, "would be all bearded out and unkempt. But you've got kind of a metrosexual thing going."

"This is your vision of us, Little Lamb."

"My vision of you? What do you mean?"

"Well," she clarifies, "each person sees us how they think they should see us. We are as you want us to be."

"Oh. So you appear in a vision and I see you how I want to see you? Wait. Am I dying? Are you here to tell me I'm dying? Am I dead? Oh, God, I'm dead. Where are the pearly gates? Is this hell? I knew it! I knew this place was hell, I just..."

"Wait, wait, slow down," Saint John interjects. "You aren't dead. You are dying though."

"Nooooo! I'm too young!"

"I don't mean right now. I mean everyone is technically dying as much as they are living, don't you think?" he questions.

"So, I'm not dying? So, I am dying? Okay, when am I going to die?"

"Oh dear," Saint Barbara states.

"Oh no he didn't," Saint John states. He covers his mouth in shock.

"Sweetie," she says as she starts to trace imaginary circles on the floor with the toes of her right foot, "are you sure you want to ask us that? We are kind of required to answer any questions we receive during one of our 'visits.' If you don't want to know, you can change your mind, otherwise we have to answer."

"Sure, I want to know."

"As you like it. You're going to die in twenty years' time."

"Wait. Twenty years? I'll be in my early thirties. How is that possible? Can I change it? Can I do something different?"

"No," Saint John chimes in. "You can try as you like, but there's no changing it. You will die the very day before your birthday in twenty years' time."

"The day before my birthday?" Johnny exclaims.

Saint Barbara rejoins, "Well, how appropriate, or apropos? I always misuse that word. Irregardless, it'll be your new 'birth' date then. You have class to go to, so let's get you to wake up. Wake up," she says as she grabs Johnny's arm and shakes him. "Wake up," she repeats.

"Wake up," Johnny hears.

Johnny's pre-teen body slumps against the wall. His eyes open, and through a blurry haze he makes out a friendly face. It's Veronica. She asks, "Are you okay?"

"Huh? No," he replies. "Why am I on the floor?" He tries to stand but topples back down as the pain from his side hits him. "Ow!" he exclaims as Veronica breaks his fall. The recent events flash before Johnny.

Sister Petunia sternly gazes at him with that unwavering line which on normal people could turn into a smile, but not on her. She poses her inquiry, "Jonathan, what are you laughing at?" Since Sister Petunia wrings the truth out of anyone who crosses her in any way, Johnny feels it is best to just state what it is he laughs at.

"I am laughing at Alicia Cooper," he says.

"Why," Sister Petunia asks, "would you laugh at another person?"

"She has blue icing all over her face from the cupcake she ate at lunch," Johnny responds innocently. "I'm sorry, Sister Petunia."

At this, Sister Petunia unleashes, "Never laugh at other people, Jonathan. We are all made in God's image and at God we do not laugh. He created you. Are you insipid? Are you?"

This boggles Johnny's mind. *Is this a trick question,* he wonders. *What does insipid mean? Should I answer* yes? *Should I answer* no? *Oh Dear Lord, she's waiting for an answer.* Her stare through those coke-bottle glasses burns hot like the flames of Hell where she surely believes Johnny belongs.

"I don't know. I wasn't being mean though. I just thought it was funny, Sister Petunia," he responds.

"And I guess that's why I'm here," Johnny tells Veronica.

"Come on," she reaches around his back and under his arm to support him, "Let's get to class."

***

Johnny steals a furtive glance at the clock. Thirty seconds from now the bell will ring. Three o'clock approaches. Freedom awaits. Johnny wonders, *Am I free? Am I crazy? Did Saint Barbara and Saint John really come to me in a vision and tell me when I'm going to die? I must have dreamt it, or whatever you do when you're thrown into a wall, and into a blackout, by a nun named after a flower.*

Brrrrrring sounds the bell. School's out for the day. Johnny follows the stream of children out the side-doors of the school, with his thumbs under the backpack straps by his shoulders. His head hunches down in thought as he walks and tries to wrap his young mind

5

around the day. Tires screech. Johnny's body careens toward the curb, propelled by the compact car whose driver runs out and toward Johnny.

"What have I done?" the driver cries. "Young man, young man! Someone please help! Call 911!"

***

Ripples of white ensconce Johnny, under him and over him. He sees ribbons of flowing white. He gasps, and his intake of breath draws the whiteness toward him, onto him, into his mouth. He coughs and grabs the white obstruction from his mouth and pulls it, over and away from his head.

He gasps for air and thinks, *I'm not dead.*

"Hello," he says, "is anyone there?"

He looks around and sees machines behind him, a clipboard by his feet, and a partially drawn curtain around his bed.

He presses the call button he finds lying on the bed. Within moments, a white-garbed nurse glides into the room. Her white nurse's cap covers a good portion of her plaited hair. She looks up and into Johnny's eyes.

My, he thinks, *she looks familiar.*

Johnny notices her name tag. Barbara.

"How are we feeling now," she begins as she checks his chart, "Jonathan?"

"Good, I guess. How did I get here?"

"A kindly good man dropped you off, I believe. I can't quite be certain, I just started my shift."

"Am I okay?"

"That's not for me to say, dear, but I will check

6

with..." she stops mid-sentence to address the man who walks into Johnny's room, "your doctor here. This is Doctor John. Doctor, this is Jonathan."

"Well, young man, it looks like someone has had quite the day so far. You young people need to be careful crossing streets, you know. After all, you're not going to live forever." He looks up and a twinkle alights in his eye.

The nurse shakes her head and wags her index finger left to right in front of Johnny's face. "No, no, no," she begins, "the doctor's right. You're not going to live forever. That's not how it works, dear. You can't change it. So, stop playing around and man up."

"I'm really just a child."

"Tom-*ay*-to, tom-*ah*-to, God created all, no matter what label you want to give. If it suits you though, then *child* up."

"That doesn't sound right," Doctor John offers.

"I agree, but let's humor our little lamb. After all, he isn't dealing well with his new information."

"He did ask for it, you know."

"One often asks for what one can't handle."

"Saint Barbara, can I go home now?" Johnny inquires.

"Precious, how precious! Did you just call me a saint? If that isn't the sweetest thing," she says as her hand lands upon her hip. "Dear, I'm just a nurse. You can call me Nurse Barbara. Saint? Did you hear that, Doctor John? What a sweet little lamb." She winks at Johnny.

"Quite precious, Nurse Barbara. Now, Johnny, you will be released home but you really must take care of yourself. You're not going to live forever, but you do have plenty of time left."

Nurse Barbara mouths, "Twenty years," and quickly places her right index finger over her lips. She dramatically pantomimes, "Shhh."

Doctor John moves closer to Johnny. "Johnny, I cannot stress this enough: you have a long life ahead of you." He uses his hand to form and flash the numbers two and zero in front of his chest. "And trust me, you're not going to leave this earth one day sooner than you're supposed to, come hell or..." A thunderclap shakes the room which momentarily darkens. "It's just an expression!" he pleads as his eyes widen toward the ceiling. He turns to Johnny, "But, seriously, and I mean this, not one single day sooner than planned."

Doctor John stamps a red "released" on Johnny's paperwork and closes the manila folder.

Johnny's mom enters the room, a bag of cookies in her hand. "I got you some cookies," she cheerily exclaims as she presents the bag to Johnny. "Is he all ready to go now, Doctor?"

"Depends on how you look at it."

"Come again?"

"He's officially released from the hospital. You may take him home."

"Thank you, Doctor." She takes Johnny's hand as he gets to his feet. "Come on, kiddo, you're ready."

Johnny looks over his shoulder at Barbara and John. He mouths, "I'm not ready." Just as he finishes his words, Barbara and John vanish before his very eyes.

2 TO-DO LIST

"I can't believe you're back at school already." Veronica punctuates her statements with her hamburger which cuts the air between her and the bespectacled student on her right. "I mean, you were hit by a car yesterday. By the way, which do you think weighs more, the car that hit you or Sister Petunia? I say we get a bumper sticker that says 'extra-wide load' and leave it on her chair sticky-side up."

Johnny responds with a small smile to Veronica.

"You must still be upset. I'm not trying to make light of what happened yesterday. I'm just trying to… I don't know. I thought..."

"It's not you, Ronnie. Yesterday was just… weird is all. I'll get over it."

A few seconds of silence pass. Veronica separates the top of her hamburger bun from her hamburger. A suction noise comes from the separation of burger and bun as the phlegmy, off-white goo stretches into strings. Veronica's face conveys the revulsion of having a closer look at what she regularly ingests.

"Honk if you're horny," Johnny says.

"Huh? Honk what?"

"The bumper sticker for Sister Petunia's chair. Honk if you're horny."

"Classy," she states, topless burger in her palm. Her hand disappears under the table. A *thwak* sounds from under the table as it jars ever so slightly. Veronica pulls her hand smoothly out from under, and only has the bottom part of the bun in her palm. "Voila! Let's see if it's still there tomorrow. If it sticks under the table for a day, imagine how long it sticks inside you."

***

Mr. Huxley begins a list of prepositions on the blackboard. Johnny surreptitiously begins his own list in the back of his English notebook. He titles his list: *T minus twenty*. "What do I need to accomplish over the next twenty years?" he wonders. He brainstorms a list of the things he wants to do before his twenty years are up. He writes his list:

My first kiss.

Sex (whatever that is).

Slap someone (real good though).

Johnny pauses to think about the slap. He doesn't necessarily want it to happen with a glove, like in a swash-buckling movie. Actually, he would rather it be without a glove. Full hand-on-face contact. The sound is important. It has to have that slap sound like in the movies.

He peruses the list as a whole and takes in its contents. "Doesn't sound that impressive," he says aloud to himself. Then again, he wonders, *Who does it have to impress?*

"Doesn't what sound impressive, Jonathan?" Mr. Huxley asks. He extends his hand and, with his index and middle fingers, presses under the words 'My first kiss' on Jonathan's list. He underlines them with his fingers. "Care to discuss this with the class, Jonathan?"

Johnny shakes his head no.

"I can't hear you, Jonathan."

"No, sir."

"Would you like me to read your... understandings to the class?"

"No, sir. I believe I need to pay more attention before my responses are shared with the class. I'm sorry, sir."

Charlie Casso

3 MANN, OH, MANN

Time for confession. Johnny considers the options. Face-to-face? Or through that screen-window thing? His eyes go back and forth between the door for the screened room and the door for the face-to-face confessional. *It's always hot in there*, he rationalizes. *They can tell who you are anyway; it's not like it's really anonymous. It's a screen, and duh you can see through a screen. Father Mann is kind of hot. Wearing that tight white t-shirt of his and his cute little earring. Face-to-face, I'd be able to get a better look at him. Who does that though? The man's a priest. The man's a man first.* Johnny wonders, *Is it true that Father Mann reads* Playboy *when he is in the confessional and no one's there? That can't be true, because who would know that? It's still kind of hot either way.*

Johnny moves forward and reaches out for the hard knob. He slowly moves his fingers over it, traces its roundness with the outside of his index finger. He delicately tickles the underside.

"Pull it hard," Father Mann urges over Johnny's shoulder. His breath warms Johnny's neck. "This door always sticks, sorry about that. Come on in." Father Mann holds the door open for Johnny to enter and take a seat in the face-to-face confessional.

"Young Jonathan," Father Mann begins, "tell me, how have you been feeling? I heard about what happened yesterday."

Johnny's cheeks darken a shade as Father Mann's concern washes over him. "I feel okay. I mean... normal." The lines of worry on Father Mann's face relax and almost disappear altogether when Johnny notices and adds, "Well, almost normal. Definitely not completely back to normal."

"What do you mean," Father Mann's eyebrows furrow and he inches closer to Johnny, "when you say you're not back to normal? Can you describe how you feel, or what's different?"

"If you only knew, Father Mann."

"I want to know, Jonathan. Please. You can trust me."

"I feel dizzy," Johnny lies. "And short of breath. It's been happening a lot."

"Does anything happen before you feel this way? Is there maybe a trigger that causes it?"

"That's the thing, Father Mann, it just comes out of nowhere. One minute I'm fine and the next... Oh, Father, the next I am just about to pass out. But, I'll be all right. The Lord will provide, right?"

"Well, yes, but you really need to address your dizzy spells and such. Perhaps it's best to take a couple of days off from school, just to make sure your recovery is up to par."

"You are right, Father Mann. I mean, what would happen if I passed out here at school? I could just, like, die on the floor."

"Young Jonathan, we would never let that happen. Should an incident occur, you would surely be taken care of. First, there's a phone in every room to call for emergency help: an ambulance, fire department, medics… you name it."

"Oh, that's a relief then."

"Second, everyone here, all of your teachers, the clergy, pretty much every single adult in the building, has taken CPR classes in the event of an emergency like the one you described."

"Everyone?"

"Everyone. Jonathan, your well-being, and the well-being of every pupil here, is paramount."

"That's very reassuring. Thank you, Father Mann."

A few seconds of silence elapse. Johnny breaks the silence, "You know what, Father?"

"Yes?"

"We didn't get to the confession part yet."

"True. I was waiting for that."

"Well, Father, what would you like to confess?"

Father Mann shoots a deadpan look at Johnny. Johnny demures. He offers, "Sorry, Father," but can't help but absorb Father Mann's gaze for another second. He looks even hotter when he's being serious.

Johnny makes the sign of the cross. He moves his right hand to his forehead, "In the name of the Father," chest, "and of the Son," left shoulder, "and of the Holy," right shoulder, "Spirit," and then clasps the hand with his other. "It has been one week since my last confession."

"Tell me, Jonathan, what are your sins?"

How presumptuous, Johnny thinks. *Oh, right*, he realizes, *this is confession*. He racks his brain for his sins. *Impure thoughts, those should be confessed.* But, no, Johnny resolves not to mention his impure thoughts. "Give me a second," he says to Father Mann. *Lying to a priest about feeling ill, that's got to be a sin.* He can't confess that either though. *A-ha! The honor your mother and father commandment! That's an easy one.* "I did not honor my mother and father, Father."

"Young Johnathan, you must always honor your mother and father."

"I know, Father Mann, and I am truly sorry."

"Are there any other sins you would like to confess today?"

Johnny scans his mind for an appropriate response. He also scans the room for the rumored copy of *Playboy*. No dice.

"No, Father, I think that's about it."

"Very well. The Lord forgives you for this and for all of your sins, in the name of the Father, and of the Son, and of the Holy Spirit. As penance, say ten *Our Fathers*."

"Thank you, Father."

Johnny and Father Mann stand to leave the confessional. Johnny pauses. He reaches an arm to the wall, breathes in heavily, and collapses to the floor face up. He appears lifeless.

"Young Jonathan!" Father Mann shakes Johnny

but receives no response. He tries for the door, but Johnny's body blocks the exit. He bends down to determine whether Johnny breathes or not. He holds his hand in front of Johnny's nostrils to check for a sign of life. "He's not breathing!" Father Mann exclaims.

He places his hand on the nape of Johnny's neck, the very same place Sister Petunia had touched. Father Mann pulls upward ever so slightly so it gives Johnny's head the proper angle for resuscitation.

God is good, Johnny thinks. He holds his breath and keeps his eyes closed in wait of his first kiss.

Father Mann straddles Johnny. Johnny feels the presence of Father Mann over him. *Even better than I thought*, he thinks. Hands on his face. His lips pry apart as Father Mann's fingers enter to open the passageway. *Tastes salty*, Johnny notices.

"Come on, Jonathan." Father Mann pinches Johnny's nose, puts his mouth on Johnny's, and blows. Johnny's cheeks fill with air. His mind reels. Father Mann blows again. "Ouch," Father Mann says.

Johnny coughs and brings the back of his hand to his forehead with a flourish. "What happened?" he asks.

"You bit my lip," Father Mann replies.

Johnny quizzically eyes the situation and asks, "Did I pass out or something?" Father Mann, for the moment, still straddles Johnny.

"You stopped breathing. I had to give you CPR."

"Thank God you were here, Father Mann. I needed that."

"Like I said earlier, that's what we're here for,

Jonathan."

A sense of self-satisfaction comes over Johnny and he thinks, *Item one, check! Now about that second item...* Johnny's eyes dreamily absorb Father Mann.

Johnny walks down the aisle toward the exit of the church. He ruminates over the past hour of his, up until recently, uneventful life. He considers, *He kissed me. No, he didn't kiss me, he gave me CPR. No, no, he kissed me, his lips were on mine, he kissed me. I felt his lips on mine. It was my moment. Eh, not so much. Yes, it was my moment. Father Mann kissed me square on the lips.* Yes, it was Johnny's moment and there was nothing and no one of this earth that could take it away from him.

"Hisssssss."

Johnny stops in his tracks. He pivots his head to the rows of pews on his left and gives a sideways glance. No one is there. He continues his walk down the aisle.

"Hisssssss."

He stops again, this time on the balls of his feet. He slowly descends his feet flat against the floor. Johnny deliberately and carefully turns himself around while he takes in his surroundings and looks for anything or anyone that could be the culprit, the source of the hissing sound.

"Hello?" he offers. He receives no reply. He waits for something, anything. But nothing. He calmly rotates toward the direction of the exit doors again and commences his walk. With his left foot mid-step, an unnaturally loud "HISSSSSSS" deafens him from each and every statue in the church, all of which suddenly seem to resemble either Saint Barbara or Saint John.

"Oh, I know you're not hissing at me. It's not like I had sex with him," Johnny yells at the statues. And he adds oh so quietly, "Yet."

Charlie Casso

4 PETUNIA AND THE GIGOLO

With his eye on the prize, Johnny sets about doing his own thing until he reaches the age of 18, at which point he feels all is fair in love and war. Additionally, he feels he won't go to hell for seducing a man of the cloth. He enters the parish he had frequented as a youth. He inhales the familiar scent of incense. He feels the familiar eyes of the statues that used to stare at him.

Sister Petunia kneels, lost in prayer, in the first row of pews. Her lips move in silent prayer. Her hands hold the rosary so tenderly one would swear they could not be the very same hands that once tormented Johnny. She hears the doors of the church close and knows someone shares her space. Sister Petunia turns her head in a measured, deliberate, barely perceptible manner and casts a sideways glance toward the door. She spies someone, a young man, a brazen young man. He wears a tank top, blue jeans, and a baseball cap in this, the house of worship.

She rotates her upper torso and casts the stare

she has perfected after countless years serving the Lord, the stare that stops people, young and old alike, dead in their tracks. This young man, however, proceeds toward the altar.

Sister Petunia's chest inflates with air and her cheeks fill with the redness of anger, for her blood boils within. The young man becomes larger in her eyes with every step he takes down the aisle. Sister Petunia grips the pew in front of her to support her weight, to assist her up from her knees. She stands upright, pulls at the sides of her dressing to maintain orderliness, and bellows, "Young man."

"Sister Petunia? Is that you? Girl, you are looking fierce!"

Sister Petunia strikes at the face that grins before her. Johnny slides back though, and all that strikes him is a breeze of air. "Older, Sister. Older and wiser now."

"You brazen thing. Who are you to come in here and address your elders such?"

"Sister, it's Jonathan." He tries to shake off his amazement at not being remembered. "It's only been four years."

"One does not come into the Lord's house dressed like a common gigolo."

Johnny removes the baseball cap from his head, revealing dark brown, shoulder length hair. He tucks the bill of the baseball cap into his back pocket. "Oh, Sister," he begins as he plunges both hands into the basin of Holy Water, "I know I've got some fixing up to do," he continues as he uses the water to dampen and slick back his hair. He shakes his head, just enough to free the drops of water that cling on. "And that's what

I'm here for," he claims as he stretches out his arms left to right, "to fix up what needs fixing in myself, with the Lord's help of course."

Sister Petunia's mouth drops open a fraction of an inch. She realizes Johnny mimics the image of Christ on the cross behind him. The muscles in her face tighten. Her mouth draws shut. The upper corner of her lip rises in disgust. "Insipid lump of humanity."

"Sister, haven't we passed all that? I'm back. It's been so long." He looks down, a moment of self-contemplation. He looks back up, into Sister Petunia's eyes. "I need Him. I need Him inside me. I'm willing to let Him in. I want to offer myself to Him, completely."

"I don't believe you."

"I couldn't be more sincere, Sister." He nods in affirmation of his sincerity. "I really need to serve Him."

Sister Petunia's eyelids shutter halfway. She glowers at Johnny.

"This is something I can't do on my own, though," Johnny offers as he turns in the direction of the confessional. "Excuse me, Sister, there's something I need to take care of." Johnny walks off, toward the confessional.

"May I come in, Father?" Johnny announces once he raps on the door of the confessional.

"Please, enter."

Sounds promising, Johnny thinks.

He enters the face-to-face confessional and sees Father Mann, the picture of salacious heaven-sent man with a devil's grin. He still wears his tight white t-shirt. The Lord's been good to Father Mann; he hasn't aged a day.

"Hi, Father Mann," Johnny beams.

"If it isn't Young Jonathan." Father Mann extends a welcoming hand. Johnny and he shake hands. Johnny pulls Father Mann in closer and envelops him in a hug.

"Bring it in, Father. It's been too long." Johnny inhales Father Mann's scent during their embrace. His lips nearly brush the hollow of Father Mann's clavicle. The familiar scent soothes and invigorates Johnny.

"I haven't seen you in years! You must be… how old are you now, Jonathan?"

"Eighteen, Father. Just turned eighteen," he confesses. He bites his lower lip, looks at Father Mann's belt buckle, then back up at Father Mann. "Oh, Father. I need you."

5 YOU'D BETTER WORK

"Johnny, you're going to have to get a job." Father Mann closes the utensil drawer of his and Johnny's shabby, not-so-chic studio apartment.

"Me? You're older, you work." Johnny watches Father Mann busy himself with mundane chores around the apartment, and does not offer to help.

"Ummm... I got excommunicated. My 'job,' as you like to call it, is gone forever." He swipes the countertop with a paper towel.

"Oh, and it's my fault? The counter's clean, by the way."

"Johnny, we had relations in the confessional."

"That was five years ago. You can get your job back. Isn't 'turn the other cheek,' like, the church's motto?"

"You really have no concept of what it means to be excommunicated, Johnny. We committed sodomy. Hmm...," He searches for a way to phrase it so Johnny will understand. He continues, "We had sex in the confessional. The church doesn't just turn the other cheek for that."

"We made love." Johnny gently removes the paper towel from Father Mann's hand, tosses it in the trash bin, and coos, "God would like that we made love."

"That's not at all funny."

"God likes love."

"That's not untrue, but…"

"God loves love."

"Well, surely, but…"

"God *doesn't* want me to love you?" Johnny comes closer to Father Mann, nee David.

"Of course God wants you to love me."

"Let me show you how much I love you," Johnny offers. He gets to his knees.

"Unless you're about to pray you find a job soon, don't bother getting on your knees."

Johnny winces. "That's a tad harsh." He gets up.

"My savings are almost completely gone. You're getting a job."

"Yeah, well, you're not getting any. At least not in the foreseeable future."

"You know, this all would've been avoided if you'd have told me Petunia was right outside the door."

"I'm supposed to know she would have nothing better to do than listen to what was going on inside the confessional? The SUPPOSED TO BE PRIVATE confessional?"

"Johnny, normal people don't scream 'Good Lord, I'm coming' in a confessional."

"They don't?"

David tilts his head and gives a look that begs the question 'seriously?'

"Ok, maybe not most people," Johnny concedes.

"They definitely wouldn't yell, 'Bleep me, Father Mann!'"

"Really? 'Bleep?' You can say f…"

"Young Jonathan!"

"Even though that still gets me hot, you can stop calling me Young Jonathan. Johnny does nicely now."

"I'll have to see how the name looks in writing. On a resume, perhaps?"

Charlie Casso

6 SAINTS AND A SINNER

I have to get a job. Johnny considers, *Pounding the pavement because I pounded Father Mann. I guess an eye for an eye is also one of those church things.* Johnny muses over the idea he has ten years left to live, at least according to his run-ins with Saint Barbara and Saint John. Ten years left to live and he has to get a job so he can afford to live in the shoddy lifestyle to which he has become accustomed. Johnny wonders, *What can I do, what can I do?* A memory of Saint Barbara and Saint John flashes before him. He has ten years left until that supposed doom date. And what has he done so far? He had his first kiss. He had sex. He wound up moving in with Father Mann, most recently known as David, what with the excommunication and all. He's had to live in the cramped studio apartment David could afford since Johnny's own parents kicked him out once they found out about his indiscretions. The gay thing likely wouldn't have bothered them. It was more the 'with a priest,' 'in a church' thing that got to them.

His eyes alight on a *Help Wanted* sign in the window of a local diner. Johnny pictures himself working at the diner. He envisions himself in a dirty white smock, speckled with food remnants, his hair in a small bun trapped inside a hairnet, sweat and grease drips from his forehead. *Not Mexican enough,* he notes of himself, and continues his walk down the street. He sees the bath and body product store, actually he smells it first, as the scent of strawberries and peaches permeates the air. He pictures himself dressed like one of the worker bees of the store, in head-to-toe white, crisp and clean. His face is freshly shaven, his complexion flawless. *Would you like to sample our newest line of kiwi guava follicle enhancer?* He imagines himself pandering to the 'clients' of the store. He shakes the thought off. *Not gay enough,* he thinks. It's not like they have a *Help Wanted* sign anyway.

Johnny walks into an office supply store. He navigates his way around the stacks of paper and locates the average looking guy wearing the red shirt that distinguishes him as the assistant manager. "Excuse me," Johnny addresses the man, "are you hiring?"

"We are always 'actively looking,'" he responds. He gives Johnny the head-to-toe size up. *Presentable enough,* his eyes indicate. "What work experience do you have in the office supply industry?"

"I've both seen and been in offices. Does that count?" He smiles a playful smile.

"No, actually it doesn't. Listen kid," he looks aside, bored almost, "this isn't just a job. This is a lifestyle. You need to eat, breathe, and sleep paper."

"That's literally impossible."

"And another thing, learn it now or learn it later, the word 'impossible' does not exist."

"But… you just said it. It clearly exists."

"I can tell this would never work. But I thank you for your interest in *OfficeGear*."

"You're really turning me down for a job at *OfficeGear*?"

"It would appear that way."

"I'm smart though," Johnny states, more as an attempt at affirmation for himself than to convince Mr. Red Shirt.

"Okay, smart guy. Here's your last chance: What's paper made from?"

Seriously? Johnny thinks. *Paper comes from wood, from trees! Wait, no. That sounds awful stupid. He can't mean that, he must mean the chemicals in paper, or something. He wants me to say paper comes from trees so he can laugh at me. What's paper really made from? There's probably bleach somewhere in the process, to make the paper white. I know,* Johnny considers, *I've got it!*

"Paper," Johnny responds, "is made from soybeans."

"What?"

"Bleached soybeans?"

"Trees. Paper is made from trees."

"That was a trick question."

"The only tricky part of that question, for you, was that there was a right answer. Listen, you're a good looking kid. You'll find something that's more suitable to your… Well, something that's more suitable."

Deflated, but not defeated, Johnny leaves

OfficeGear and squints in the brightness of the sun. The heat from the sun bores into him. He can smell his own skin, the slightly burnt smell that emanates from his pores. For a moment, he thinks he may burst into flames. *Why are you doing this to me?* he questions the heavens. The chimes of an ice cream truck at the curb interrupt his thoughts. Johnny strolls over to the truck. He considers, *Why not get an ice cream cone? It's a pretty nice day, even if I have to look for employment. Might as well enjoy these moments while I can.*

Johnny peruses the candy-colored menu of frozen treats adhered to the side of the truck. He decides on an ice cream sandwich. "Can I get an ice cream san…" Johnny's voice trails off while his brain registers the fact that the ice cream purveyors are none other than Saint Barbara and Saint John.

"C'mon!" Johnny protests. "I can't even get an ice cream? Why are you tormenting me?"

"Sir," the stranger next to him begins, "your ice cream sandwich is right in front of you. Are you all right?"

"I'm fine," Johnny responds. "*They* are the problem."

"Young man," Saint Barbara responds, "we are merely here to give you what you want. Is this," she holds out the ice cream sandwich to Johnny, "not what you want?"

"No, it's not what I want. I want my old life back."

"Did he not just ask us for this ice cream sandwich?" she asks Saint John. "I clearly recall him saying he wanted an ice cream sandwich."

"Yes, he did, he clearly did," Saint John responds to Barbara. "But it's really no worry. The young man seems to be going through some issues."

"I can hear you," Johnny chimes in.

Saint Barbara and Saint John continue their conversation with each other. "Maybe a recent breakup with a girl," Saint Barbara surmises. She gives Johnny a coy look.

"A death in the family! The poor thing may be suffering the loss of someone near and dear to him," Saint John pretend guesses.

Johnny clenches his jaw and stares hard at the back right tire of the truck.

"The poor thing needs a job!" Saint Barbara exclaims. The revelation startles Johnny. He focuses on Saint Barbara and Saint John once again.

"Yes, you've got it correct, Barbara," affirms Saint John.

"You know," adds the stranger, "that dirty little diner over there has a *Help Wanted* sign in the window."

Johnny's face, particularly the curl on his lips, denotes his displeasure with the thought of working at the diner.

"Judge not lest ye be judged, young one. It seems you need a job and there is one ready for the taking right across the street," Barbara offers. "Young man, you are going to be left with a mess if you don't act soon."

"What?" Johnny asks.

"You're going to be left with a mess if you don't act soon. Your ice cream sandwich is starting to drip. Please take it."

Johnny takes the ice cream sandwich and responds, "Oh, right."

"Would you like to pay now?"

"You know you have to pay," Saint John adds.

"I have to pay?"

"Hey," the stranger interjects, "if he gets free ice cream I want free ice cream."

"No, no, dear," Saint Barbara responds, "everything comes at a price."

7 A ROSE BY ANY OTHER NAME

The bells above the door of the diner jingle and announce Johnny's entrance. His slow shuffle inside, however, announces the reluctant aspect of his entrance. Johnny takes a skeptical glance around. The sheen of grease on the counters is evident. A long strand of brown hair drapes across the tray of cookies, so prominently displayed there that it almost appears intentional, a sort of *look how long this strand of hair is* arrogance.

Johnny sidles up to the counter and takes a seat on an empty bar stool. He tries to make eye contact with someone who works there, anyone who works there, but no one even looks in his direction. A waitress saunters about, refills an iced tea, and semi-slams it on the counter in front of a customer who thanks his waitress with a mere grunt as gnarled tidbits of cheeseburger escape from the side of his mouth.

"Whaddaya want?" The waitress seems to ask Johnny this question, but, then again, she doesn't even look in his direction. She slices a piece of cobbler and in one swift motion has it plated and sliding across the counter to its suitor. "You gonna take all day, Peaches?"

"Are you talking to me?" Johnny asks.

"Guess your name's Peaches then. Yes, I'm talkin' to you. Whaddaya want? I don't have all day."

"I saw your *Help Wanted* sign in the window."

"You're gonna sit in my section and not order anything?"

"I just wanted to know if…"

"Information ain't free, Peaches." For the first time, she makes eye contact with Johnny. "Mama's got rent to pay. Mama's got bills. Let's see, mama's got 'lectricity, mama's got… mama's got gas-- well, mama's got a gas bill, mama don't have no gas-- now, mama's got…"

"Coffee. I'd like a cup of coffee, please."

"That's better. It's a start. Have your coffee and then we'll talk more." She semi-slams the cup of blacker than black coffee in front of Johnny. He winces at the smudge of lipstick he sees on his cup. He opens his mouth a fraction to say something, then thinks better of it. He closes his mouth, rotates his cup around, and settles the cup down on its saucer. He sighs at the sight before him: lipstick stains decorate this side of the mug as well.

"Can't be that bad, buddy," the patron two stools over from Johnny says. "Have a cookie." He nods his head in the direction of the plate of cookies.

"Thanks for the offer, but I don't think my stomach can handle that."

"You're not drinking your coffee, Sugar Peach," the waitress addresses Johnny. "You too good for it?"

36

"No, it's not that. I just wanted to know if…"

"If you could get a job here at this here fine establishment?"

"Yes. Well, no. Well, yes. You make it sound so…"

"Truthfully dishonest? Listen kid, I got no time to sugar coat things. The place ain't great but it's a living and it's all I got. So, yeah, I call it like I see it."

"I never really worked before, but I have to find a job if I want to continue having a roof over my head. People barely talk to you once they hear you have no experience."

The waitress walks out of Johnny's sight, through the swinging doors to the kitchen.

"Pretty much just like that," Johnny continues more to himself than to anyone else. Johnny pulls three singles out of his pocket, drops them on the counter, and gets up from his stool.

Mr. Weatherby two stools over, the one who drops more cheeseburger bits than he eats, interrupts Johnny with one of his eloquent grunts.

"What?" Johnny, with barely a shred of patience left, asks.

"I said…" and he makes the grunt noise once more.

"I really have no time for this."

"Sit down." He gives Johnny a no-nonsense glare. "I said sit down. You think Flo over there dismisses people? You think she doesn't care? She has no heart? A minion, that's what you think. Well, she's not and she does and she wouldn't and not in that order."

"Her name is Flo?"

"Does she look like a Susan to you?"

"No, but… Flo?"

"It's short for Florence."

"I thought you were pulling my leg. You know, Flo the waitress from that old TV show where…"

Mr. Weatherby cuts Johnny off. "In my day we read books. Your generation with your fancy televisions and your video machines and your floppy disks and computers. Books, boy, that's where it starts and where it ends. Now I said sit down and I'm not gonna say it again. You show that woman some respect."

The waitress pushes through the doors and carries three plates that bear heaps of fries, onion rings, and chicken tenders. She delivers them to a nearby booth as Johnny reclaims his seat.

"Sugar Peach, what are you good for?"

"What?"

"What kinda job are you looking for? Ok, let me break it down. What do you do well that you'd be able to do here?"

Johnny gives a sheepish grin and responds, "I really don't know."

"Then, kid, there's nothing I can do for ya." She starts to walk away.

"Listen, Flo, I'm sure I can do something."

She turns around to face Johnny. "I'm sorry, did you say you wanted an ass kicking? 'Cuz I swear I thought you said when you walked in that you wanted a cup of coffee. Now I hear you want an ass kicking."

"I did want that. The coffee, I mean, not the ass kicking."

"When you call me Flo you're ordering an ass

kicking."

"Your name's not Flo?"

"You little shit, get out." She points at the door.

Johnny sees her nametag indicates *Rose* and gasps. He turns to Mr. Weatherby and exclaims, "You told me her name was Flo!"

"The gall on this one," the waitress responds. "Kid, this one here," she points at Mr. Weatherby, "is a functional mute. Comes in every day, rain or shine, gets the same thing, but never says a word. He can't, he's a mute. That's what mutes do, or don't do."

"He's not a mute, he spoke to me. He told me your name was Flo and that I should stay and you'd help me."

"That's a doozy, kid. You also get visions of the Virgin Mary and stuff?"

Johnny hears the music of the ice cream truck. He looks out the diner window and sees the ice cream truck. Saint Barbara and Saint John wave cheerily at him.

"I'm sorry, I guess I have an active imagination sometimes. I really apologize if I offended you. I have to be honest, I need a job badly. I don't steal, or anything like that. If you give me something, any job, I can try my best and if you don't like it, or me, well then neither of us are any worse off, no?"

"If you really are as desperate as you're saying, then we might be able to work something out. There is one position needs filling. Our mopper up and quit on us. It's not as glamorous as all that. Mopping's the most luxurious part of the job, I'm sure, but it's something. If you're spry and young and got a bit of muscle on ya you'll be all right. Gotta clean every floor in the place, constantly. We can't have the department of health coming in here and shutting us down 'cuz someone dropped a ham sandwich and it stayed on the floor. Gotta keep things neat. Neat and tidy. Can you handle that?"

"I'm sure I can."

"Don't ya wanna know what the pay is?"

"Sure, what's it pay?"

"Hell, I don't know, you think I own the place?" She stares at Johnny for a good few seconds of uncomfortable, for Johnny, silence. "Sally," she yells as she cocks her head in the direction of the kitchen, "Sally, we got a new floor boy. Come and meet him." She looks at Johnny and imparts, "Sally'll set you up with your pay and all. My work here is done." As she begins to move away from Johnny, she adds, "Seriously, my work here is done. Clean this up."

8 WORKING BOY

"Mister Mann, I got a job," Johnny greets David as he bounces into the room.

"You did?"

"Yes, I did. I am officially the bread-winner of this household. I'm also the bread-sweeper, I guess."

"That's terrific! What's the job? And what's a bread-sweeper?"

"I'm working at the dirty little diner a few streets up."

"You can't even boil water."

"I'm not the cook. I'm more of the cleaning staff."

David raises an eyebrow and asks, "You clean?"

"Yes, I clean. I take offense to that."

"I've never seen you clean around here."

"That's not the point. That doesn't mean I *can't* clean, it just means I *don't* clean. There's a difference."

"Six of one, half a dozen of the other."

"It's six of one, half a baker's dozen of the

other," Johnny counters.

"No, it's not. Where would you get that from?"

"I have a job now, David, I'm not stupid. Six is the same as half a dozen. You have the saying wrong. It's six of one, half a baker's dozen of the other. That's what makes them different."

"Johnny, that's the point! There is no difference between six and half a dozen. That's the whole point of the saying, that no matter how you say it, it's the same thing."

"Well, that just makes no sense at all. And I think you're wrong. Can we get back to the point here? I got a job. It's not going to be enough though, not enough for us to live on. And it doesn't look like the Lord is going to provide the rest of the money we need for rent and food, so I think you need to, I apologize for the pun, man up and get a job."

"After all we've been through, after we lived off of my savings for years, you just turn on me like that and tell me to 'get a job'? I had a vocation. I was meant to be a priest, that was my life. Granted, I did things I probably shouldn't have…" Johnny darts a reproachful glance at David, but David continues, "and I'm not saying I regret any of the things I did, particularly where you were concerned. I don't regret. I just made choices that made life more difficult for me. For us. But, for better or worse, I'm glad for everything. I think I merely require patience, patience to deal with the cards we have been dealt. Patience to sort them out and adjust to the hand before us. I will get a job, of course. I will provide, just as the Lord would have me provide. I will do right by you and we will have a nice long life ahead of us."

Johnny's mind wanders at David's mention of their long life ahead. He thinks of Saint Barbara and Saint John ten years ago when they told him he'd have a mere twenty years to live. He's already used up ten of those years and look at where he's landed: on the verge of homelessness, abandoned by his family, his lover has been excommunicated from the church, from his very livelihood. And where did this all come from, he wonders, why has this all started? All because he feels an impulse and acts on it. If only he hadn't acted on his carnal feelings for David, or Father Mann as he was called back in the day.

But that wasn't it, Johnny reflects. Johnny would surely have been able to control his desire for Father Mann. He had been quite the respectful, humble child. He was driven to act. Driven by the saints! Driven by his vision! It was the fault of Saint Barbara and Saint John. They tell him he has twenty years left and he makes that ridiculous list of items to accomplish before he dies. It is all their fault. *A vision of Saints*, he thinks, *that's what caused this*.

A memory flashes before Johnny's eyes. It's of him sitting on the ground, a young heap of life on the floor. His eyes about to close as the plain black leather shoes carry their menacing clomps away. *Sister Petunia*, Johnny realizes, *she caused this. Sister Petunia is the party responsible for my descent. As such, she needs to pay for what she has done. After all*, he thinks, *an eye for an eye and a tooth for a tooth*. "Isn't that, like, the church's other motto?" he asks aloud.

"Isn't what the church's other motto?" David asks.

"Huh? Oh. Sorry, I was just daydreaming."

"Of course. I pour my heart out to you while you daydream. Sounds about right."

"No, no. It's just… there's something I need to do." And with that, Johnny removes himself from the presence of David with a lone thought in his head: *Vengeance*.

9 PLUCKING PETUNIA

The long gray tendrils pull out of the water, toilet water, and not the perfume kind. Actual toilet water. Johnny pushes from behind again. The mounds of gray spread out in the water, somewhat tenderly for such an aggressive push. She fights for air as he presses her down into the porcelain bottom of the bowl. Bubbles of various sizes come to the surface of the water. *You deserve this*, he thinks.

A rap sounds at the door, *knock knock knock*. A strange voice calls, "Is everything all right in there?"

Johnny turns to the door. A mixture of concern and daze paints his face. "Yeah," he stammers, "be right out."

He turns back to the toilet bowl and releases his vice-like grip from the neck of the lifeless mop. He pulls the mop out of the toilet and the long gray tendrils scatter drops of water onto the floor. He lifts the mop by the handle into the yellow mop bucket and uses the contraption to wring the water from it.

Knock knock knock.
"I said I'm coming."

***

"Peaches, hehe, I like that name for you,"
Veronica says, air-poking her hot dog at Johnny.

"First of all, my name's not Peaches."

"But she," Veronica motions to the waitress,
"calls you Peaches, or Sugar Peach. Personally, you
remind me more of a banana. All tall and doo-da-doo,
da-doo-da-doo-doo."

Johnny shakes his head.

"Some of us have work to do, Ronnie."

"That's why I'm here. I'm gonna finish this fine
hot dog over here and then go make a Jackson Pollack
outta that bathroom. Keep you employed."

"That's ten shades of gross. Please don't."

"I'll think about it. How's Mister Mann?"
Veronica playfully caresses the underside of the hot dog
bun. "Mister May-uhn."

"He's actually looking for a job, too, now. Or at
least that's what he's supposed to be doing."

"That's not distrust I hear, is it? How can you
not trust a priest?"

"You have to stop with those 'not' questions.
They're virtually impossible to answer. 'How can you
not trust a priest?' How can I answer that?"

"Tomato, tomato," she enunciates, each word
exactly the same way.

"You want tomato?"

"No, tomato, tomato. Same thing." Veronica

looks at Johnny, and tries to gauge how stupid he can be. "Has no one ever told you tomato tomato?"

"It's tom-*ay*-to, tom-*ah*-to and," he has a flash of his initial interaction with Saint Barbara and Saint John, "yes, actually they have."

"So, you know what I'm talking about then. You have to trust David, he's a priest."

"Was. He was a priest."

"I think the priestery is one of those things that, once you're in it, you're in it for life. It's like a gang, but like a really intense gang with, like, God as the leader."

"Priesthood."

"I never thought of it that way before, but priest," she slices the air with the remaining inch of hot dog, "hood probably does make sense." Two shreds of sauerkraut fling to the floor. Johnny's eyes follow their descent.

"I have to clean that, you know."

"We all have to clean up messes now and then. Sometimes they're our own messes and sometimes they're someone else's."

Johnny sweeps around Veronica's feet. He moves the shreds of sauerkraut behind the counter and leans on the end of his broom. He gazes at Veronica who finishes the last bite.

"Anyway, you should trust him. The man is, or was, a priest."

"And how'd that work out for him?"

"So, because he was dishonest in his dealings with the church, you think he's going to be dishonest with you?"

Johnny doesn't answer Veronica. Instead, he lets

his eyes drift to the couple who sit in a corner booth, on the same side of the booth, as they feed each other french toast sticks. Veronica pinches together a small clump of the sauerkraut that litters the countertop. She settles the clump on her index and middle fingernails, held in place by her thumb. She releases her thumb from holding the two fingers, the fingers flick outward, the sauerkraut projects at Johnny's forehead and *splat*.

"Earth to Johnny, hello," she waves at Johnny. Johnny takes a napkin from the counter and wipes off his forehead. "Well?"

Johnny thinks for a moment. *I don't think he's going to be dishonest with me necessarily. I just feel like I didn't sign up for this. I didn't ask to be twenty-three, sweeping floors for a living, supporting, at least for the time being, my older boyfriend, without any parental guidance or assistance at all.*

What, in life, do you sign up for? Not much. A lot of what happens just happens. Whether it's good or bad, you just have to deal with whatever goes down and move on. Then again, I'm only twenty-three, so what do I know? We have the rest of our lives to figure this out.

Some of us have the rest of our lives to figure it out, Johnny thinks, *but not me. My circumstances are quite different from Veronica's. Whatever remains left for me to accomplish in my life needs to be accomplished, and fast.*

As if sensing his thoughts, Veronica asks, "So, what is it you intend to do with the rest of your life?"

Johnny takes his broom in his hands and begins to sweep away from Veronica. While he tries to free a french fry from its hiding place between the runner and the door, Johnny mutters, "I have to work."

"I'd like a cup of coffee, please," Veronica addresses the waitress.

While Veronica receives her coffee and begins her ritual of adding sugar, tasting the coffee, adding a bit of milk, tasting the coffee, adding more sugar, tasting the coffee, and on and on until she finds the coffee perfectly to her liking, Johnny busies himself with his broom and the already swept floor.

A lifetime of monotomy. Monotomy, he muses, *wait is that right? Sounds right. I'll be with David and I'll be stuck in a rut while I sweep and mop the same floors day after day. The only thing that'll change will be that there will be one less day left for me.*

"Ronnie, I have to ask you something serious." Johnny waits for a signal from Veronica to proceed. She leans in a bit. "I was wondering, do you ever think about Sister Petunia?"

"I told you, Johnny, while I appreciate the beauty of women I am not a lesbian."

"I said serious, Ronnie."

"I am serious. Aside from that one time right out of high school, I..." she trails off right as she notices Johnny's downcast eyes.

"You *are* serious. Sorry. No. I, well, she hasn't crossed my mind really. I'm not sure why she would. She was a meanie, for sure. I guess I don't think about her because, well, out of sight out of mind?" She phrases the last part as a question. "What's on your mind?"

"It's just, sometimes I think about how cruel she was to us. We were just kids. What kind of person does what she did, and to kids? I don't know. She crosses my mind sometimes. It's like a part of me wants some kind of revenge."

"What's black and white and red all over?" Veronica asks.

"A nun falling down a flight of stairs?"

Veronica retorts, "Obvious answer. Other acceptable responses include a nun with a sunburn, a nun with a paper-cut, and, my favorite, a nun during menses. Feel better?"

"A tiny bit, only because in each of those instances, as long as the nun was Sister Petunia, she'd be in pain of some sort. Even if it's just a little, just so she could see what she put us through."

"It sounds like you want closure."

I want her in a closed casket, Johnny thinks.

"Well," Veronica continues, "maybe we can get some closure for you. Would you be willing to have a sit-down with her? Maybe we can invite her here for a meal."

"What, so she could see what a great person I've become, what a master of the trade of... of... mopping I've become? No thanks." *Besides*, he thinks, *she didn't even remember me when it was only four years after graduation, never mind now. That's it! She won't have a clue who I am when she sees me. She will never know what hit her.*

"Then what do you propose?"

"I think I'll have to turn to the Lord for guidance on this one."

10 TRUST

Johnny opens the front door to his apartment and notices
the light that emanates from the bedroom. David must be
in there, hopefully looking for employment online.
Johnny settles his keys on the table, takes a quick swig
of water from the fridge, and goes in to greet David. The
door to the bedroom pushes open with a loud creak.
David's hand jumps to his heart as he exclaims, "Make
some noise when you come in. Don't scare me like that."
All the while, it seems as if David closes windows on the
computer screen in front of him.

"Whatcha doing?"

"Looking for a job, of course."

"Find anything interesting?"

"Well you know, there's a lot out there. This
may take a while. I'm older than you, so it might be
harder for me to find a job than it was for you. You have
time on your side."

Johnny asks, "It looks like you had a bunch
more windows a minute ago. What happened?"

"They were all dead ends and pop-ups. You know how it is."

I don't, Johnny thinks. *What is he really up to?*

"Chin up, I'm sure you'll find what you're looking for. I'm just going to get changed. Maybe we can go out for a libation tonight?"

"You know I don't drink."

"You know the Blood of Christ wasn't really blood, right?"

David sighs.

***

Inside the bar, four men in various stages of dress, and undress, surround Johnny and David. "So," one of the men addresses David, "you were a man of the cloth. Do you still have the uniform?"

"You can't ask him that," another one chimes in with a chuckle. "But since you did…"

"It was years ago. I doubt I still have the clothes from then," David responds.

"That's not a no! I'll take it!"

Johnny looks on, not at all amused by the men who hit on David. He stirs the ice in his glass with the little black straw. One of the men directs his attention to Johnny and asks, "How long do you know David?"

"We've been together for a few years now."

"Nice. Glad to hear it," he lies. His focus remains on David while he speaks with Johnny. He undresses David slowly. He works his way from top to bottom removing every piece of clothing with his eyes. "Glory be," he whispers.

"How do you know the other three guys?" Johnny inquires.

"Well, the two on the left of your man I met out and about a couple of years ago. God, I don't even remember where. We just kept running into each other places and finally became friends. Well, more like 'going out friends.' Most of the times we see each other is at night in bars, but it's planned."

"That's pretty nice."

"Yeah, it definitely works for us."

"And what about the other one? The one on the right."

"Sal? Sal's… well, Sal and I kind of, sort of, briefly went out. And we stayed in touch."

"That's a lot of qualifiers you have there. What's with all the hesitation to say you went out? Love unrequited or something?"

"No, not at all."

"You still seem hesitant. Spill it."

"Okay, fine, I blew him but I don't want to talk about it."

"You don't want to talk about it? You can't do that. You already started."

"It's just… It just. Well, it was," he shudders, "it smelled like rotten meat."

Johnny remains completely silent.

"I figured since his tongue was so scratchy when we kissed, I'd rather blow him than kiss him. And then when I went to, it smelled disgusting. I tried to do it but I had to keep stopping because it smelled so bad."

"What did you do?"

"I told him it smelled. What was I going to do? I

couldn't just stop. And besides, how could you let someone blow you knowing that you smell like raw meat?"

"What did he say?"

"He said it's a 'real-man' thing, that he doesn't wash down there because he likes it to be natural. Have you ever heard of that? Never in my whole life have I heard of something like that. He's a pig. We're friends now, and I can have a pig for a friend, but not for a lover."

"Classy approach. I believe there's an Oscar Wilde or Virginia Woolf quote that addresses the very same point."

"Are they friends of yours?" he asks Johnny. Before he can get an answer, he's interrupted by the onset of a new thought. "Hey guys," he addresses the group, "I have an idea. We have the suite tonight and it's only a few blocks from here. Why don't we take the party there?"

"You're staying in a hotel tonight?" Johnny asks.

"Yeah, we don't come out too often so, way I see it, it's worth it to do it right when we do. I know the manager so I get a nice gigantic suite when it's available."

Johnny arches his eyebrow and shakes his head no at David. David responds with a shrug of his shoulders.

"Do you guys need a moment to discuss? We aren't having a sex party or anything, if that's what you're worried about. I just figured you seem like good people, especially with this one here being a former man of the cloth. We have a nice space, free booze and whatever. Your call."

"Give us a minute," David directs. He approaches Johnny face-to-face. He tells Johnny, "It's your choice whether we go or not, but it would be nice to spend the night together doing something different. Nothing funny is going to happen."

Johnny thinks to himself for a second and decides that, if it's his choice, he should trust David enough to take him at his word and go to the hotel. If Johnny decides not to go, then it looks like he doesn't trust David, and, well, that's not good for the relationship.

"All right," Johnny responds, "we can go. I just worry about ulterior motives is all."

***

The group arrives at the hotel and it is, in fact, a luxurious suite. Johnny and David get comfortable on the couch. Sal goes to take a bath, which Johnny thinks is highly appropriate given his situation down under. Apparently, someone joins Sal in the bathtub, at least that's what one of the other two passes along.

On the couch, Johnny and David start to make out. A few minutes elapse as they lose themselves in each other. Someone walks right up behind them, crosses his arms and rests them on the ledge of the couch, then rests his chin on his arms, and stares at Johnny and David. He wears a white wife beater and visible Keith Haring tattoos and, by the want in his eyes, is completely enraptured in his two new friends. Johnny notices him through the corner of his eye, but does not let it break his focus from David.

Keith Haring Tattoo Guy inches closer to Johnny and David. This time, David's concentration breaks. He looks at Keith Haring Tattoo Guy and then looks back at Johnny. He continues kissing Johnny. Keith Haring Tattoo Guy comes in even closer. David turns to Keith Haring Tattoo Guy, places his right hand behind Keith Haring Tattoo Guy's neck, and draws him in for a slow kiss. David gazes at Johnny through the corner of his eye as they swap saliva. He stops. He realizes aloud, "Johnny's not into this." Keith Haring Tattoo Guy walks away, dejected.

Johnny calls him to come back over to where they are, pulls him close by his wife beater, and makes out with him briefly. Johnny releases Keith Haring Tattoo Guy's shirt and pushes him away. Johnny directs, "You can go now." Keith Haring Tattoo Guy walks away again, this time dejected and confused.

"How do you like it?" Johnny asks David.

David responds, "What do you mean? You kissing him?"

"Yes. Does it bother you?"

"Of course it bothers me," he says with a pained expression of lust and trepidation.

Johnny counters, "I can't tell it if bothers you in a 'that upsets me' way, or in a 'hot and bothered' way, but I have my suspicions. And, either way, I'm leaving." Johnny feels sure David loved it. But, in the moment, Johnny hopes there is some semblance of truth in the jealousy department. Johnny also feels a sense of odd relief in that now his eyes are open regarding David's lustful ways. *Isn't lust a sin?* Johnny wonders. *If it isn't then it should be.*

"I'm obviously not staying here without you," David offers. "Let's go home."

Charlie Casso

11 FATHER FIGURE

"Ronnie, would you sit down? I can't talk to you with you walking all around the place looking for dust."

"Johnny, I know it's only a studio apartment but if I don't keep it clean no one else will. It's just me here."

"I know, but this is really important."

"One second. Make that fifteen seconds. Let me just clean this mirror here and then I can give you my undivided attention." She cleans the mirror with the rag she just used to clean the toaster oven, and leaves the mirror dirtier than it was only seconds before. "Perfect. Now what's your plight, sodomite?"

"Please don't refer to me as sodomite."

"Come on, it was a cute rhyme."

"No."

"Fine. What's up?"

Johnny describes to Veronica the events that transpired between him, David, and the guys from the bar. He manages to retell the events in a fairly objective manner, which is no small feat. When he is done, he remains silent while Veronica assesses the situation.

"You did seem like you suspected something. Maybe you were right. It's possible David wants to sew the oats he never got to sew when he was all priestly."

"He's too old to sew his oats now, Ronnie."

"Men. They are oats, not eggs. Your oats don't dry up like lady eggs. They're not even literal oats. If they were then they could dry up, but they're not. So they can't."

"You're losing me. What's your point?"

"My point is he may want to do the things he could never do before. Man sex. Ha ha, that's funny. Man sex, like, Father Mann sex."

Johnny glares at Veronica.

"Okay, okay, but you get my point, right?" she asks.

"He should have sewn his oats with me. He doesn't need some barfly for that."

"We're jumping to conclusions anyway. It was one of those things that happen. You were invited somewhere, you went… it was the spur of the moment. It wasn't premeditated or anything. He may have just been in the moment. Completely harmless."

"You're right, I didn't think of that."

"That's not to say he's completely innocent. It's just… proceed with caution. Make sure everything's on the up and up."

Johnny considers the weird occasion when David was supposed to be looking for employment online. He tells Veronica, "I noticed the other day he was being weird about the computer. It's like he was supposed to be looking for a job online but when I walked in the room he was a little shifty and I saw him close some windows on the computer screen."

"You men and your porn. Priest porn. Nun porn. I can't decide if that's hot or gross."

"Actually, I hope that was it. It was just weird that there would be a bunch of windows. It's not like you'd watch multiple porn videos at the same time."

"Do they still have chat rooms? Or online hookup places?"

"Well, yeah, I'm sure, but…"

"What are the account names he gives himself when he logs into things?"

"You mean his email address?"

"No, like your user name for an online store or something. One of the ones you make up that you can remember. You know, sometimes people see them and sometimes they don't. Maybe one you use to make comments on someone's blog."

"Oh! Oh, I don't know his user names."

"Not all of them. This is like pulling teeth. My guess is he uses names like 'GodsGift,' 'FallenOne,' names of that nature."

"Actually, I have seen him use 'Thumper.' It always sticks out to me because it has the whole Bible thumper meaning and it also has the cute Bambi reference."

"So we're pretty much looking for names with some kind of biblical or holy reference in them."

"We are? Where are we looking for these things?"

"Chat rooms, silly. You're worried that David's

lust is getting the better of him and, well, there's only one way to find out if you have a reason to worry."

Veronica shakes the mouse on her computer to wake it from its slumber. She does a search for hookup sites and, to no surprise at all, finds three that seem quite popular.

She opens up all three, each in its own browser window. She clicks on each of them, one by one, and peruses the list of participants currently in each. What she notices is either very odd or highly coincidental. She points to the name "FatherFigure" in the first window. She points to the same name in the second window. Finally, she locates the name in the third window and underlines it on the screen with the tip of her finger. A person who calls himself "FatherFigure" is active in each hookup site, and each has the same generic torso pic in lieu of a face. She turns her attention to Johnny, who looks blankly ahead, mouth agape.

"What do you want to do?" she asks.

Johnny shakes his head in response. His curiosity has been piqued. He considers bringing up the subject to David and having accusations fly, but then he reconsiders. Johnny decides to do what any rational lover would do in such an instance: He resolves to create an online alter-ego to investigate the matter.

"Ronnie, get your Gemini on, it's time to create some alter-egos."

"I didn't see that coming, but game on."

"You're faster, you do it."

"Just because I lost my virginity first, doesn't mean I'm fast."

"I still can't believe you did it with your step-brother Marvin. I mean, even if he wasn't your step-brother, the name Marvin should've turned you off."

"He was my step-brother and we were never that close anyway and you know it."

"If I remember you correctly, Marcia Brady, the farthest apart you were was about eight inches, so, I'd say that's pretty close."

She backs away from the computer and states, "Here I thought you wanted my help but if you're going to…"

"I'm sorry, I'm sorry. Seriously, though, you are fast. On the computer I mean! Please?"

"Fine. User name?"

Johnny thinks for a moment, his eyes shift left and right. "PreyOnMe. P-r-e-y on me. So it'll look like this person wants guys on him, but it has the double meaning of pray," Johnny moves his hands together as if they are in prayer, "on me. What's good for the goose is good for the… other goose."

"I like it. All right, we need some stats. And pick stats you can stick with because we want to use the same for each site we use. You don't want him, or anyone else for that matter, to notice inconsistencies. If they do then our cover's blown."

"Let's make PreyOnMe an inch shorter than me, ten pounds lighter, dark hair, brown eyes."

"So that's…"

"6'1, 175, dark brown hair, brown eyes."

"Ethnicity?"

"Italian. He likes Italian. If you want to catch fish you have to use the right bait."

"Anything else?" Veronica asks.

"Yes. Tonight, I'm serving snapper," Johnny replies.

"No, you boob, anything else regarding body specifics?"

"Body specifics?"

"Body type. Slender, athletic, a few extra pounds…"

"Put athletic."

"And then there's body-part specifics like…"

"Oh, no way. Notwithstanding what happened recently, David is way too prudish to be attracted to someone who would list specifics about their…"

"Lovestick?"

"…sure, on a public profile."

"K. I'll leave that blank then. Now just let me copy and paste this info to the other sites. And then we are all… we are not all set. A picture. We need a picture. No one is going to talk to anyone without a picture."

"I am sure you can think of a person you've talked to online who's 6'1 or so and has dark hair."

"The things I do for you. Give me a minute." Veronica pulls up files on her computer and rapidly clicks through the images. "This guy lives in England now, so I don't feel bad using his pic. You like?"

"Cute. I approve. Yes, please."

Veronica clicks away. "Uploading. Uploading. Uploading. All done!"

"Now what?" Johnny asks.

"Now…" Veronica continues to click away on her computer. She adds PreyOnMe as an active participant to each of the hookup sites. Upon successful completion, she finishes her statement with, "we wait."

Johnny's heart beats faster, and with a more thud-like pound, as he wonders about what may happen. "We got a bite," Johnny exclaims as a message pops onto the screen.

"Give it a minute," Veronica responds. "You're fresh meat. Just watch."

Within seconds, a dozen additional messages spring onto the screen. Johnny eyes them and starts to close each message. He notes, "Does anyone know how to speak to anyone else with more than 'sup' as their point of entry?"

Barely a minute passes and, to his horror, Johnny sees a new message pop up. It's from FatherFigure. He stands up from his seat, for no other reason than he simply cannot sit at this point.

Not knowing what to do, he turns to Veronica. "Ronnie," he frantically blurts, "David just messaged me. He said 'Sup?' How dare he cheat on me!"

"We don't even know if this person is David. He could just be a daddy looking for a younger guy. You don't know yet, but there's only one way to find out."

"Do I call him and ask him why he's in the chat-room? Do I break up with him? What do I do?"

"Johnny," she says pleadingly, "don't do anything until you have proof it's him and proof he's up to no good. Without proof, he can deny until kingdom come and say he wasn't going to do anything and that he would never do anything. Just sit still and see what happens," she advises.

As per her advisement, and the fact that in this state of panic Johnny really shouldn't rely on his own instincts or judgments, he sits back down and waits to see what happens. He doesn't have to wait long, as a new window pops up on his computer screen; it's another message from FatherFigure, this time from the second hookup site.

"Ronnie, he messaged me again! What do I do?" he exclaims. She asks what he has said, to which Johnny reads, "Sup?"

Veronica urges, "Johnny, keep calm. You need to stay calm to do this right."

"What do I do? I'm going to call him right now," Johnny decides.

"Johnny, don't. Don't call him. Talk to him online as PreyOnMe and see what he wants, then at least you have proof. Until you have proof of what he wants online, you do not call him."

Johnny responds to FatherFigure, and Johnny reads the conversation aloud to Veronica as it transpires.
FatherFigure: Sup?
PreyOnMe: Sup?

Veronica remarks, "*Sup?* Et tu Brute? Are you really *that* guy now?"

"Apparently, there's not much you can say to 'Sup?'" Johnny replies.
FatherFigure: "Not much, just relaxing. You?"

"He typed 'not much' instead of nm. I bet it's him," Johnny adds.
PreyOnMe: "Same. Wish there was something to do. I have all this energy but nowhere to go."

Veronica wonders aloud, "Sounds like you've done this before."

"It's just," Johnny takes his time finishing his sentence, "I don't want to scare him off by being the one to suggest we do something. He's going to be skittish if it's David."

FatherFigure: "I'm sure we could think of something."

"That son of a… Judas! Wasn't he the traitor? How could he do this to me? That's it, I'm calling him right now."

"No, Johnny, he hasn't done anything yet. You have to set it up, place and time. For right now he's only talking to someone. Set it up before you decide anything."

PreyOnMe: "Any suggestions? I'm game."

FatherFigure: "Several. I have to travel though."

"You'll be traveling all right, directly to HELL!" Johnny screams at the computer screen.

FatherFigure: "Can you host?"

"The only 'host' he should be concerned with is the communion host at mass. What happened to him that now this is the kind of 'host' he's concerned with?"

"I don't know, Johnny, but you need to respond to him. And you can't host here, he knows where I live."

PreyOnMe: "Yes. I know it sounds lame, but can we maybe meet outside first in a public place? I don't do this often, and I'd rather meet in pubic first, just for safety's sake."

Veronica remarks, "Nice touch!"

FatherFigure: "Of course. That's quite understandable. Where shall we meet?"

PreyOnMe: "You know the Poisoned Ivy Bar and Grill?"

Veronica asks, "That place is still in business?"

"Yeah, I'm always surprised when I pass it."

Johnny looks at the computer screen. "He responded!"

FatherFigure: "Yes. Be there in fifteen minutes."
PreyOnMe: "Perfect. See you soon!"

Veronica directs Johnny to be strong and reminds him he can do this. He tries to breathe, and tries to compose himself. He picks up the phone with his sweaty right hand, and dials David's cell phone. David picks up after three rings and it sounds like he is on his way out the door. Johnny does his best attempt at nonchalance and asks him how his night is going. David complains that he just got a phone call from his aunt who feels a little under the weather. His aunt supposedly has asked David to go to the drugstore to pick up some over-the-counter medicine and bring it over. Johnny surmises this is supposed to not only make it seem that David is not off to a booty call, but also make it seem like David is a really good person and a really caring, family-oriented man. Ah, but for the dichotomy of the difference between seeming and being.

Johnny counters with an offer that, maybe after David drops off the medicine, he and Johnny can grab a bite to eat, dessert or something, since he's all done at Veronica's. David quickly shoots the idea down. He claims he is afraid his aunt may want him to stay and keep her company since she's not feeling well. As such, he doesn't want to make plans, knowing it would leave his aunt in a lurch. Speaking of which, David mentions he needs to get going. Johnny concedes the matter, and hangs up, knowing that within fifteen minutes things will get a lot more interesting.

12 ORDER'S UP

Johnny and Veronica inhabit a booth in the back corner of the Poisoned Ivy Bar and Grill. They share a paper tray of fries due to societal constraints that demand they make a purchase in lieu of merely sucking up the free air conditioning. Also, they are hungry.

"What are you going to do if David walks through that door over there?"

"I don't think that's something I can plan out, Ronnie. I think I just have to deal with it in the moment."

Veronica places a fry on the table in front of the tray. "I say you smash him." To illustrate her point, she makes a fist and smashes the fry flat; its insides spread out in all directions. "Trust me," she adds, "nothing tastes better than revenge." She licks the potato fragments from the underside of her fist.

"Look, Ronnie," Johnny motions toward the windows, "he's outside." David stands on the sidewalk. He checks his phone, most likely to see if he's on time.

"What do I do?" Johnny asks Veronica.

"I don't know. I didn't think this far ahead. I mean, I really was hoping it wasn't David, or that if it was David he wouldn't show up. I wasn't expecting this."

"Stay here," Johnny directs.

Johnny shakes the potato particles from his clothes and realizes Veronica really needs to curb her food propelling ways. He moves toward the door with both a heavy foot and a heavy heart. He puts on a brave face as he pushes through the door.

"David?"

"Johnny! What a surprise seeing you here!" David's face reddens.

"Ronnie and I were bored so we figured why not grab a bite. You were going to your aunt's anyhow. Hey, why aren't you there?"

"Oh. Umm, I, well I didn't know what to... I mean what to do if she had nothing in her stomach. I ordered some food and am waiting for it. You know, feed a cold and all."

"Why don't you sit with us while you wait for the food? Come on." Johnny waves David in.

"Oh. Okay." David follows Johnny inside. He stops at the counter while Johnny walks ahead. Johnny notices David does not follow so he doubles back to find out what the matter is.

"I'll be back in a sec. I was just checking how much longer it would be for the food," David tells Johnny.

The waitress asks, "You want a burger and fries?"

"Yes, that's it," David tells her.

"Give me five minutes."

"What happened to your order?" Johnny asks.

"They gave it to someone else or something.
Phone orders, you know how they go. Speaking of
going, I'd better hit the restroom while I'm here."

Veronica makes a quizzical face at Johnny from
the booth. Johnny, as he leans against the counter, shrugs
and shakes his head in response. David returns from the
restroom. The waitress holds the grease-stained brown
paper bag out for David. Order's up. David gives his
thanks, and payment, and tells Johnny he'd better motor
to his aunt's.

"No worries. Glad to run into you here. Hope
your aunt gets better soon."

"Thanks, Johnny." David turns to leave.

"I'll have to PreyOnMe," Johnny adds.

David stops.

"Did I say PreyOnMe? I meant pray on it."

"Young Jonathan, are you… you're not…?"

"What if I am?"

"How could you do that? How could you test
me?" David questions.

"How could I test you? How could you fail?"

"Young Jonathan, I don't like the fact that you
are testing me."

"Well, I don't like the fact you were about to go
have sex with a complete stranger."

"Testing me. That's really horrible, Johnny.
How could you do that? Where is the trust? I don't think
I like this. I have to go."

"Wait," Johnny extends. David does not turn

around. "David, wait," Johnny extends once more with feeling. David about-faces to meet Johnny. David's face meets the flat of Johnny's right hand. David's world spins. More accurately, the Poisoned Ivy Bar and Grill spins, or seems to spin, as David's head whips right from the impact.

"It stings!" Johnny cries as he massages his right hand with his left one. "They don't show you that in the movies."

David regains his composure. He stands in front of Johnny again and presents the right side of his face to Johnny. "Care to try the other side?"

"You're only asking because you know it hurt me more than it hurt you, proving once and for all that the 'turn the other cheek' motto is nonsense. You'd never really turn the other cheek if you didn't get some sick kind of self-satisfaction out of it."

David shakes his head in response.

Johnny replies, "On that note…" Johnny leads with his left elbow, whips his forearm up and back, flicks his wrist, thrusts elbow, forearm, and finally wrist forward and, *Smack*!

"Much better!" Johnny chimes.

13 JUST WRONG

David successfully turns the tables on Johnny and makes him feel as if he is the one in the wrong. Over the next few days they address the issues at hand, or the issue at hand, because apparently David's wanton behavior is not an issue. Rather, the issue is Johnny's mistrust of David. They decide to work things out, let the past be the past, and move forward. Johnny vows to forgive David, however he makes no mention of forgetting.

Another month of uncertainty regarding David's fidelity is all Johnny can take. Johnny's inner voice incessantly pesters him and tells him David cheats. The voice grows so loud it starts to seem audible in the real world, like someone else talks to Johnny and tells Johnny to beware of what David is up to. While Veronica warns Johnny not to trust David after the last incident, this voice is one that is not hers. It is definitely from within and, at its persistence, Johnny addresses the issues with David once again by creating yet another online persona.

Welcome the ever-so-explicit Hard4now. Completely driven, Johnny doesn't merely go to any online hookup site, he goes to one which specializes in extreme fetishes. At Veronica's apartment, his new persona approaches people whose profiles list interests in bondage and scat. While he weeds through the undesirables, a.k.a. those who are too short, tall, fat, thin, and / or old, he receives messages from a few members he needs to block because he can tell they will not be a good match for David. He needs to find someone who is good looking but who also has a hardcore kinky streak.

When someone's screen name is "BrownUrChest" that can pretty much mean only one thing, or so Johnny prays. He messages BrownUrChest and asks not only what he's up to, but also what he's into. BrownUrChest responds that he is into scat. Not knowing what the terminology is for those into scat, Johnny has to find out if he likes to do it on others, or if he likes others doing it to him. BrownUrChest explains that, as per his screen name, he likes doing it to others, on their chest. Johnny tells him he's never done it before but he really wants to try it; he's fantasized about it for years and it is about time the fantasy comes true. Johnny details how he's discreet, in the closet, good-looking, can travel, and would love for BrownUrChest to sit on his chest while being serviced and then, as he's being serviced, have him do his thing on Johnny's chest while holding Johnny's hands behind his head. Johnny explains he wants to be dominated and used, to which BrownUrChest eloquently replies, "Hot."

Now that BrownUrChest is in, Johnny must get David on board a.s.a.p. He messages David, who of course is online, still as FatherFigure, and, not surprisingly, gets him to agree to a meeting tonight. The back and forth between David and Johnny and BrownUrChest and Johnny isn't nearly as confusing or hectic as Johnny imagined. Johnny gets the whereabouts of BrownUrChest and gives them to David. Johnny gives the description of David and what he's wearing to BrownUrChest. The meeting time and place is set for tonight in about forty minutes at a location which is pretty much equidistant between the two of them.

Before logging himself, or rather Johnny's new persona, offline, he makes sure to confirm with BrownUrChest that he will release his bowels on David's chest. Johnny asks him to not let him know when he is going to do it either. He just wants him to do it. Johnny explains if he lets him know he may chicken out, and since he's been fantasizing about a hot guy doing this on his chest for so long he doesn't want to sabotage this opportunity.

BrownUrChest reassures Johnny he will not get off him until he has fulfilled the obligations inherent in his name, and namely shat on his chest. Johnny tells him he can't wait. And this is the honest truth, Johnny simply cannot wait. That's what David gets for shitting on Johnny, figuratively speaking.

"Johnny," Veronica stands in shock, "I can't believe you are really going through with this. It's kind of…"

"Smart? Inventive? Karmic?"

"Gross."

"It's up to David to go through with it or not. He told me to trust him. This is on him now."

"Yeah," Veronica adds, "but he has no idea what'll be on him later."

"Gives new meaning to 'holy shit' now doesn't it?"

"Holy shit, indeed."

***

Although Johnny doesn't find out what exactly happens, he has a pretty good hunch, because at night he finds David in the worst mood ever. "What's the matter?" Johnny inquires.

"I don't want to talk about it."

"David," Johnny responds with feigned sincerity, "I used to tell you everything. People used to share their deepest, darkest, most inner secrets with you on a daily basis, and you can't tell me what's wrong?"

"I just had a shitty day."

Don't laugh, Johnny tells himself.

David continues, "I need to reevaluate my priorities, get my life in order a bit. This sheep seems to have lost its way from the herd."

"Sounds like a good plan. You still need a job last I checked."

"Yes, I know. I was actually thinking, since I'm having quite the difficult time finding employment, perhaps I should see about something more... humbling."

"Humbling?"

"Yes. Still a job, but more a job than a career."

Johnny's response is an inquisitive look at David.

David continues, "There's this business that I keep seeing when I'm outside and I, at first, would never entertain it as a field of opportunity for me. But then, earlier this week, I saw a *Help Wanted* sign in its window. I thought it might be a sign."

"You thought the sign was a sign?"

"You make it sound stupid."

"No, I'm just asking for clarification," Johnny states in a way that makes it hard for David to discern whether he is being earnest or derisive.

"Yes, I thought the sign was a sign. A sign from God," David adds for clarification.

"Did he have nice handwriting?"

"Did who have nice handwriting?"

"God. If God's sign is a sign I'd expect it to be amazing. Flowing cursive, luscious loops,…"

"You *are* mocking me."

"Anyway, tell me more. Where was this sign of which you speak?"

"I'm not telling you anything if you can't be serious."

"I promise I'll be serious," Johnny pledges. He presses his right hand against his heart and holds his left palm outward and flat to signal his sincerity.

"It was in, or on, an ice cream truck."

Some moments of silence pass. Johnny's face registers several thoughts and emotions. First, confusion, as per the lowered left eyebrow, the slight squint in the eye, and the crinkled space between his eyebrows. Next, shock, as evidenced by the shift in the mouth, lips parted, lower jaw lowered, and eyes opened wider. Finally, poise. Johnny closes his mouth, stands up straighter, and takes a deep breath.

"What's with the reaction? You look as if you've seen a ghost," David addresses Johnny.

"It's just unexpected." Johnny's mind reels. He searches for the right response. "I just never really saw you as an ice cream truck kind of guy."

"It wouldn't be my life, or my career, but it would be a good way to make some money. It wouldn't even have to be on my resume or anything. I'm sure it's off the books. And it would be kind of nice to see all those happy faces. Who isn't happy when they get ice cream?"

"So, a former priest, excommunicated for having… relations… in the confessional, is going to roll around town in an ice cream truck and serve ice cream to kids. Are you just trying to get on Megan's list?"

"I thought you were going to be serious."

"I am."

"We both know I needed a job and the people on the truck were so nice and welcoming, I thought what a great opportunity, even if it's just for the time being."

"What people on the truck? I figured," Johnny wants to say *hoped*, "it would just be one person on the truck plus you."

"This nice couple who own the truck. Barbara and John, great people. They said they were looking for an extra set of hands on board, since it helps keep the lines down when they are busy. I was inside and everything and those trucks are roomier than you would think by looking at them."

"It sounds like you've done more than think about taking that job."

"I just didn't know what you'd think of me working on an ice cream truck."

"What will happen come winter?"

"This is not a permanent stop, Johnny. Hopefully, I'll have a better job soon. For now, though, it's something."

"It is… something. When do you begin?"

"Tomorrow."

"Congratulations," Johnny envelops David in his arms. Unbeknownst to David, Johnny's face conveys his angst. A series of questions unfurls in Johnny's mind. *Why are they involved? What do they want with David? Are they trying to get to me? Is this about me?* Johnny's arms no longer hold David, instead they hang loosely around him. David notices the limpness of the arms, the dead weight they put on him, and frees himself from the hug's remnants. Chimes distract him from his thoughts. The ice cream truck is on the block, David realizes. Johnny stiffens as the same realization trickles up his spine.

"They're here!" David exclaims.

"By coincidence or on purpose?"

"On purpose, of course. I knew I would tell you by now, and so I asked them to come over to meet us at home. It's the right thing to do, don't you think?"

"I don't see how what I think has any impact on the situation now that you already invited them."

"You don't want them here? You don't even know them yet."

If only that were true, Johnny thinks.

"We're here!" chime Barbara and John before the doorbell begins to ring. It rings, only to re-announce their arrival.

Driven by anger, Johnny goes to the door. Barbara and John wave wildly on the other side of the screen. "Hi there," they beckon, "you must be this Young Jonathan we've heard so much about."

Johnny winces. *You very well know exactly who I am*, he thinks.

"Exactly who Young Jonathan is, Barbara, we don't know," admits John.

"Oh, but, Little Lamb, we'd love to find out," adds Barbara.

Johnny reddens with anger.

"You look flush, Little Lamb. Are you okay?" inquires Barbara.

David, behind Jonathan, moves in and pushes the door open for Barbara and John. "Jonathan, where are your manners?" David directs, "Come on in. Barbara, John, this here is Young Jonathan."

"Pleased to make your acquaintance, Young Jonathan," they say in unison.

"Likewise."

"Let's have a seat in the living area," David directs.

Barbara approaches Johnny for a closer look at his face. "My," she extends an arm toward Johnny's face, "you seem familiar. Might we have met before?"

She can't do this, Johnny thinks.

"Now that you mention it, Barbara, this young man definitely seems familiar," John adds. He rubs his chin for a pensive effect.

Johnny muses, *Fine, you want to tell him how you know me, more power to you. You'll be the ones who look crazy, not me, which is the only reason I haven't told him.*

"I know this sounds crazy, but I really do think I know this young man. Where, oh where, oh where have I seen him though?" Barbara beats her foot against the floor to create a rhythm with her question. "Oh, I know!" she exclaims. "Yes, you're the ice cream sandwich! Isn't that funny, I picture you as a giant ice cream sandwich right now, which you're not, of course."

"No, he's not an ice cream sandwich," adds John. "If he were, we'd have to eat him!" He feigns three large air chomps.

Kind of disturbing, Johnny assesses.

"That must be where you know me from. It's hard to resist the occasional ice cream sandwich," Johnny admits. David watches the interaction, completely unsuspecting.

David rings in, "Isn't it just the best? A simple ice cream cone, sandwich, or what have you, can bring people together. Good people, no less."

"Peachy," adds Johnny.

"Peach ice creamy," add Barbara and John simultaneously.

David's expression mirrors the sentiment he offers, "You two are so similar, you must be related in some way."

"Nope," John replies, "we are just bringing goodness to the masses."

"Doing God's work, if you will," Barbara tops.

David blushes at the mention of "God's work," turns away and offers, "Would anyone like a cold beverage?"

"I'd love a soda pop," Barbara replies.

John adds, "Sure, count me in for one as well."

"Anything for you, Johnny?"

"I'm all right."

David absconds to retrieve the beverages. Barbara turns to Johnny and pinches his cheek. "Eat you up!" Johnny pulls away from her pinch. He rubs his cheek as if her touch dirties him.

"Little Lamb," John begins, "is all copacetic in the house that Johnny built?"

"All is not copacetic in the house that Johnny built and I think you two are very well aware all is not... copacetic."

"It is now, and that's why we're here. David has employment, a sense of purpose. Isn't that what you wanted?" Barbara queries.

"That's not what I wanted."

"That's not what you wanted?" Barbara asks.

"That's not what he wanted?" John whispers.

"Well, yes, that's not what I wanted."

"The boy is confused," Barbara directs to John.

"Assuredly confused."

"I'm not confused. I wanted David to find employment, yes."

"And he has employment, no?" John queries.

"No," Johnny answers.

"No?" Barbara queries.

"Well, yes, but I didn't want him to work in an ice cream truck."

"David's too good to work in an ice cream truck. The lamb has a point," Barbara mocks agreement.

"Yes, David is too good to lower himself to such

depths," John verbally agrees, while his face says otherwise.

"You know, dear," Barbara moves in toward Johnny, "you are the reason why he has to work in an ice cream truck."

"Be more specific. Tell him," John urges.

"You are the reason," Barbara continues, "David has fallen on hard times. Your little conquest. Had it not been for that, he would likely remain a man of the cloth. Instead, he's fallen from good graces."

"Me?" Johnny rages in a whisper. "My fault?"

"Your fault," John abruptly responds.

Barbara leans in to cock her head left, right, and left again to emphasize the three words she quickly adds, "All your fault."

"You all," he motions to the two before him, "came to me. You all," he motions again, "told me I had a limited amount of time left. You all," Johnny jumps up and down like a small child throwing a tantrum, "made me what I am."

"We saved you," John remarks.

"Did not!"

"Did too."

"Children," Barbara intervenes. "Let's not behave like children. Johnny, we did save you. As for why you'd think otherwise, I haven't the foggiest."

"Saved? You destroyed! You don't tell someone they are going to die."

"Did you think you were going to live forever? Sweetie," Barbara condoles, "there are no such things as vampires."

"I didn't think I was going to live forever but I

didn't need to know when I was going to die."

"Then why did you ask?" John questions.

Johnny scours the recesses of his memory in search of the answer. "I don't know," he responds. "The heat of the moment?"

"See, Lamb," Barbara condoles, "we only answered because you asked. Quite pointedly, too."

"We didn't destroy anything," John adds, "we simply gave you information. What you chose to do with it was your own doing."

"Here we go," David announces as he moves in with his guests' beverages. So what's the topic of conversation we are up to?"

"Well," Barbara begins, a sparkle in her eye, "since you asked, we were discussing the wildest thing. If someone said to you, I can tell you the exact day you will die, would you want to know?"

David crinkles his nose. He replies, "That's somewhat morbid."

"What do you think?" Johnny asks David.

"I think it's a morbid topic, can we switch subjects?"

"Surely. Let's talk about lighter, fluffier things," John enlivens.

"How about we discuss the field of ice cream purveying?" Johnny suggests.

"That's a tad offensive, Young Jonathan. I wouldn't call it light and fluffy. It's a career. It's a life choice."

"Would you say it's a career?" Johnny directs to the two guests.

"Well," John responds, "I would wholeheartedly call it a life choice. Everything in life that happens is about a choice. One must be careful not just what they wish for, but what choices they make. Every decision, no matter how innocuous or monumental, impacts one's life as much as one's life, no matter how innocuous or monumental, impacts one's decisions. Johnny, what life choices have you made? What do you do for a living?"

"I work at a diner."

"Talk about light and fluffy!" Barbara exclaims as she slaps her thigh. "Diners serve the lightest, fluffiest ice cream anywhere."

"Pancakes, Barbara," John remarks.

"Oh?"

"Pancakes. Diners have light and fluffy pancakes. Well, not all diners, but most. You're thinking pancakes, not ice cream."

"You can take the girl out of the ice cream truck, but you can't take the creamy white goodness out of the girl," Barbara offers.

Johnny winces. *Gross visual*, he thinks.

"I digress!" Barbara continues, "You work at a diner, how very nice. Another person who likes to serve the public, just like us."

"I wouldn't say 'just like us,' Barbara, Johnny is a bit younger. He has his whole life ahead of him. We are relics in comparison. We, on the other hand, are older. But we do have open roads ahead. Roads paved with people craving cold candy confections."

"Speaking of which," Barbara adds, "tomorrow is David's first day on the truck with us. How exciting! I remember my first time like it was only yesterday."

"Tell me about it please, so I know what to expect."

"It's quite endearing," John offers.

"Yes," Barbara affirms, "Yes, it is. First you're driving down the street on a sunny day. You look to the sky and admire all the fluffy cotton candy clouds which appear to suspend there against the bright blue sky, just for your enjoyment. Then, you listen to the call of the birds. Tweet, tweet. Tweet, tweet, they call." Barbara searches left and right, for effect. "Where are you, little birds? I hear your calls but do not... oh, there you are. And you spy with your little eye the winged ones. They perch themselves on tree branches, balustrades, phone poles... It just takes a while to see them, to actually... see them. You realize it would be rude to not reply to them. You commence the distinct call of the ice cream truck. The call reaches the birds, and it also reaches everyone else. Children and adults, both young and old, all delight in the sound of the ice cream truck. The call liberates the child in each and every single one of us. It makes even the most jaded feel childish again. Exuberant. Gleeful. AhhhHHHH!" She ends on a high note and extends her arm upwards as if she elevates the people she speaks about to a higher level.

She's nuts, Johnny judges.

"Isn't this one just the most special? Such passion you have, Barbara. I am sure that, by your side, my days will be most splendiferous."

"Trust me, they will," John adds. "With Barbara along for the ride, every day's a treat."

"Speaking of every day being a treat, I have to be at the diner early in the morning, so if you don't mind, I have to get to bed."

"It is getting late," John concurs. He pats Barbara on the knee, a signal they should go. They both rise. "We shall part ways until tomorrow. Rest up for one of the best rides of your life."

"Will do," David replies as he opens the door for Barbara and John. "Thank you both for coming!"

"Our pleasure," Barbara replies. "Believe me," she makes eye contact with Johnny, "our pleasure completely."

Charlie Casso

14 BRUISED PEACH

Johnny blinks the foggy sleep from his eyes. He makes out 4:16 on the alarm clock. He lumbers himself out of bed and makes it to the clock to depress the alarm's off button before the time changes to 4:17. Unusual time to set one's alarm, he's well aware, but he prefers the oddity of his wake up times.

He pads his way to the restroom, washes the sleep from his face, brushes his teeth, and moisturizes. *After all*, he reminds himself, *moisture is the difference between a grape and a raisin*. He pads over to his small stack of clothes for the day and dresses himself in the standard black pants, polo shirt, and sneakers that work necessitates. He opens the front door and lets himself out into the remnants of night, the pale quiet time that buffers the night owls from the early birds.

Johnny traipses toward work with a mind mostly void of thought. It's too early to ponder much. A recollection occurs to him, however. He hears Barbara's voice repeat, "Our pleasure, our pleasure completely."

He wonders, *Why it is their pleasure to visit me? What is the purpose of their visits? Why do they invade the personal space I call my life? Is it to remind me of the limited amount of time I have left to live? Likely not, since they didn't mention it at all last night.*

He taps a key against the glass pane of the diner's door to get the attention of the manager on duty. He's let in with a low groan of "morning" from the manager. Johnny readies the diner for the day ahead while Barbara's voice still echoes in his head. He wonders, *Is it all to give me direction in life? I've always had direction, but has it been the wrong direction? But if you're traveling the wrong way on a one-way street, you're still getting somewhere. Yes, but there'll be accidents, pile-ups even. But maybe there wouldn't be; sometimes a street is empty. If the street's empty and one travels on it the wrong way, might they not get to their destination quicker, maybe even more efficiently? Have I been traveling on the wrong road? Going the wrong direction? Headed into a pile-up? Or getting to where I'm supposed to be, but getting there quicker? Why aren't they telling me what to do? Why aren't they giving me some direction? Is it only because of Sister Petunia that they visit me and that I'm aware of what I'm aware of, or would I have been visited regardless? Why must I examine my life like this when the sun has yet to rise and the even the birds remain at rest?*

Johnny dutifully polishes, scrubs, and sweeps. His routine is so engrained in him he works with precision and diligence although his mind meanders far away. *David begins work today, with them. Are they going to tell him who they really are and why they're here? Seems unlikely, but so does meeting them in the first place. I have only so much time left and here I am, stuck in a rut. Are they going to drive me crazy or drive me toward a goal or something?*

A tapping on the door breaks Johnny from his thoughts. He turns to see what patron wants to come in for the first coffee of the day. It never astonishes him how routine people can be. It's five o'clock in the morning, time for the diner to open, and someone's already at the door. He discerns the outlines of two figures. He imagines they are the figures of Barbara and John. *That can't be them*, he tells himself and walks over to unlock the door.

"Good morn…" he begins to welcome but draws the last word to a stop right in the middle when he realizes they are, in fact, the figures of Barbara and John.

"Good morn to you too, kind sir," John remarks.

"Good morn, yes, good morn, it sounds so very regal," Barbara quips.

Give it a rest, Johnny thinks.

"You have a nice rest last night, young one?" John asks.

"It was undisturbed, if that's what you mean. No weird occurrences, no strangers invading my dreams or my space. So, yes, it was nice."

"Is that harshness we hear?" Barbara asks John.

"Why, I can't tell. My ears hear it, but my heart does not believe it. Why would one speak harshly to another?"

"Yes, why? Why, Little Lamb, why speak to us with such a tone? Have we done you wrong?"

"Do we do you wrong? Do you want to slap

us?" John asks.

"No, I don't want to slap you."

"Talk about slaps, that slap you gave to David, Little Lamb… it nearly deafened all the angels from here to Palo Alto."

"Palo Alto? That's oddly specific," Johnny remarks.

John explains, "She just likes saying Palo Alto. Sometimes she repeats Palo Alto over and over to see how many times she can say it without getting tongue-tied."

"One hundred and forty-nine, my all-time record," Barbara confesses. She beams with pride. "Palo Alto," she adds.

"Wait, you know about the slap? What?" Johnny questions.

"Ever hear the expression, 'Angels we have heard on high' before?" John asks.

"Of course."

"Well, 'Saints we have heard on higher' just never took off. It doesn't have the same ring, I suppose."

"You're watching me. Why are you watching me?"

"Now, now, young man, don't be so self-centered. We watch lots of people. Don't we, Barbara?"

Barbara responds with, "Hordes."

Johnny asks, "Do you watch whores or hordes?"

"My dear, I said we watch hordes."

"Again, I can't tell which you're saying. Hordes, I'd understand, but I feel you're calling me a whore. I'm not a whore."

"Why would I ever call you a whore?"

"Because of what I did with David back when he was Father Mann."

"Lamb, if that's the verdict you place on yourself for what you've done in the past, please don't put it on us. We watch over people to ensure they are doing their best to lead fruitful, productive lives."

"And if they're not, that's when you get involved?"

"No one said we get involved, but we do watch over people," John admits.

"Like guardian angels?"

"No. There are angels and there are saints, but there are no 'guardian angels' exactly. They're a man-made construct to make people feel better, feel like they're being watched over by a higher power."

"But I thought you two watched over people. Isn't that the same thing?"

"We watch over people but they don't know it."

"That's not true. I know it."

"You may know it, but others wouldn't believe you even if you told them," Barbara adds.

Johnny tries to put the information together, to process it in a way he understands. "So what exactly are you two then, if you watch over people, don't get involved, and aren't guardian angels?"

"We are saints," John admits.

"We are saints, indeed," Barbara confirms.

"But, Johnny, we told you this when we first met. You know we are saints. Barbara and I were very direct and honest with you."

"I do believe he's right, Johnny. If we weren't watching you, we'd think you had suffered a head trauma to forget who we are." She extends her arm and caresses Johnny's temple with her fingertips. He sways back an inch or so, just enough so air moves between his head and her fingertips. Barbara notices and frowns.

"Why the long face, Sugar Plum?" breaks the privacy of their hushed conversation. Rose touches Barbara's elbow and offers, "Come, let's get you settled in a booth. Maybe some coffee running through your veins will perk you up." Rose shows Barbara and John to a booth.

"That's so kind of you. Thank you," Barbara remarks.

"Be right back with two coffees, figure out what you wanna eat," she directs as she slides two menus on the table.

Rose pivots around, retrieves two mugs and saucers, and asks Johnny, "Hey, you know those two over there?" She nods in the direction of Barbara and John.

"I've seen them around."

"Never seen 'em before. Nice polite people to be up so early. Usually it takes a few hours for manners to set in."

"Yeah, I guess. I don't know. Maybe they're from out of town?"

"You just said you seen 'em around. How can they be from outta town if you seen 'em around?"

"Extended stay?" Johnny attempts a sincere look, a slight smile broadens his face.

"Glad to see you smiling, Peaches. Sometimes you just look so... so... bruised. Sometimes you're my bruised peach, that's what you are. And you're too young a peach to be a bruised peach." She pinches Johnny's cheek. "You think you got it bad," she empathizes, "working here every day, mopping up ketchup, scrubbing the toilet, making your hands raw from all the chemicals you use to clean this place. Over and over you do the same thing because it never stays the way you make it. It always gets dirty again. It's the nature of the beast, Peaches, the nature of the beast. Don't let it get to you though. I'm too old to be slinging hash and taking orders from people I don't know. Peach, I don't take orders from people I *do* know. You realize how hard this is for me? But I do it. Believe me when I tell you this, and you better believe me, I'm older, and with age comes wisdom. And saggy tits. But wisdom's what I'm going for here. Believe me, you might think you got it rough but smile through it. Fake it till you make it, Peaches. But until then, go wipe down their table for 'em."

Johnny grabs his rag and plods over to the booth. Barbara and John look at Johnny expectantly. "Just cleaning the table," he offers. He makes circular motions with the rag on the table's surface.

"You didn't suffer a head trauma, did you?" John asks.

"No."

"Not on our watch," Barbara prides.

"Still confused." He looks over his shoulder to make sure Rose is not within earshot. "So, it's a no to guardian angels, but a yes to saints. It's just you act like guardian angels, or at least what they are supposed to act like." He moves the rag to a different section of the table.

Barbara looks up from her menu. "Lamb, people get so confused about us, we can't blame you. It's like the whole Saint Valentine debacle."

John adds, "To take Saint Valentine and call him Cupid, and assign him a baby's face... It's all such nonsense. So what, the guy likes to have a little fun with people and their love lives. That's no reason to change his name and appearance."

"Right? And this fictitious Cupid person gets all the credit while Saint Valentine's name lies in obscurity eleven months out of the year. It's not right," Barbara offers. "And he's not that cute. He has fangs." She clutches the sides of the open menu in front of her.

"He doesn't have fangs and you know it. He has sharp incisors."

"Same difference."

"Anyway, we understand your confusion. We, as saints, only interact with you in dire circumstances."

"But you've been interacting with me a lot lately."

"Things are a lot dire for you," John admits. He closes his menu.

"Truer words were never spoken," Johnny concedes. He fists the rag as Rose approaches with the two coffees in hand.

"Decided?" Rose asks.

Johnny plods away while Rose takes the first of many orders of the day. *Things are a lot dire for me*, he thinks, *at least I'm not the only one to notice*.

***

"They certainly love their pancakes," Rose comments to Johnny. "Ordered 5 different types of pancakes between the two of 'em."

Customers drip in from the darkness outside. A general bustle enlivens the diner the more crowded it gets. Before Johnny realizes it, Barbara and John exit through the front door, not a trace of pancake left on any of their plates. He watches as they disappear from the view the windows provide.

"Sugar Peach, get under those tables over there," Rose directs Johnny, as he sheepishly resumes work. "And smile, Sugar, it's a new day," she adds.

Johnny brings his broom over to clean, as Rose directed, and jars with a new thought. He reaches down under the table, grabs at thin air, and shuffles toward the door. "One of them dropped a wallet," he exclaims, "I'll be right back!" He runs out of the diner and to the right, in the same direction Barbara and John had gone. He runs for a good fifty feet and realizes they are nowhere to be seen ahead of him. *How the devil did they disappear so quickly?* He stands stock still for a moment, exhales a defeated sigh, and pivots to face the direction from which he came.

"Looking for us?" Barbara surmises.

Johnny startles back. His hand jumps to his chest. "You left your wallet," he offers his right hand and realizes there is no wallet. "Nevermind. There was no wallet. I just needed an excuse to get out of there to speak with you. I need more."

"You need more what?" John asks.

Johnny responds with silence and punctuates his response with a lack of any movement on his part.

"You need more what?" John repeats.

More silence. Johnny's hands completely rest down at his sides. His shoulders slump a bit. His eyes linger down toward the floor.

"I…"

"You can tell us," Barbara offers.

"Don't…. know." More silence passes. "I followed you out here for answers but I don't know what the questions are." He takes a moment to consider. "You said things are dire for me, and I know they are. Yes, I've probably made them that way myself, but, if there's no way of changing what's going to happen, if I'm still going to go when you said I will, well, why shouldn't I do what I want to do?"

It's Barbara and John's turn to respond with silence.

"Is this your way of telling me I should do what I want to do?"

More silence.

"I guess I have been doing what I've wanted to do," Johnny realizes. "Well," he adds, "I haven't been doing everything I've wanted to do. But I'm going to. And now that I know you two can't stop me, well… things are going to get interesting." Johnny's head bobs ever so slowly and slightly up and down. "Very interesting." He walks forward, right between his two companions, toward the diner.

Barbara and John pivot their bodies and watch Johnny make his way back to work. "That boy is in for a world full of hurt," Barbara confesses.

John nods his head in agreement with the accuracy of Barbara's appraisal. "I couldn't have said it better myself."

Charlie Casso

15 HIATUS

"And have yourself a creamy day, young lady," David offers as he waves goodbye to yet another friendly patron. The young lady walks away, ice cream cone in hand, as her honey colored pigtails sway at her shoulders in stride with the bounce in her step.

He turns to Barbara, "These customers are delicious. Each one is more pleasant and bursting with life than the next. It's amazing the personalities that are attracted to ice cream. I haven't seen a single disgruntled customer yet."

"What you're attracted to is often a reflection of who you are. Sweet people, sweet things. It's that simple."

"Interesting," David muses, "I always think one looks for what complements them, what makes them complete."

"According to your calculations, then, a disgruntled person, as you put it, is one who would seek out the completing nature of ice cream as it would offset their… disgruntledness."

"Precisely."

"That's not accurate. You are what you eat. The phrase might be trite, but it is accurate."

"Hi there," beams a young lad from about a foot below the truck's window.

"What can I get you, little one?" David inquires.

"Vanilla cone, please," the little one responds with an ear-to-ear smile.

"See what I mean?" Barbara prods David.

David lowers the cone down to the little one and retrieves the two dollars the child holds in the air. "Be careful with that; it's gonna melt out there."

"Okay, mister," the little one licks his cone in agreement and skips away.

"I see what you mean," David gives in to Barbara. "Johnny, then, he's a reflection of me. He doesn't complement me?"

"David, I barely know Johnny at all. Why, you and I met only days ago. I can't judge whether he's a reflection of you or if he completes you in any way. That's for you to do."

"What attracts me to him if it isn't that he complements me, completes me, or makes me whole?"

Barbara makes wide eyes at David.

"I'm sure he's not a reflection of me. He's pure of heart. I've done bad things, surely, but not he. He's been the bystander to my devious ways." The ice cream truck sings its siren song while David continues. "Why Johnny?" David stares blankly at the silver ledge of the ice cream truck window. He doesn't notice that three customers gather in front. They wait for a signal to place their orders. Barbara taps David's shoulder and successfully breaks his distant gaze. "Oh, right. My apologies." He offers to the first customer he sees, "How can I help you this fine day?"

***

"You can't break up with me, David. Between the two of us we barely have a pot to piss in or a window to throw it out of."

"Please don't talk to me in such a way, Young Jonathan. Matter of fact, we do have those things you mention. We have both. We have a pot and we have a window."

"Forgive me, Father," Johnny begins with mockery, "*we* may have a window to throw it out of, but only *I* have the pot. The cookware is mine, lest ye forget."

"I assumed the pot referred to a toilet, not cookware."

"How is it I know these things and you don't? Does that even make sense to you, to say a person can throw a toilet out a window? What kind of person would be capable of doing something like that? Toilets are heavy."

"Someone strong, I assumed," admits David.

"No, it's a pot to piss in or a window to throw it out of. A real cookware pot. Because, in olden days, people used to have to go to the bathroom in a pot, before they had toilets. Then, they'd empty its contents out the window."

"Maybe you do complement me after all, Young

Jonathan. You're a reservoir of information, the types of which I have been deprived."

"No, no. You were just breaking up with me. Don't go getting all googly-eyed now. Besides, that was a total tangent. You don't decide to not break up with someone because of a tangent in a conversation."

"You are correct, my smart Young Jonathan."

"If you don't want to be with me, it had better be for a legitimate reason. I'll accept a legitimate reason. I won't accept staying with you, though, because of a tangent in a conversation."

"Fair enough. I had a thought in the ice cream truck today."

Johnny thinks, *There's a sentence no one's ever heard before.*

"I thought, why are we together? You don't complement me."

"I may not compliment you now, but I used to compliment you. I used to compliment you all the time."

"Comp-lah-ment, Young Jonathan. Comp-lah-ment."

"Oh, like an angle."

"That's right, Young Jonathan, like how angles complement each other to create a whole. You and I don't complement each other in a way that creates a whole. I thought further about it. I thought, well, if he doesn't complement me, does he reflect me, does he offer me a version of myself I can be with?"

"Do I reflect you?"

"Not a bit."

Johnny registers the remark.

David explains, "Not a bit in the traditional way.

You reflect me the way a funhouse mirror reflects an individual. You present to me the way I could be given another reality, given different circumstances. And I don't mean externally, I mean internally. You are a good person, for the most part. There was a time I saw that in myself. Now, when I look at you, I see myself in you, but I see myriad others in you as well."

A twitch disturbs Johnny's left eye as his mind reels. He puts his left hand to the side of his face and presses his middle finger against the side of his eye, right where the twitch just made itself known. "You totally made my eye twitch!" David leans against the kitchen counter as Johnny continues. "A funhouse mirror? Really? I'm some distorted, demented version of you? And don't think I didn't catch that *I see myself in you* bit, because, you know what, you're never going to see yourself in me again, at least not in the literal sense."

"I didn't mean funhouse *bad*, I meant funhouse *different*."

"And believe me, I know the myriad others you want to see in me as well- I was at the hotel with you and those skanks in case you forgot. Not happening."

"That's not what I meant, Jonathan."

"It's never what you meant. It's never what you meant, I'm so tired of hearing it."

"You're catching me on semantics."

"Yes, I'm catching you on *some* antics. I think the only part about us breaking up that breaks me up is that you are beating me to the punch. I carried you. Where would you be without me, Father? Seriously, where would you be?"

David stands on his own, without the support of

the counter. He crosses his arms in front of his chest, stares into Johnny's eyes and states, "I'd still be the Father you condescend to call me. I'd remain Father Mann, if it hadn't been for you. That's where I'd be. You deride me for working in an ice cream truck, yet you're the one who derailed me from my vocation."

"Okay, fair point. But still, I support you."

"It's easy to pick up what you are responsible for making fall in the first place."

"Blame, much?" He stares at David to give him time to absorb the realization. "You know something," Johnny continues, "you know that poster you like with that poem on it, the one about the footprints and the sand you like so much? You like it because you associate with it. Except it's not the Lord carrying you, it's me! You're on my back!" He slaps himself on the shoulders for effect.

"I'm not... well, it seems we have a lot to consider. Maybe this wasn't the best time to discuss our situation. Would you be amenable to a hiatus?"

"What does a hiatus entail?"

"A break."

"Oh, Lord," Johnny decries.

"A regular break, nothing extreme. Not a break up where we date other people, merely some time to think about what we value in life, where we want to be, and what we want to do. Would you be amenable to a hiatus of that sort?"

"I guess. I should still break up with you though, if for nothing else than the fact that you were about to break up with me and if there's anyone breaking up with anyone it's going to be me breaking up with you. But fine, a hiatus. Until when?"

"Can we make it open ended?"

Sure, Johnny thinks, *because I have all the time in the world.*

"No," Johnny replies.

"What do you propose then?"

Johnny considers the fact that his time left, at least according to Saint Barbara and Saint John, is quite limited. He acknowledges he will need to either make amends with David or completely separate and move on. But, either way, it needs to be done quickly. "One month," he blurts out as soon as it occurs to him.

"Rather quick, I suppose, but all right, one month it is. A one-month hiatus from all relationship-oriented activities and discussions. One month from today we will convene and debrief regarding our relationship, or lack thereof."

"Awesome," Johnny manages.

16 THE LEG BREAKER

Johnny's chin rests on his hands which flop over the top of his broomstick. He rocks ever so slightly left and right while he conveys his newest woes to Mr. Weatherby, his mostly silent therapist of sorts. Typically, patrons tell bartenders their woes but, unsure of the social mores of janitors and diners, Johnny assumes he can't be too far off the status quo. Rose shakes her head and rolls her eyes as she passes Johnny and sees he shares his life with the one she knows as "the mute". Once she's completely out of earshot, Johnny divulges, "I really think I could get him back into the good graces of the church somehow. I have to. He blames me, whether he admits it or not, for his being excommunicated. I need to fix it then. I blame, and I'll admit it, I do blame Battle-axe Petunia for my lot in life. I'll get to her soon enough, somehow. I just don't know where to start. Isn't excommunication, like, final?"

"Get thee to a bookery, boy," offers Mr. Weatherby.

"Come again?"

"I forgot your generation likely doesn't even know what this is, but I'll give it a try. It's called a library. Get thee to a library."

"You said 'bookery,' not library."

"You don't read much, do you? You with your fancy computers and your…"

"Not that again," Johnny interrupts.

"Go to a library and you'll find out all you need to know about excommunication. Maybe there's a way it can be reversed."

Rose pushes through the doors with plates heaped with food. She delivers them to their respective places, while Mr. Weatherby chomps another bite into his cheeseburger. "It's okay, Peaches, suck up the air conditioning. That's what it's for, so you can stand around and look pretty and not sweat. Me? Hey, Rose can sweat it out, busting her ass." She gives Johnny elevator eyes. "Wanna clean up that two-top over there, or should I just have the next people eat the leftovers off the plates there when they sit down?"

Johnny shakes his head off his hands and back into his work. "Sorry, Rose. A little dazed today. David almost broke up with me."

"Almost? Did ya kill him before he finished?"

"We settled on a hiatus."

"You kids today make things so complicated. You know what a hiatus is?" She does not give Johnny even a moment to answer. "It's a break up. How can I put this delicately? It's a pussy way of saying break up."

Mr. Weatherby bows his head down further into the cheeseburger he grips a few inches above his plate.

He watches Rose through the corners of his eyes.

Rose continues, "You kids today, instead of breaking up you say you're taking a break and thinking things out. Think this!" She uses her right arm to push up her breasts. "Take a break? Let a man tell me he wants to take a break. I'll give him a break: I'll break his legs. Both of 'em! Then he can take all the time he wants to figure things out, like how much he misses me, and how much he misses the use of his legs. But you kids today. I tell ya, it's a whole different generation. This one over here," she motions toward Mr. Weatherby, "even he'd agree. Cheeseburger's good right?" She smiles at him. "Peach, wake up. I say this because, I was gonna say I love ya but well, I really don't know ya that well, so I say this 'cause, just 'cause I can't mind my own business I guess. He's gonna distance himself from ya. He's done, he just doesn't want you gone yet. He wants to get used to you *being* gone. If I were you, I'd scram. I'd also cut my hair, but I'd scram too."

"Thanks for the advice, Rose. Sometimes it's hard to hear, but you're probably right."

"And thank you, Peaches."

"Thank me? For what?"

"For cleaning that two-top over there."

"But I didn't…"

"That's right you didn't, what are we gonna chit-chat all day over here? Let's go, Sugar Peach, shake the fuzz off." Rose retreats to deliver ketchup to needy diners.

Johnny swings past Mr. Weatherby toward the dirty two-top when he hears Mr. Weatherby confess, "That woman intimidates me."

111

We can all be intimidating, Johnny thinks.

17 UN-EXCOMMUNICATION INFORMATION, PLEASE

Johnny and Veronica walk toward the Public Library as Johnny leafs through his wallet and rattles off the forms of identification he has brought with him in order to attain a library card.

"You might not even need one. I'd imagine what you'll need will be mostly reference material, and they aren't going to let you walk out with reference material. I brought change for photocopies if you need."

Johnny pulls the door open for Veronica who enters before him. The ice-cold air hits them and evokes goose bumps along their arms.

"Let's see what they…" Johnny begins.

"Shhh, inside voice," Veronica hushes.

"Let's see what they have," Johnny whispers. "Where do we start?"

Veronica, in lieu of a verbal answer, walks to the information desk planted square in the center of the floor. The bespectacled purveyor of information seems both pleased to have a visitor in search of knowledge and nonplussed at the same time.

"What's wrong?" Veronica asks the person who mans the information desk.

"The question is too general, miss. What's wrong with what?"

"Your face."

"Ronnie!" Johnny remarks.

"Shhh," the library visitors resound.

The informant, Veronica and Johnny decide to call him, purses his lips in response to Veronica's accusation. "There's nothing wrong with my face, miss."

"I meant you look confused."

"I'm the information desk, clearly I'm not confused. You've come to the information desk. If one of us here is confused it's clearly you."

"Ronnie, drop it, please. We need info," Johnny admits.

"We do need info, Mr... Informant. Can we call you that?"

"If you must."

"Let's start small. Why'd you look confused?"

"Ronnie, drop it," Johnny pleads in a whisper.

"I typically don't get information requests from your age group. Your age group typically doesn't set foot in the library, to be honest."

"Leave it to us to stand out from the rest, I guess. Well, now that that's settled, we really do need your help, Mr. Informant. We need to know if a person who has been excommunicated from the Catholic Church can be un-excommunicated. I'm not even sure if that's a word, but you know what I mean. We need a real answer, too, not a guess or whatnot, but a good, reliable answer. Please say you can help us."

"I can help you," answers the informant. "I'm not winging it here, so you know. I hold the much coveted, yet vastly underrated, Master of Library and Information Science degree. I can help you find the answers to almost anything your heart desires." He blinks at Veronica and Johnny and waits for their reply.

"Just the un-excommunication information, please," Veronica urges.

"But that's amazing about your degree, congratulations. Your folks must be very proud of you," Johnny chimes lowly.

"I'll tell them that when I go home today," Mr. Informant replies as he reads Johnny's face. "Yes, I still live at home, young man. And, before you say anything, yes, I'm a little old to live at home, but that's the price you pay for securing a Master of Library and Information Science degree. Literally, that's the price you pay. I couldn't afford the degree and to live on my own. Baby steps."

"There's nothing wrong with that," Johnny reassures. *This guy has issues*, Johnny thinks. "And remember, don't elephants gestate for like nine years or something? Imagine how long those baby steps take."

"Johnny, baby elephants walk as soon as they are born," Veronica offers.

"You're thinking deer."

"You're thinking fawn."

"I'm thinking Bambi, to be honest, call it what you want."

"Anyway," Mr. Informant interjects, "let's see what we find regarding your request." He strikes away at his keyboard. He peers over his glasses and strikes the keys a few more times. "Sweet Mama Cass!" He looks back and forth between Veronica and Johnny. "I'm going to set you two up on a computer with a list of the references you need to consult. You will find all the answers you need. Should you require printouts, each computer is attached to a printer which accepts credit and debit cards for your convenience." He takes a printout from his printer and walks around his desk to show Veronica and Johnny to their station.

Moments later, they are set up with a list of resources literally at their fingertips. Veronica mans, or *womans*, the keyboard while Johnny looms over her shoulder. "Go to the next one," he directs, "this one's too general." She peers up at him over her shoulder.

"I can feel you breathing down my neck, Johnny."

"You don't need to be dramatic."

"I'm not. I really feel you breathing down my neck. You're making me sticky with your hot breath."

"My breath's not hot enough to make…"

Johnny's sentence finds itself interrupted by the "Shhh" that choruses from the library visitors.

He continues in a breathy whisper, "My breath's not hot enough to make your neck sticky, you drama queen."

Veronica swerves her neck away from Johnny. She hushes, "Ick, that's even worse, it's like you're spraying me with humidity. Back off a second, or at least tilt your head away from me while you breathe. Breathe through your nose, pretend you're having oral sex or something." Across from Veronica, an older gentleman at his computer gawks at her with something between a grimace and a smile on his face. "I know what you're thinking, old man, and it's not gonna happen." He jerks his head back to his computer screen.

"That's the one," Johnny enlivens. He points toward a line on the screen. He reads, "'Excommunication is resolved upon repentance.' Print this screen, Ronnie, this is what we need. Repentance must be a long process, but let's find out what it entails."

"Good spotting, Johnny. I was distracted by the horny man across from me. I think he's looking at porn." The man looks at Veronica. "Hey, keep your hands where I can see them, playboy."

"Well, I never," the older man grumbles.

"You look like you have, though."

"Ronnie, just print. Please," Johnny pleads.

Johnny retrieves the printouts and he and Veronica relocate to a clean, empty table in the center of the library. He spreads the pages out on the table while they take a closer look at the paragraph headings on each sheet. They scan through the titles: *Excommunication in the Catholic Church, Communion and Excommunication, Ecclesiastical Office and Excommunication*, and finally *Excommunication and Absolution*.

"Excommunication and Absolution," Johnny reads aloud. "This is it. He needs absolution. Let's see how he can get absolved and if he can secure his position in the church again."

"Are you sure you'd really want him back

there?" Veronica asks.

"He blames me, Ronnie. I'll fix what he claims I broke. But, if, no I take that back, *when* I fix what he thinks I broke I'm going to make sure I'm not the only one to fix what they broke."

"What does that even mean? Who else broke something?"

"Ronnie, what's black and white and red all over?"

"A newspaper," Veronica responds.

"Good answer. Not the one I was looking for, but a good answer nonetheless. I'm glad you said that. This way you won't ever be seen as an accomplice."

"An accomplice to what?"

"Exactly." Johnny takes the papers, folds them into a neat little rectangle, and pockets them. He nods in the direction of the exit, and he and Veronica gather their belongings to leave. As he pushes the door open, Johnny turns to Veronica and intimates, "Forget I said anything. Seriously, forget I said a word."

18 BLOOD ON A ROSE

Johnny lays the single yellow rose and the single red rose across the papers that rest on the dining room table. *One for friendship and one for love*, he thinks. He sits patiently on the dining room chair that faces the front door and waits. A glance at the clock reveals it's a little after ten. Children are likely to be safely within the confines of their own homes by now, so surely David should walk in at any moment. Some twenty minutes pass. Johnny considers whether David purveys ice cream at this time of night or if he, perhaps, takes advantage of their little "break." His fingertips drum against the wood surface of the table. His pulse quickens a bit, enough that he notices, yet not enough to cause alarm. He takes a deep breath and splays his hands out on the table to push him up from his seat when he hears David's keys jangle in the front door. Johnny composes himself and remains in his chair.

"I'm home," David announces. Johnny, in turn, waves two fingers at David. "What are you up to, Young

Jonathan? Oh," he notices the flowers, "are these for me?"

"It's an apology, David. I thought about what you said and I want to make amends."

"Very thoughtful of you. You never get me flowers."

"The flowers are actually the smaller part of the gesture. The papers underneath them are the main part."

"Did you finally get a star named after me?"

"No, I didn't register a star in your name for you. It's better. At least, I hope it's better. You can be un-excommunicated. I still don't think that's a word, but you know what I mean. You can be absolved. I did the research. It's not even very difficult. The main part is that you are sorry for what you did and you recognize it and are willing to admit it and make amends. You can get your position back in the church. You can be who you once were. It can be like old times again. Goodbye to the ice cream truck. Goodbye to your hand-to-mouth existence."

"Goodbye to you, too, Young Jonathan?"

"What?"

"Would this be goodbye to you, too?"

"Why would it be?"

"If I ask the church for forgiveness and seek absolution, I assume it is to join their good graces and bid farewell to what dropped me from them. I surely cannot be with you and them at the same time. That would be an exercise in insincerity."

"If you need to say goodbye to me in order for the church to accept you, then that's what you may need to do. I'll be okay. Did you know you could seek absolution and possibly get your position back?"

"I was aware, but it's not as easy as it sounds. It means cutting ties, showing allegiance, and starting anew, and I'm not quite sure I'm ready for it. I'd even have to serve in either a church that's a new construction, and you know there are no new churches going up, or one that's closed for reconstruction, renovations, upkeep, or what have you, and being reopened."

"You showed allegiance in the past. I don't think it's the allegiance part that's causing you hesitation. And what does it matter if the church is newer, older, or in between? If you're concerned about cutting ties with me, I think you're already on the right path. We are on a break and all."

"A break for one month."

"We wouldn't be on a break if we weren't broken."

"You think we're broken, Jonathan?"

"Individually, no. Together… yes. But that's not to say I won't help you get back where you belong. There are two roses in front of you, one red and one yellow. The red rose is for love, the yellow for friendship. The choice is yours, but I know there's only one right choice. And you know it, too."

David places his hands in his trouser pockets. He maintains the posture of someone about to pull those pockets out and show the world their emptiness. He appears forlorn, on the brink of giving up. He removes his right hand from his pocket. He takes one step forward, closer to the table. He leans forward, reaches down and fingers the stems of the two roses. The bottoms of the stems rest between his index finger and thumb and he rolls his thumb over them. He gently pushes one stem off his index finger and it descends to the table's surface. He grips the remaining stem between his two digits, lifts the flower upward and grips the stem in his hand. "Ouch!" he exclaims. He opens his hand enough that a bulbous bead of blood drips down the rose's stem to its very bottom, hangs there for a second, and releases toward the table. The single drop of David's blood lands perfectly in the center of a petal of the rose that remains on the table. And, had Johnny not seen it with his own eyes, he would never have noticed it, because it is the exact same shade as the flower on which it lands.

I knew you'd make that choice, Johnny thinks. *But if you react that way to a single drop of blood, grab a tourniquet and a washcloth because there's about to be a bloodbath.*

19 A GOOD OLD-FASHIONED SMOTING

The siren song of the ice cream truck plays across the night air. The tune sneaks in through the partially open window and lands upon Johnny's ear. He bites his lip in wonderment and halts for a second. He holds the stack of shirts he intends to place in his closet as his eyes meander toward the window. The song plays on. He mindlessly deposits the clothes onto a shelf and creeps toward the sound. He looks outside and sees Barbara and John's ice cream truck, distinguishable by the stuffed animal, a giant brown teddy bear with angel wings, tied to its front bumper. Johnny raps the knuckle of his index finger on the window and realizes the futility of his attempt at an interaction with them.

Once outside, he looks both ways and crosses to the truck. Barbara and John peer down at him. Johnny stands on the tips of his toes and searches for David. He floats down to the flats of his feet as he finds there is no

David in the truck. Barbara looks behind her to discover what Johnny searches for. She turns back to Johnny and proposes, "Ice cream sandwich?"

"Not today," Johnny responds.

Johnny inches higher again in another vain effort to find David in the truck.

"There's a menu right here," John offers as he pats the outside of the truck with his hand.

"That's not what I'm looking for. You know what I'm looking for."

"Do you know what he's looking for, Barbara?"

"I couldn't even fathom a guess."

"I'm looking for David."

"David," John starts, "David... name definitely rings a bell," he attests.

"You know who he is," Johnny urges.

"If, by David, you mean the one who worked here with us for a few short months and then up and left us, if you mean that David, why, no, we haven't seen him lately," Barbara offers. "If, on the other hand, you mean David the one who at one point, how can I put this delicately, had been known as a man of ill repute but who recently worked his way back up into God's good graces," Barbara continues, "why, no, we haven't seen him lately either."

"You guys must get some sick pleasure out of torturing me," Johnny accuses, hands on hips.

"Anger is an ugly pose on you," Barbara retorts.

"I'd strike that pose from your repertoire," John agrees.

"I don't need advice on attitude adjustments from the likes of you two."

"Watch your tone, Little Lamb, before you get sheared," John threatens.

"Really? A couple of saints are going to rough me up? I'll believe it when I see it." The sky darkens to a shade of purple against which the mounds of clouds press. The clouds gather together, as they absorb and echo the purple hues, and descend to the earth. Johnny can almost reach out and touch them. While Johnny practically chokes from the suffocating closeness of the clouds, other passers-by seem not to notice anything out of the usual. "What are you doing to me? Are you smoting me? I thought only God smote people. I thought that was a verb only God could use. Are you smoting me? Can you smote because you're God-adjacent? Come on, I didn't do anything smote-worthy. I mean, really I didn't." Barbara and John narrow their eyes on Johnny. "Okay, maybe I did, but I don't deserve to be smote. There are people much worse than me. Smite them."

"He cowers," Barbara notices.

"Nothing more unsettling than seeing a little lamb cower. Don't fret, Little Lamb," John reassures. A clap of thunder jars Johnny's nerves. He falls off his feet backward, and lands on his hind, legs spayed out like a rag doll abandoned by its adoptive parent. The clouds lower further and block the top of the ice cream truck from Johnny's sight. He can't see Barbara or John, but he can hear them clear as bells. The clouds cleanly and clearly transport the sounds of the saints to Johnny.

"He's scared," Barbara states.

"He deserves to be scared."

"He deserves to be happy."

"Everyone deserves to be happy, Barbara, that's

why this young one needs to let go of David and begin anew."

"He's never going to begin anew. His time left on Earth is limited and he knows it. He's going to finish what he started, whether we like it or not."

"Not if God smites him, he won't. The lamb may be able to crawl on all fours right now, but that's about it. He certainly can't see otherwise. He can't see with his head in the clouds. He is this close to being smote. Maybe if we chant for it, God will smite him. Let's try!" Barbara starts the chant, "Smite! Smite! Smite!"

John joins in the chant, "Smite! Smite! Smite!"

Johnny hears their chant. It booms to the beat of his heart. He rolls to the ground, vertebrae by vertebrae, as the clouds inch downward. The clouds trap him against the ground. He crosses his arms, his hands cover his face, and he shields his eyes from the clouds about to overtake him. He gasps for air as the physical closeness of the clouds mentally suffocates him. "Smite! Smite! Smite!" booms at him.

In Johnny's ears, the sounds evolve to "Might! Might! Might!" He hiccups for air. He takes some into his lungs, exhales, and inhales again, deeper this time. "Might! Might! Might!" He slowly pulls his hands away from his face. They settle for a moment at his neck. He uncrosses his arms and moves them to his sides, palms against the ground. He opens his eyes enough to confirm that the clouds loom directly above him. The tip of his nose suspends them in mid-air.

He presses his hands against the floor and gradually returns himself to his abandoned rag doll position. He blinks but doesn't know if he blinks. His world is blankness in the depths of the clouds. He stands. "My time has not yet come," he speaks into the clouds. His sounds, however, barely register in his own ears. The sounds of "Might! Might! Might!" dominate. "My time has not yet come," he repeats. He competes with the other sounds as he bellows, "My time has not yet come!" At his exclamation, his nerves tense and his fingers start to curl. The clouds swirl into his palms, slowly at first, and then progressively more rapid, until all of the clouds disappear into Johnny's balled fists. He stands there, stock still, in front of the ice cream truck.

"Sweetie," Barbara begins, "your time has come. You're next. Would you like your normal ice cream sandwich?"

With a twitch of his head, Johnny snaps himself to attention. "What?" he asks.

"You said your time has not yet come and, well, thank you for your patience, your time has come, you're next in line. Would you like your normal ice cream sandwich?"

Johnny remains, perplexed. "Sure," he resolves, "one ice cream sandwich, please." He licks the ice cream from the center of the sandwich as he walks homeward. *Was I just told to keep firm in my resolve, to have strength, to have might?* Johnny wonders. *If God can smite me, then why doesn't He? Even at their encouragement, God didn't smite me. How rude, by the way, for saints to chant 'smite' like that. They'd probably chant 'jump' if they saw someone on a ledge. I'd expect more from a saint. Wait, they chanted 'smite' and I was almost smited, but I wasn't. I was right, it's because my time hasn't come yet! They said in the hospital that I wouldn't go even one day sooner than expected. He couldn't smite me if He tried!* A clap of thunder resounds along with a closer cracking sound from above. A tree branch lands across the sidewalk in front of Johnny's feet. The thickest of it crashes through the driver's side window of the car parked on Johnny's right. *That's right, resort to scare tactics. I call your bluff.* Johnny pauses, looks in the direction that will lead him home, then looks in the direction that will lead him to church, to God's home. *I think it's time I pay you a little visit now.*

20 WHAT HAVE I DONE?

The heavy, gilded doors creak closed behind Johnny. The weight of the doors as they close on the backs of Johnny's shoes propels him forward a few inches. He looks behind him, the same look he would give to someone who had pushed him. Johnny turns his gaze forward, down the aisle. *Empty as usual.* The distinct sound of a button brushing against a pew catches Johnny's ear. *Someone's here.*

He inches toward the pews, self-aware so as to not make any noise that would disturb the would-be denizen of the church. He peers around the column that obstructs his view. He takes in the familiar garb: penguin-wear. Peeking out the front side of her habit, Johnny notices the silver-grey tuft of hair. *Evil doesn't die,* he tells himself.

He shuffles himself into a pew and lowers the padded bar to kneel. He kneels and joins his hands together in mock prayer. His head bows downward and his eyelids almost shut. He remains in this position for what seems like an interminable amount of time. Creaks from the front of the church reach him. *She moves. Stay still. Oh, if I could be like a chameleon and blend in with these pews right now.*

A light thud, a light scraping. Another light thud, another light scraping. Yet another light thud, and yet another light scraping. Sister Petunia ambles down the aisle. Her left hand falls on the back of each pew as she makes her way down. Her fingernails scrape each pew and create the menacing sounds that so perturb Johnny.

The sounds stop. Johnny peers through his eyelashes but only sees the seat of the pew in front of him. He shuts his eyelids and waits. *Please say she has passed. I am not ready to see her yet.*

"You brazen thing," startles him.

Sister Petunia.

"Get up," she snarls.

Keep your eyes closed. Keep your head lowered. Don't make eye contact and she'll go away.

"Get up," she snarls, louder than before.

She can't scare you anymore. Don't give her that power. You're not a child anymore, she has no power over you.

A vice-like grip captures the nape of Johnny's neck. It yanks his shoulders and upper body up before his lower body can manage to react. Sister Petunia's grip, unrelenting, yanks Johnny off the floor and into the aisle. He lands on his feet but stumbles backward into the side of a row of pews and onto the floor. His hand instinctively presses on the pew-slammed section of his back.

"Insipid lump of humanity. Useless bump on a log. Heathen." Each statement from her is that, a statement. She doesn't scream them as exclamations, rather they are facts that roll out of her mouth. "Your body isn't fit to touch the floor in this house. Get up." She kicks Johnny's foot from under him as he tries to stand. He lands on his knees and palms. "Like the dog you are," she goads him, "you should be put down."

Johnny tries to scramble to his feet but Sister Petunia extends her leg and delivers a hard, heavy-heeled kick to his lower side. Johnny flips over and lands flat on his back. "Bet you never thought you'd be on your back in this church again," Sister Petunia gloats. "Miracles do happen." She plants her right foot firmly along one side of Johnny's ribcage and her left foot along the other side. She squeezes the sides of his ribcage between her ankles. "Now," she begins as she lifts her left leg over Johnny. She presses her foot down on his upper chest, "why are you here?"

"I seek forgiveness."

"Liar!" she sneers. She travels her foot closer to Johnny's throat. "I should crush you."

"Murder is a mortal sin," Johnny squeaks.

"How dare you deign to inform me about sin. I've given my life to the Lord and, as surely as I've devoted my life to Him, you must pay. If I can give a life I can take one too. You took a life. You took Father Mann's life, you took his livelihood. You took a life, a good life, from God Himself. You took His child and you tainted him. You seduced him. Sodomite. If no good deed goes unpunished, why, then, should the bad ones?"

She presses her heel into Johnny's throat. He feels his throat push closed by the force of her weight. His eyes roll back in his head.

"Sister, no," he tries to plead, but to no avail.

Hands splayed at his sides, his body jerks under her hold, yet she remains in control as death slowly moves in on Johnny. His fingers spread and reach in the direction of his throat. They surround Sister Petunia's ankle and squeeze with every drop of might Johnny has. His fingernails dig into and rupture her skin. Blood flows down onto his throat as she screams. She steps all her weight onto Johnny's throat to get him to release his grip, but slips on her own sleek blood, off Johnny, and onto the floor. Johnny gasps for air and instinctively puts his hands to his throat. He presses with his fingertips. *No rips. I'm alive. And this bitch is crazier than I thought.*

He scrambles to his feet, away from Sister Petunia who remains on the floor. She shakes off the impact of her fall. Johnny retreats down the aisle toward the exit and swears to himself he will not return here. One hand reaches each push-bar to open the doors, and he is paralyzed by a blow to his spine. His body flings forward into the closed doors.

"We are not done yet, young man."

Immobilized by the blow Sister Petunia delivered with the aid of the gilded metal pastoral staff, Johnny's body slithers down from the door to the floor. Sister Petunia takes him by the ankles and drags him down the aisle to the altar of the church. She releases his ankles and they thud the ground while she heaves a few breaths at the base of the altar.

"Flip over," she directs. "I said flip over." She

132

kicks the side of his leg but he barely moves. "Useless lump of humanity." She grabs one of his legs and with one swift motion lurches it in such a way that his body flips to the desired position.

Johnny sees her above him and he knows he is powerless. *She's going to win after all. It was inevitable. Evil always does win.*

A sinister sneer shows itself on her face. She reasons, "I know it's your member that causes you all of your troubles, and everyone else's troubles, so let's remedy that first."

She's going to castrate me.

She bends down, arms extended, exact intent unknown but Johnny gets the gist.

Might? Johnny pulls his knees inward and kicks with what little might he has. He makes contact with Sister Petunia's stomach and propels her away from him. She stumbles over the two steps behind her and tries to regain her balance. She totters and, for an instant, resembles an actual penguin tottering back and forth. On the brink of composure, she trips over an obstruction behind her, the base of the baptismal pool. On her way to the floor, her skull cracks against the decorative concrete statue of Saint John. She lands and cracks her skull one more time, this time against the marble floor.

"Sister Petunia?" Johnny asks from his place on the floor. He cranes his neck to see what has become of her. He eyes her, motionless. "Sister Petunia?" He receives no response. The black and white heap morphs as blood pours from Sister Petunia. The heap becomes black and white and red all over as an iron-like scent wafts to Johnny's nose. *What have I done?*

Charlie Casso

21 COLLATERAL DAMAGE

"I can't believe you killed her." Veronica leans in over Johnny's hospital bed. "I mean, we dreamed about it, sure, but you actually did it. Like, *on the news* did it. We used to laugh about the stupid people who make it on the news, now we *are* the stupid people who make it on the news."

"Ronnie, first of all, we'd laugh at the people on the street the reporters ask for comments, not the actual people the news stories are about. Second of all, I still laugh at them. Third of all, I didn't kill her; it was self-defense. And, fourth of all, we really shouldn't talk about it. I was told not to talk about it with anyone until I'm fully cleared."

"Are you in a lot of pain?"

"I'm in a hospital bed. What do you think?"

"I think I wonder how many people died on that bed."

"You must have been a candy striper in a

previous life. Your bedside manner is… well, it's something."

"Did they at least give you the good stuff? A little something to ease the pain?"

"Stuff? Yes. Good? I'm not so sure."

"You want some?" She reaches for her purse from the side chair.

"Don't make me laugh, it hurts too much."

"Sorry."

"Excuse the interruption, young lady, we need to check on our injured bird here. If you would be so kind as to wait in the hall," the doctor motions in the direction of the door.

"No problem," Veronica assures. "I'll be right outside."

Johnny shrinks in his bed, aware that, although he can't see their faces obscured as they are by their masks, they will assuredly reveal themselves as Barbara and John.

The nurse draws the curtains around Johnny's bed as she narrates, "Let's have us some privacy."

"I'm sorry," Johnny remarks.

"I said, let's have us some privacy."

"I meant I'm sorry I killed Sister Petunia, not I'm sorry as in I couldn't hear you."

"Our main concern here is your physical health, but if you'd like to speak with someone regarding any emotional issues you may be dealing with, I'm sure we can get you a referral," the doctor assures.

"But you *are* who I talk to. Aren't you mad at me for what I've done? I killed a nun. She's, like, almost one of you."

The doctor and nurse remove their masks. They are merely a doctor and a nurse, and Johnny has never before seen either of them. "Oh. That's disappointing. You're just regular people." The doctor and nurse exchange concerned glances.

"He may still be in shock," the nurse empathizes.

"We are going to give you a little while to rest and restore your faculties. We'll be back in a few," the doctor adds.

Veronica re-enters the room and pulls back the curtain from around Johnny's bed. "So, what did they say?"

"They said I need rest."

"That's it? Everyone needs rest. There has to be more than that."

"I must have seemed confused. They said they'd come back. I think I was just too flustered to make much sense. It's all too much."

"I can understand that. You want me to let you rest a bit? Don't answer that. I'm going to let you rest, whether you like it or not. No distractions for you. I'll check on you later but, in the meantime, if you need anything you know how to find me." Veronica departs from the room and Johnny turns his gaze to the ceiling.

Just fall on me, ceiling, just drop down and crush me flat like a pancake. I can take it. I've certainly taken much worse, especially if you include the pastoral staff to the spine. If I spend the rest of my life in jail, well, I won't be too surprised. Kill a nun, life in prison. Seems about right. Who is ever going to believe my side of the story, the only side of the story? Joke's on them though, because even if I get life in prison that's only a few months. Joke's on me though, because if I'd have never asked when I was going to die then I wouldn't know I only have a few months left and I possibly wouldn't have made the choices I made to get myself here. If I could do it all over again, I wonder if I...

Footsteps pad toward Johnny's bed. The doctor and nurse return to check in with Johnny. "We've been holding up nicely I assume," the nurse coos.

"As nicely as a person could, I guess. Given the circumstances and all," Johnny replies. "I think I would definitely like to speak with someone. It's probably one thing to kill someone in self-defense, but a nun? Kind of intense."

"We don't take the blame for her," the doctor states as a matter of fact.

"Why would you?"

"That certainly takes some of the pressure off," the nurse admits. Relaxed, she removes her mask, as does the doctor. Barbara and John smile at Johnny. "So glad you're not upset."

"You two?" Johnny acknowledges as he tries to settle his feelings about them. *Should I be upset with Barbara and John because of Sister Petunia, since she was supposed to be a servant of the Lord, yet was so downright evil, or should I be scared of them because I recently took the life of a nun and they may not take too kindly to that?* "Are you mad at me?"

"Little Lamb, no. We're not mad at you one bit. Why would we be?" Barbara inquires but does not await a response. "You think we harbor anger because dear Sister Petunia cracked her skull open and died in the house of God?"

"Yes."

"No," John offers. "If anything, we are angry that she hoofed her way through life stomping on anyone and anything in her path, for no good reason whatsoever. She wasn't molding individuals, young men, young women, tomorrow's future today, none of it. She bellowed her way through life, belittling others to buoy herself. To make it worse, she did it all under the ruse of being a servant of the Lord."

"So you're not angry with me."

"Anger's an emotion for the red-of-face and black-of-heart. You see how anger served Sister Petunia. No, we are not angry. We are, though, sorry you had to get hurt. We would never have expected someone to use a pastoral staff in such a manner, especially not a nun."

"On the bright side," Barbara offers, "you weren't impaled."

"I could have been. I really don't know what she was going for but I definitely know it had something to do with my nether-regions."

"I doubt she would have impaled you. Impaling is quite difficult, to be honest," Barbara offers.

"She kicked me while I was down, in the most literal sense, tried to crush my esophagus, attacked me with the pastoral staff... do you really doubt she would have impaled me? Does everything else seem so easy, breezy? Do I need a safe word with you two now?"

"Touchy," John notices. "We should write that on his medical record. I think they label patients like him 'difficult.'"

"I think I reserve the right to be touchy. I think I

earned that right. I think it's my God given right for as long as I remain on this earth to be touchy."

Barbara purses her lips. John clears his throat. "Speaking of how long you are to remain on this earth…" John begins.

"What now? Did you give me the wrong date or something? What?"

"We just wanted to make sure you were aware that your time's coming to an end. If there are any loose ends you'd like to tie, or goals you'd like to achieve, this is the time."

"My end's never been loose, for one, and my goal, for now I guess, is to stay out of prison. Although, if I do wind up in jail, I may very well get impaled in the end. Wow, that sounds worse out loud than I thought it would."

"There's a nice goal for you, Little Lamb, stay out of jail." Barbara nods her head in approval, "I like that goal, I do."

"You have very little control over whether you go to jail or not. You do realize that, don't you?" John asks in a fatherly tone. "What's done is done, and your word can't exactly be taken as gospel. You are, after all, the accused here. Your legal woes are going to have to sort themselves out with very little involvement from you. You're merely a side effect, a casualty perhaps."

"John, the boy's in a hospital bed recovering from a nun gone rogue. You might want to go a little easy on him."

"I am. I merely need him to be aware of the gravity of his situation."

"I think he's quite aware of his situation."

"It's grave," Johnny admits, "I get it. You know, there's a chance I won't even recover in three months. She really took it out of me."

"Why is it you were there in the first place? What brought you to the church?" John inquires.

"Are you going to interrogate me now?"

"You are quick to blame Sister Petunia for what happened, yet no one knows why you were in the church in the first place. If it was another church it would be more understandable, but to return to the same church David once served at and was excommunicated from, it seems… well, I'd rather not come right out and say it."

The room remains void of sound, save for the beeps of the medical apparatus behind Johnny's bed.

"Premeditated. There, I've said it," John continues. "You wanted a confrontation with Sister Petunia. You sought one out after all these years. You knew you had only so much time and you couldn't bear the thought of not having it out with her. You wanted her to pay for what she had done to you. Face it, if she hadn't knocked you unconscious all those years ago you would never have seen us. You'd have never discovered when you were going to die. You'd have lived your life naturally, without the end of it always locked in your sights. The only thing that gets in life's way is death; for everything else one has only one's self to blame. You were too slow to realize that, and blamed her for your choices. You chose to confront her, to accuse her probably, and torment her no doubt. And we all know how that went."

"I did. You are right, I chose to confront her. I chose to go to the church, to *that* specific church, in hopes of seeing her. But then, when I did, I changed my mind. I really did, I changed my mind. I just sat there in the pew, all by myself. I hoped, I prayed she wouldn't notice me there because I didn't want a confrontation anymore. I had willed myself to move on and drop the grudge I carried with me. All the negativity wasn't worth it. Misery loves company but if my company was going to be the likes of Sister Petunia, then misery wasn't for me. I was willing to let it all go, I really was. Apparently, Sister Petunia was not ready to let it go. I killed her, I did, but it was self-defense. She was about to kill me."

"There, there," Barbara coos. She gingerly pats Johnny on the head. "Lamb, I know this has been chaotic and traumatic for you, but I really do need to ask, what part of 'you're not going to die one day sooner than planned' was confusing to you?"

"Huh?"

"Dear, which part of 'you're not going to die one day sooner than planned' was confusing to you? Some part surely confused you, because Sister Petunia's death was not part of the plan. You seem to have thought your life was in peril, peril enough to send a nun to her death, yet I am at a loss to understand why."

"Let's see, what part of 'she had her foot on my throat' did *you* not understand? Did you expect me to lie on the floor and wait, just have faith that you were right?"

Barbara's and John's eyes alight at the word "faith."

Johnny continues, "And I didn't die a day sooner than expected, did I? No, I didn't think so. Maybe Sister

Petunia's the side effect, maybe she's the collateral damage here. Ever think of that?"

"It wasn't her time to die," John states.

"So, people can only die when it's their predestined time to die?"

"No, that's not what I'm saying, it's just preferable is all."

"Preferable? Preferable, yes. Preferable like as in I prefer not to get kicked, stepped on, violated... by a nun. That kind of preferable."

"You don't have to use sarcasm," Barbara admonishes.

"Bad things can happen when a person dies before their time, is all. As such, it is preferable that people not go sooner. What's done is done, I suppose. What we need to focus on is the three months you have left. Get your affairs in order."

Johnny reflects for a moment about what John has just said. He realizes, "But the only affair I've ever had that would need attention is..."

22 CAREFUL

"David."

David about-faces at the sound of his name. He searches for the source of the sound. His eyes find it in the light given off by the stained glass windows.

"Young Jonathan, is that you?"

"Yes, David, umm, Father Mann. It's me, as I live and breathe." *For now*, he adds in his head.

David steps down from the altar and takes a few paces toward the first pews. "Come in, Young Jonathan," he directs. "I was just going over my next sermon. I find practice makes perfect, don't you think?"

"Practice does make perfect. So do lowered expectations."

"I miss that tongue of yours."

"Careful, Father."

"I meant your cunning way…"

"Careful, Father."

"…with words."

"That's better," Johnny agrees. "I wanted to come," Johnny begins.

David interrupts, "Careful, Young Jonathan."

He continues, "to say goodbye."

"We said goodbye at the apartment when I moved out. You mean you've come to say hello."

"I know what I said and I know what I mean. They are one and the same. I've come to say goodbye."

"Where are you going? Come closer, Young Jonathan, it's hard to hear from here with all the noise from the crew outside. The renovations here never seem to end. Thankfully, they are working on the façade, so maybe that means they'll be done soon."

I didn't expect him to ask where I was going. Think fast. "Different places. I thought I'd travel for a spell, visit some places where I've never been: Chicago, Detroit, Texas... The Alamo."

"You're going to visit The Alamo?"

"I'm going to visit The Alamo," Johnny replies with feigned gusto.

"But... why?"

"Life happens? I've been tied here so long and the ropes that bound me weren't ropes at all."

"You were bound," David asks as his left eyebrow slowly rises, along with a certain appendage, "with ropes?" He swallows.

"Yes," Johnny continues, oblivious to the effect he has on David, "but those ropes, as tight as they were..."

"Go on," David pressures.

"...were made of licorice."

"Licorice?"

"Licorice," he nods sheepishly.

"What color?"

Johnny winces, confused at the question. "What color? I never really thought what color. Black."

"Nice," David utters.

"And the thing is, all the time I've been tied down and I just now realized the ropes were made of licorice. There was nothing of real substance tying me down. Sure, I had a job, and a job can keep you where you are, but I worked at a diner cleaning the floors. I could do that anywhere. I finally realized all I had to do was take it in my mouth, and even if I let it just sit there it would melt away. I could swallow it or spit it out, but the end result would be the same: I would no longer be bound by artificial ties."

David pulls at his collar, his face is flush. He reaches forward and moves his hand around the base of Johnny's neck. He brings him in and overtakes Johnny's face. Fast and voracious, his tongue explores the landscape of Johnny's lips.

Johnny neither returns David's kisses nor opens his mouth to accept them. He squeezes his hand between himself and David, and presses his palm against David's chest. "Whoa, whoa, whoa," he leans back as David leans forward. David continues to lap at Johnny's lips. "Easy boy." He extends his arm and moves a foot back to create space between aggressor and prey. David pants.

"What has come over you?"

"No one lately. It's killing me." David reaches out, grabs Johnny by the front of his shirt, and pulls him in again. Johnny's lips pay the price for David's ravenous needs.

This is like face rape. He's totally raping my face right now. Show me where the bad man touched you, show me where the bad man touched you. No.

"David, no," Johnny reprimands. David moves in again. "David, no," Johnny repeats. He does it a third time and draws out the command as if David were a child, "David, noooo."

"Come on, Young Jonathan, just one last time for good measure. Let's christen the confessional."

"Let's not and say we didn't."

"Young Jonathan," David drawls.

"That's not going to work on me."

"You've been a bad, bad boy, Young Jonathan. Let's get you on your knees in the confessional. It's time to make amends." David grabs the front of Johnny's pants and tries to pull him toward the confessional. "It'll only take a few minutes and it won't hurt at all. Unless you want it to."

"David," Johnny tries to get David to listen to him. "David!" Johnny digs himself into the floor as much as he can. "Listen to me." David stops pulling at his Young Jonathan. "I really came to say goodbye."

"You can't really be going. Besides, it's so much better when you're coming."

Johnny returns this remark with a scowl.

David continues, "I didn't forget your birthday's in what, two days? You remember the last time we were in church and your birthday had just passed? You turned eighteen and came to visit me. You remember what we did, don't you?"

"I'm turning 33 now. That's a lifetime of difference."

David extends a hand to touch Johnny. Johnny prevents it from its reaching its goal. "David, I have to leave," *I'm being forced*, "to explore difference places," *most likely Hell*, "and do different things," *burn, char, turn to ash...*

David tries to interrupt, "But..."

"But nothing. This is not up for debate. It's predestined, if you will. But I loved you once and I owed it to you, and to myself, to say goodbye."

"Is this supposed to be a 'parting is such sweet sorrow' moment? Because, if it is, there's nothing sweet about it."

"I think what's supposed to be sweet about the parting is that we will meet again. But we won't."

"Yes we will, we'll meet in Heaven. Should I not run into you at The Alamo, of course."

I don't know what's sweeter, that he believes I'm really going to The Alamo or that either of us will make it to Heaven.

"Of course," Johnny echoes.

"Can I give you a hug goodbye?" David asks.

"I wouldn't have it any other way."

David and Johnny embrace. David's hands press into Johnny's back as they work their way slowly up and down.

"David, I can feel your erection pushing into my thigh," Johnny exclaims as he pulls away from him.

"God is good?"

"Some things never change. At least I tried." Johnny storms toward the church doors and pushes through them. As the doors to the church reach their most open position, Johnny looks over his shoulder at

David and corrects, "And for the record, my birthday's tomorrow."

"Watch out, guy!" A voice from above, an angel? A saint? God? No. A construction worker shouts from the top of his scaffold. Johnny's eyes dart upward but he's blinded by the sun and again by the crushing weight of death that falls on his head like an anvil.

From inside the church, David screams, "Johnny!" and runs toward the lifeless heap on the floor. "Johnny!" David falls to his knees and cradles the lifeless body in his arms. "Johnny, this can't happen. This can't happen." David sees the culprit of the crime on the floor. He looks up, toward the sky, the construction workers, and God, and accuses, "You dropped an anvil on my Young Jonathan!" He cries. "Who does that?"

Johnny watches the scene as his legs dangle over the edge of the cloud on which he sits. "You killed me with an anvil?"

"Having died, you'd think you'd have learned from your mistakes by now," Saint John answers.

"He's right," Saint Barbara attests. "Enough with the blaming. Do we look like the type to drop anvils on people? The answer is no, we don't."

"Well, I certainly don't appreciate it. David clearly doesn't appreciate it. You know what, though? Ronnie will find this hysterical. I can live with that."

"Too soon," Saint Barbara and Saint John say in unison.

"Oh, I didn't mean live with it, like *live* with it. I'll have to work on that. Will he," Johnny nods toward David, "be all right?"

"I'm sure it'll take a while, but things will work out the way they are supposed to. It may not be for the best, things don't always work out for the best, you know, but they will work out the way they are supposed to. That's for sure," Saint Barbara promises.

"Guys," Johnny begins, "speaking of the way things are supposed to work out, what would have happened to me had I not known when I was going to die? I mean, I didn't know exactly when or how, but I knew the day. I'm just wondering, had I not known, would I have done things differently? What would life have been like?"

Saint Barbara and Saint John cast disconcerted expressions at each other. Saint John sighs. "The boy certainly picks opportune times to barrage us with questions, doesn't he?"

"What does that mean?" Johnny asks.

"You see," Saint John begins, "we had to answer you when you asked when you were going to die because we approached you in a vision and, rule is, we have to answer if you have a question you really feel needs answering. So we did. This isn't a vision you're having anymore though. You've entered the afterlife."

"Is that good?"

"That's very good," he continues. "Since your mortal life has just extinguished, we are required to address any concerns you have. Death is quite the harrowing experience for some."

"So that means you can show me what life would have been like had I not known when I was going to die?"

"In a word," Saint Barbara draws out, "yes."

The cloud on which they perch swiftly descends to the earth. During its retreat, Johnny's face, body, and whole being warp backward through time. The cloud bounces to a float mere feet from the ground and Johnny, tender, young, and thirteen years old, bounces off the cloud and onto his feet. He shakes his head and opens his eyes. He finds Sister Petunia before him.

She grabs and balls the collar of Johnny's shirt at the nape of his neck, and seethes, "We are all made in God's image and at God we do not laugh." Drops of spittle project from her mouth, two of which find a resting place on Johnny's lower lip. His eyes cross, his head spins, and his feet lift off the ground. Sister Petunia keeps Johnny's shirt in her grip, and the youth elevates from the ground because of it. The right side of his body slams against the chalkboard. *Crunch* emanates from his hip as it crashes into the ledge where the chalk rests. Johnny's world goes black.

23 INTO THE LIGHT

"Wake up," Johnny hears as he regains consciousness.

Johnny slumps against the wall, his eyes open, and through a blurry haze he makes out Veronica's friendly face. She asks, "Are you okay? It looks like you were hit with an anvil or something."

"Huh? No," he replies. "At least I don't think so." He tries to stand but topples back down as the pain from his side hits him. "Ow!" he exclaims as Veronica saves him from his fall. Johnny flashes back to how he ended up on the floor.

Sister Petunia sternly gazes at him and inquires, "Jonathan, what are you laughing at?"

"I am laughing at Alicia Cooper," he responds.

"Why," Sister Petunia asks, "would you laugh at another person?"

"She has blue icing all over her face from the cupcake she ate at lunch. I'm sorry, Sister Petunia."

Sister Petunia unleashes, "Never laugh at other people, Jonathan. We are all made in God's image and at

God we do not laugh. He created you. Are you insipid?
Are you?"

"I don't know. I wasn't being mean. I just
thought it was funny, Sister Petunia."

"And I guess that's why I'm here," Johnny tells
Veronica.

"Come on," she reaches around his back and
under his arm to support him, "Let's get to class."

***

The sound of pencil brushing up against loose-
leaf paper, as it darkens the white to a silvery shade of
grey, keeps Johnny from falling asleep. He fills in the
remaining space of the final bubble letter in his eloquent
statement *English Sucks.*

"Tomorrow we start with prepositions, class.
Tonight, memorize all of the words on your handout.
They are in alphabetical order and I expect you will be
able to recite the list by heart. Do not disappoint," Mr.
Huxley directs. The bell signals the end of school for the
day.

A steady stream of students flow out from the
school, Johnny amongst them. His head hunches down
in thought as he attempts to wrap his mind around the
day. *I should really speak with someone about Sister
Petunia,* he thinks. *If I talk to mom, though, that could
be a disaster. I don't want her flying off the handle and
saying anything to Sister Petunia. She'll just get worse.
They always say speak to an adult if you need help. What
adult at the school would be willing to... Father Mann!*

Johnny stops in his tracks. His thumbs tug at the

backpack straps by his shoulders. He turns himself around and marches back to the school. He walks around the perimeter, to the front of the church. He peers up the steps that lead to the front doors. *I wonder if he's even in there.* He considers turning away. *There's only one way to find out,* he resolves. Johnny takes each step with trepidation until he's finally at the top. He reaches out and pulls the right door open. The cool air rushes into him as incense invades his nostrils. He enters, and the doors close to separate him from the outside world.

He dips his index and middle fingers into the small pool of holy water and crosses himself. *Give me strength.* He gingerly makes his way up the aisle and peers around the empty church. The confessional, to the right of the altar, could be manned or empty. The church is void of sound. If someone else was in there seeking absolution, there'd be at least some noise. Johnny moves forward anyway. Since he's here already, he might as well check if there is a Father present.

Johnny moves into the screened confessional. He closes the door behind him, kneels, and pulls the screen open. It creates the distinct grating noise sinners fear the moment before they unburden their souls. The screen remains closed from the other side. He waits. The grating noise recommences, this time from the other side of the confessional. The light from the priest's side of the confessional casts fragmented shadows onto the lower part of Johnny's face.

"Forgive me, Father, for I have sinned. It has been about a week since my last confession."

"Tell me, what are your sins?"

Johnny takes his time as he forms his response.

"Thing is, I am not really here to confess my sins."

"You are aware you're in a confessional?"

"Well, yes, but, no, well, see I, I've come for advice."

The Father adjusts himself in his seat. He vies to discern who kneels on the other side of the confessional. He can see Johnny's lips move as they form the words he releases into the air. "That's all I need, Father, advice."

"Young Jonathan, is that you?"

"Yes, Father, it is." Johnny lowers himself a bit and tries to see who it is on the other side of the screen. "Father Mann?"

"Yes, Young Jonathan. Young Jonathan, come around. Let's have a talk." Johnny's face is shadowed as Father Mann stands up and moves outside the confessional. Johnny gets off his knees and opens the door to find Father Mann welcoming him, hand extended. "Young Jonathan, so nice to see you." They shake hands, adult and child meeting in the middle. "Come on in," Father Mann offers as he puts his hand on Johnny's shoulder.

I feel better already, Johnny thinks as he registers the heat from Father Mann's hand.

Once inside the face-to-face confessional, Father Mann pulls the door closed behind him. "For privacy, of course," he verbalizes.

"Of course," Johnny assents.

Father Mann and Johnny take their respective seats on chairs that angle in toward each other in a non-confrontational stance of sorts wherein the occupants might be more prone to share, yet maintain, their own personal space.

"Now tell me, Young Jonathan," Father Mann begins, "you say you seek advice." He extends his hand and rests it on Johnny's knee. "How may I be of service to you?"

Johnny tells himself, *Don't misinterpret. He's a priest and, even if he weren't, he wouldn't want me anyway. For one, he's not gay. For two, I'm lanky and scrawny and have as much sex appeal as a bucket of paint. For…*

"Earth to Young Jonathan," Father Mann squeezes Johnny's knee. He moves his hand up an inch and pats. "You said you seek advice. What can I do you for?"

Johnny's mouth opens enough to accommodate his tongue which feels swollen, tied, or both at the moment. His young, confused mind remains at a loss for how to respond. *What can I do you for, he said. What can he do me for?* Johnny's mouth opens further for him to speak and simultaneously stick his foot in it when he manages to respond, "Hours." *You can do me for hours.*

"Our what, Young Jonathan?"

"Our… Father, who art in Heaven, hallowed be thy…"

"Something's clearly bothering you. There, there, Young Jonathan," he pats again. "I'm going to refrain from speaking for a bit and leave the floor all to you. You take your time and tell me whatever is on your mind. I promise to help you as best I can."

Johnny nods approval. His hands clasp each other atop his lap. Father Mann removes his hand from Johnny and sits back in his chair. Johnny eyes Father

Mann's black pants. They appear suitable for a man of the cloth: plain, nothing fancy, a little used as per the soft appearance of the fabric. Johnny's eyes follow the flow of the fabric up Father Mann's shin, over his knee where the fabric appears even more worn, to his thigh. At his thigh is where the fabric shows the taut muscle underneath. The pants secretly want to rip open and reveal the body they shroud. Johnny's eyes continue their journey. *Hi, crotch,* he thinks. *Don't stare!* He averts his gaze and looks Father Mann in the eyes. *Tender, yet strong.*

"The reason I'm here," Johnny begins, *the reason I'm here is because I'm totally in love with you and want to see what your kisses feel like, how your scruff feels against my neck, and how your arms feel around my body.* "The reason I'm here is because I do need your help. I'm being bullied."

"Oh my, that's quite troubling. I'm so sorry to hear that. Are you all right? What am I saying, of course you're not all right. Thank goodness you've come for help in time. Young Jonathan, I'm so proud of you for coming forward. No one ever deserves to be bullied. Teenagers can be so cruel. I'm so sorry."

"Thing is, it's not a teenager."

"You're getting bullied by a younger student? I'm not surprised in the least, to be honest. Don't let it get to you, you'll grow into your frame, it's nothing to be daunted by. You just have to eat a little more is all."

"I'm not getting bullied by a toddler, thank you very much for the vote of confidence."

"No? Then what is it? Who bullies you? This is a safe space, Young Jonathan. I will protect you."

"That's very reassuring, Father Mann."

"Now tell me," Father Mann begins as he leans in to Johnny and places his hands on Johnny's legs directly above the knees. His fingers cradle around the sides of Johnny's legs. He continues, "Who is it that hurts you so?" He stares into Johnny, a soft stare, a stare that fixes eyes upon eyes yet welcomes instead of intimidates.

Johnny's pupils dilate. He takes in more of Father Mann's countenance. The warm tone of his skin, the scruff, just a day or two's worth, enough to make Johnny want to brush the side of his face against it and revel in its roughness.

"Trust me," escapes Father Mann's lips, the tender, billowy lips, with the soft glisten from the occasional lick. Johnny entertains how he would like to be the one to give those lips their sheen.

Emotions collide within Johnny. His heart beats for Father Mann, yet his loins retreat at the thought of Sister Petunia. It amazes him how the thought of her could make his privates shrivel up.

"Sister Petunia," Johnny confesses.

"Sister Petunia?" Father Mann repeats for clarification. That name from those lips wreaks havoc upon Johnny, his heartbeat, and his nether-regions.

"Yes. Are you mad at me?"

"Jonathan, I could never be mad at you. You are so courageous, coming to me with this. I can't tell you what it means to me to know you trust me enough to share your concerns with me. You poor thing." He stands up and puts his arms out for Johnny. Johnny stands and leans himself into Father Mann's comforting embrace. Father Mann's scruff scratches against the top of Johnny's head. Tingles surge through Johnny. His arms prickle with goosebumps. *I could get lost here,* Johnny thinks. They break their embrace and take their respective seats once more.

"Now, tell me, what has Sister Petunia done that has caused you to feel scared, intimidated… unsafe maybe?"

Johnny answers with a blank stare.

Father Mann continues, "Sister Petunia scares and intimidates a lot of students now, doesn't she? Adults, too, for that matter."

Johnny nods in agreement.

"Let me rephrase then. Is there a specific incident you would like to discuss?"

"She knocked me unconscious today."

"She struck you?" His hands search along Johnny's face for bruises and finally rest at the base of his neck.

"She didn't, like, punch me in the face if that's what you mean."

"What happened then?" Father Mann asks. He pats Johnny's upper back with the fingers that rest at his neck and releases himself from Johnny.

"She picked me up and threw me into the blackboard today. I almost died."

"You almost died?"

"Almost."

"Do you think you're exaggerating a little bit?"

"I said almost."

"But still."

"You weren't there, you don't know."

"You're right, Young Jonathan, I wasn't there and I don't know. Had I been there this would never have happened. I'd never let anyone lay a finger on you." He rests his hand on Johnny's leg.

"I know I blacked out. Ronnie woke me up. I don't know how long I was out, but I was. She didn't even care. Sister Petunia, I mean. Ronnie cares, of course. Sister Petunia though, she just left me there. I could've died. Who does that, and to a kid?"

"Good question, Young Jonathan. Whoever would put a child in harm's way like that, well, I can't say." Father Mann's hand retreats back to its owner. "Would you like me to speak with her?"

"No, Father, no, you can't do that. She'll kill me, she'll kill me for sure."

"She won't kill you, Young Jonathan."

"Her name is Petunia, wouldn't any person with that name want to kill?"

"You have a point," Father Mann concedes. "What do you suggest we do then?"

Please don't ask me that, Johnny thinks, *because you might not approve of my answer. We are in the confessional though, in all fairness, so if I were to overstep a boundary this is definitely the right place for it. I could confess right here, presto!*

"Young Jonathan, what shall we do?"

A sea of warmth rushes through Johnny at the sound of his name, at least the way Father Mann says it. *Jonathan*, his full name. *Young*, the modifier placed formally, yet casually, before it. *Young Jonathan.*

"I guess I just wanted someone to talk to. I feel better. You made me feel better, I guess just by being here for me. The hug certainly helped." Johnny blushes five shades of red, each progressively deeper and darker than the one before, as his inner voice screams at himself, *You did not just say that!*

"That's what I'm here for. Anytime you need anything, whether it's advice, counsel, confession, even to talk, even a hug, Young Jonathan, I'm here for you."

"You are?" Johnny musters with innocence.

"I will always be here for you. I still don't feel comfortable about this incident with Sister Petunia. Maybe we should take you to the hospital, get you checked out."

The additional time with Father Mann tempts Johnny. He considers for a moment. He decides and responds, "I'll recover, no worries. I'm young, my body can take it."

"I'm sure it can," Father Mann replies. "I mean, I'm sure it can recover fine. If you aren't feeling well, though, it would be my pleasure to accompany you and make sure you are taken care of."

"Thank you. I'll be all right. I will come back, to speak or whatnot. You can count on it."

"I look forward to you coming."

The confessional absorbs the last words and echoes silence. Father Mann stands and Johnny follows suit while Father Mann opens the door.

"Thanks again, Father," Johnny offers sheepishly.

"Of course." Father Mann ruffles Johnny's hair and pulls him in for a hug. "One last hug for the road," he narrates. Johnny tilts his forehead in toward Father Mann and lowers his chin down toward Father Mann's chest. He feels the bristle of scruff once more. *Heaven,* he thinks. *Like I've died and gone to Heaven.*

Charlie Casso

24 GIRL TALK

Steady *beeps* invade Johnny's ears. *Beep, beep, beep, beep, beep...* He opens his eyes and finds himself blinded by ripples of white. He grabs at the whiteness and pulls it over and away from his face. "Up on your feet," he says aloud. "Shut the alarm clock," he says as he depresses the nipple on the clock. "Stop talking to yourself. Will do."

"Johnny, honey," his mom yells from downstairs, "you awake?"

"Yes, mom."

"Good. Don't forget to take the bag of cookies I bought for you yesterday. They're the rainbow ones you like."

"Okay, mom," he yells down.

Johnny readies himself for school in his usual way. He brushes his teeth, washes his face, and moisturizes because, though he's young now, he realizes the adage *the difference between a grape and a raisin is moisture* is likely true. He dresses and takes a long look in the full-length mirror that adorns the inside of the door to his room. He asks himself the one question every youth asks themselves before they consider going to school for the day. Namely, *Is there anything about me today, my hair, my clothes, my face… that will cause someone to make fun of me?* While he believes he's the only one to answer *yes* on a daily basis, he shrugs and heads to school anyway.

***

"Cookie?" Johnny offers.

Veronica juts her chin in the direction of her lunch tray where Johnny deposits the rainbow cookie. She makes a face of contempt for what is in her mouth, drops the hamburger on her plate, and napkins the glob she spits from her mouth. She moves the weighty napkin to the side of her tray and tucks it under the tray's lip. Her fingers pry the top part of the bun from the burger it houses. Sounds of suction spread, as does the white goo that adheres the hamburger to its bun.

"The food in this place," she states, topless burger in her palm, "is atrocious."

"Good word, Ronnie. Ten points."

"The thought of having this vile meat inside of you…" her hand disappears under the table. A *thwak* sounds from under the table as it jars. Veronica pulls her hand from under, and now holds only the bottom part of the bun. She continues, "…is more than I can handle. Voila! If that hunk of meat is still up there tomorrow, imagine how long it sticks inside you. Speaking of hunks of meat, how did your conversation go with Father Mann yesterday?"

"Ronnie," Johnny remonstrates.

"Come on, Johnny, the man is hot. God created man and Mann is hot. Deal with it."

"You shouldn't talk about a priest that way."

"I'm not talking about him any way, I'm just saying he's a hunk of a man." She swirls a french fry in the air while she continues. "And I love his name. Father Mann. It just, like, puts it out there. All like, I'm Mann, deal with it. Hot." She dips the french fry in her pool of ketchup. "He can dip his french fry in my ketchup anytime." She licks the ketchup as it dangles off the end of the fry.

"Easy there, Lolita."

Veronica smiles in return. "I'm just saying." She gazes dreamily while Johnny shakes his head and throws his hands up having been forgotten about. Veronica notices and remarks, "Oh, sorry. So, wait, how was it?"

"It was fine. He was consolative. Consolating? However you say it, he consoled me."

Veronica arches her eyebrow. "I'll bet he did. He could console me anytime."

"Ronnie!" Johnny reprimands.

"Fine, fine. So, did he offer anything? Bricks, rope, and an alibi, perhaps?"

Johnny glares at Veronica. "Yes, Ronnie, bricks, rope, and an alibi." He rolls his eyes. "Father Mann listened. He understood. He offered to speak with Sister Petunia."

"Oh, God," Veronica interrupts.

"That was my reaction, too. Don't worry, he's not going to say anything to her. She'd be on the warpath if she knew I told anyone what she'd done."

"Oh, yeah, she seems really concerned about how others view her. You could show how the west was won on her butt. Real concerned with how others see her." Veronica pushes her french fries away from her. "So nothing changes. She goes about smashing whoever she wants against the walls. That's the plan?"

"Why mess with perfection, right?"

"Come on," She takes her tray in one hand and pops the rainbow cookie into her mouth with her other. "We'll figure something out," she mumbles as cookie crumbs sputter from her lips.

"Classy, Ronnie," Johnny acknowledges as he follows along.

25 THE PERKS OF PUNISHMENT

"Prepositions, people," Mr. Huxley demands of his students. "Prepositions are what I want. Prepositions and their objects are what you will produce. Clean sheet of paper on each desk, now. You will begin on my mark. Alicia, stop looking so confused and get it together. Ready? And… begin."

Pens and pencils scribble across paper. Each student works feverishly as they try to recall the complete list of prepositions in alphabetical order. Johnny struggles his way through his sheet of paper and adds another line of words after every fifteen or so seconds of thinking. Veronica sits to the left of Johnny. She giggles silently to herself as her pen flies across her paper. She releases her pen from her grip and it lands flat against the table just as Mr. Huxley calls, "Time! Writing implements down. Pass your paper to the person on your right. For those on the end," he addresses the far end of the room, "quietly get up and pass your paper to the person at the start of your row." Johnny scans

Veronica's paper.

> aboard the plank
> about the jugular
> above the heart
> across the throat
> after the scream
> against the wall
> along the wrists

Veronica's list of prepositions goes on and on, and they are all correct, each and every one. "You're going to get locked in the looney bin, Ronnie. You better hope he doesn't read your answers."

"They're all right. What's he going to say?"

"That you are nuts, maybe?"

"Well, how did you do, Mister Smartypants?"

"I remembered, like, ten. They are hard."

"But you turn your nose up at mine," she whispers. "At least I got all of them right. I needed something to help me remember them. Sister Petunia finally came in handy," Veronica enlivens. "I used her as inspiration."

"I see that."

Johnny jumps in his seat when Mr. Huxley booms, "Jonathan, is this the time for talking?"

"No, sir."

"You can stay after class today and clean the boards. That will make up for the time you lost today due to your talking. And make sure you clap the erasers clean." He takes one eraser in each hand from the chalkboard ledge and inspects them. He approaches Jonathan, arms by his sides, erasers in hands. "Do you hear me, Jonathan? The boards and the erasers, after class." To narrate his point, he claps the erasers against Jonathan's head. Each time they hit their target, clouds of white smoke billow out. Johnny's head becomes surrounded by a thick, heavy cloud of chalk dust which slowly falls to his shoulders and, ultimately, to the floor. "Head in the clouds, always with your head in the clouds. Take note, people," he directs to the class, "the longer you keep your head in the clouds the longer it takes you to get anywhere." The class members silently stare at the papers on their desks, afraid to respond to Mr. Huxley.

Johnny stares at Veronica's paper on his desk. He restrains his breathing so as to limit his intake of chalk dust. *Don't cry,* he tells himself, *you're face is probably covered in white chalk and if tears run down your cheeks they'll make you look like one of those sad clowns with their makeup running. Don't cry.* He bores his stare into a spot of ink on the paper until all he sees is the blackness of the ink.

He blinks a few times and realizes he's in front of the blackboard. It's after school and time for his penalty. No one else in the class, just Johnny, the blackboard, the erasers, and his thoughts. He notices a statue of a saint affixed to a wall in the corner of the room. "I'm surprised he's not making me dust you," Johnny tells the statue. "Fine, ignore me." He takes the erasers and claps them together out the window. The song of an ice cream truck reaches Johnny. "Of course! Taunt me, why don't you?" Johnny directs below to the ice cream truck. He huffs, turns around, and takes his clean-ish erasers to the blackboard to begin cleaning it.

He starts at the top left section, on his tip-toes,

and makes a nice clean sweep down to the bottom. He turns his eraser over in his hand and inspects its underside. It's white already. "Are you kidding me?" he asks aloud. "This is going to take forever." He shakes his head at the blackboard, on which remains the list of prepositions Mr. Huxley wrote after their exam was over. "Among the graves, around the neck, at the funeral... damn, she was right. It is easy to remember them this way." He looks at the underside of the eraser again, shrugs his shoulders, and takes a second swipe at the blackboard. The *shhh* sound the eraser makes against the blackboard is his only company. The sound ushers his mind into fantastical thoughts about the very prepositions on the board and their objects, at least the objects he and Veronica gave to them.

"Young Jonathan?"

Startled, Johnny spins around. The eraser projects from his hand and, as if it has had enough of being trapped in the classroom, makes its way out the open window. Johnny's back hits the blackboard, and his hip crunches as it hits the ledge where the chalk is kept. "Ahhh!" Johnny exclaims and grabs his side.

"I'm so sorry, I didn't mean to startle you," gushes Father Mann as he rushes to Johnny. "Are you all right?"

"I'm fine. That's what I get for daydreaming."

"You didn't look like you were daydreaming."

"I was multi-tasking. This class and daydreaming go hand-in-hand. It's kind of a prerequisite."

"Very well. You have my most sincere apologies. Can I look at that?" Father Mann motions toward Johnny's side.

Johnny lifts his shirt from its belted place in his pants. It's already red. It'll be black and blue by tonight. "I'll be all right."

Father Mann moves his hand onto Johnny's side and massages it with his fingertips. "Just keep an eye on it." He moves his hand away and the bottom of Johnny's shirt falls to his side. Father Mann continues, "Why are you here anyway, and by yourself?"

"Mr. Huxley."

"I see. Care to talk about it? It seems you've had a rough couple of days."

"I don't feel safe here."

Father Mann's face responds before he verbalizes his concern. His eyes narrow in on Johnny. Worry lines pop up on his forehead. "Did someone threaten you? Tell me."

"No, no. I mean I don't feel safe here, in this room, Mr. Huxley's room. I don't feel safe talking about things, with you or anyone, in this room. It's not like the confessional, or home, or the mall, or, well just about anyplace other than here. I feel like somehow someone will overhear. Worst of all, I feel somehow Huxley will overhear."

"Young Jonathan, you scared me for a second there. We can go to the confessional if you'd like to talk, anytime. I told you that. We can go right now."

Johnny arches an eyebrow at the blackboard. "*We* can't. I need to finish this. Don't worry about me, Father. Besides, isn't there some line like 'he that endures to the end shall be saved' or something along those lines?"

"Good memory. That's Matthew, actually."

"Yeah, I can endure, Father."

"I'm sure you can," Father Mann agrees. He adds, "I can help you, with your endurance. I mean, I can help you finish, with the blackboard if you'd like."

"No offense, Father, but I don't think priests are made to clean blackboards. God kind of prevented that by making you wear so much black all the time." He gives Father Mann a quick set of elevator eyes.

"And that's why man invented white undershirts." Father Mann unbuttons his black shirt, takes it off, and drapes it, inside out, over a desk.

Johnny's mouth gapes open as all thoughts flee his brain. His blood rushes elsewhere and makes thought… not possible.

"You don't mind if I help, do you?" Father Mann jars Johnny out of his stupor.

"Of course. I mean of course not. I mean thank you." Johnny tries his best to walk over to where he left off cleaning the blackboard without staring at Father Mann through the corner of his eye.

"Johnny?"

"Yep?"

"Do you have another eraser?"

"Oh." He looks at the window. "I think…" he begins. He walks over to the window, Father Mann in tow. They both lean out and look down.

Johnny looks to Father Mann on his left and admits, "I don't see it."

Father Mann looks to his right, at Johnny, and replies, "It's a *no* here as well. Young Jonathan," he ruffles Johnny's hair, "what am I going to do with you?"

Johnny thinks, *Aboard the member, about the groin, above the pelvis, across the face, after the kiss, against the wall, along the thighs, among the moans, around the tip, at the base...* "Whatever you want," Johnny responds.

"Come again?"

Johnny tells himself, *He said, "come again."*

Johnny responds, "I mean we could clean the boards if you'd be up for it. Either way it's very generous of you to offer."

"No problem at all. Let's get to it."

Johnny emits an audible, guttural sound.

"Oh, right, we need another eraser. I'll go borrow one from another classroom. Don't start without me." Father Mann offers. He removes himself from the room to retrieve an additional eraser.

"Wouldn't dream of it," Johnny responds.

Charlie Casso

26 HUNGRY

Veronica and Johnny share a hug in front of the greasy diner they normally pass by but never go into. For today's outing, they've agreed to try the greasy diner if, for nothing else, kicks. Once inside, they forego the allure of the window seats for a more comfortable booth in the back. Veronica eyes the surface of the table as she situates herself. "You can write your name on the table in the grease," she narrates as she uses her index finger to write a giant *V* on the table.

Johnny shrugs, "Well, we do refer to it as the greasy diner. At least we know we have good instincts."

"Yet we both agreed to eat here. What does that say about us?"

"That we live life to the fullest?"

"Pending e-coli or salmonella poisoning, this may be the last day we live."

"I'm not getting salmon, so that one's not going to get me."

Veronica gives Johnny a confused look. "Say

177

what?"

"No salmon. I wouldn't order fish at a diner."

"I've seen you order the McFish at McDonald's."

"McDonald's isn't a diner, that's my point."

"So what are you going to order here? Wait, let me guess. A burger."

"How'd you know?"

"You make no sense at all. Order a burger from McDonald's. Order fish from a diner," Veronica directs.

"But I don't want salmonella."

"Salmonella doesn't come from salmon. It comes from chicken."

"I don't want chicken."

"And they let you graduate high school?" Veronica asks.

"What does that have to do with anything?"

"How do you not know where salmonella comes from?"

"I thought I did," Johnny responds.

"You don't."

"Fine. But now I do. And they let me graduate high school because I is very smart."

"Hey, can you believe it's been, like, four years since we've seen Huxley and Petunia?"

"Please don't remind me about them," Johnny pleads.

"Hey guys," the waitress interrupts, "whaddaya want?"

Veronica and Johnny exchange glances that say, *Is she serious?*

"You're not ready," she continues, "I'll be

back." The waitress walks away.

"I think that was a threat," Veronica whispers.

"Should we leave?" Johnny asks Veronica.

Veronica's eyes travel the distance between their booth and the front door. "No. The exit's too far away. I think she'll tackle us before we get to the door. Just get prepared to blurt out your order when she gets here."

"All right. That's a lot of pressure just to order food. I feel uneasy now. This is what it must feel like when you're in jail before lunch or something."

"I believe you're right. I think the booths are very similar to these."

Johnny nods his assent.

Veronica continues, "The air conditioning in jail, I hear, is also pretty good. Definitely comparable to here."

"Really?" Johnny asks.

"No, you boob. Really? You think they have booths and air conditioning in jail? Don't ever get arrested. Between your misconceptions and the nightly pillaging of your town, you won't be too comfortable."

"Pillaging of my… Oh! Ronnie!"

"Here she comes, get ready!"

The waitress returns, pulls her pad from her apron and asks, "Well?"

Johnny jumps in, "I'll have a pizzaburger deluxe, no onion rings, please."

"And you?"

Veronica requests, "Can I have a grilled cheese, please? No tomatoes."

"Drinks?"

Johnny responds, "Just water," to which

Veronica nods. Johnny quickly adds, "Two waters."

The waitress makes a note of it, or doesn't, and abruptly walks away.

"She's quite pleasant," Johnny notes.

"What are the chances of her not spitting in our food?"

"Same chances of us getting any food." Johnny adds, "Hey, what were we talking about before she came over?"

"You in jail?"

Johnny considers and responds, "No."

"Oh," Veronica remembers, "it was whether or not you could believe it has been four years since, well, since we were kind of in jail if you want to refer to it that way."

"I wonder if they are still there."

"Where else are they going to go? I don't think there's a high demand for the likes of them in another field, or even in that field for that matter. They were awful."

"I concur."

"We should go back there to…"

Johnny cuts off Veronica and interjects, "get revenge!"

Veronica shakes her head at Johnny. She redresses, "No, you super-zero. I was going to say we should go back there to show them how well we have done."

"Oh." Johnny takes his own stab at sarcasm and adds, "That'd be just as good as getting revenge."

"It would be a different type of revenge. It would be a type that says, 'Look at me, I've become

great regardless of how you tried to hold me down.'
Revenge isn't just the *slap you in the face* thing you see
in movies. This would work just as well."

"And when do you propose we exact said
revenge?" Johnny inquires.

Veronica confers with the clock on the wall. Its
hands indicate a little after noon. She asks, "What are
your plans after lunch?"

Johnny confers with the clock and notices the
time. He directs his attention to the greasy tabletop in
front of him. A plate heaping with his pizza-burger and
french fries slides onto it. In front of Veronica slides her
grilled cheese. "Hope you guys are hungry," the waitress
states.

Veronica and Johnny consider the statement.
Veronica nods in response. A beat passes. Johnny begins
to nod.

27 TRUST ME

"It's so weird entering through the front door like this," Veronica states as she pulls open the front door to the school of their youth.

"Yeah. I kind of pictured you as more of a back door girl," Johnny retorts.

"Let them overhear you say that. We'll be kicked out on our butts before we even get inside." They enter the lobby of the school and gaze in wonder at the familiar, yet unfamiliar surroundings.

"If feels so much smaller," Johnny notices.

"It's probably because we got bigger."

"You think?"

"No, the place shrunk. Of course it's because we got bigger. It throws everything off. That and probably because we were scared when we were younger and we have nothing to be scared of anymore." Johnny notices over Veronica's shoulder, about twenty feet behind her, plods Mr. Huxley. Eighteen feet. Johnny blanches. Twelve feet. Mr. Huxley hasn't noticed them yet. Eight feet. It's too late, there's no avoiding it. Mr. Huxley stops behind Veronica.

"Can I help you?" Mr. Huxley asks, startling Veronica in the process. She turns around to face him.

"We're baaack," she responds.

Mr. Huxley tries to register her response. He looks into Veronica's eyes and then Johnny's, and then back to Veronica. He does not recognize either of them.

"It's Veronica," she begins, "and Johnny. Remember? It was only four years ago we graduated."

"Oh, yes, yes, of course I remember the two of you," Mr. Huxley offers, although neither Veronica or Johnny can figure out if he really remembers them or not.

Johnny stays quiet while Veronica puts them in the limelight. She asks, "Don't you want to hear how successful we've become?"

"Of course. How have you been?"

"How do I look?" Veronica coolly responds.

"You both appear to be well. Graduate high school?"

"Yes."

"Working?"

"Working on it."

"And what about you, quiet one?" Mr. Huxley asks Johnny.

Johnny wants to tell him he's recovering from the torture Huxley put him through. Johnny wants to tell him he's eagerly anticipating the weekly therapy sessions he's sure he'll have to go to in the future because of him and Sister Petunia. "Where's Sister Petunia?" Johnny asks.

"You're never going to believe it," Mr. Huxley starts.

"She's dead?" Veronica guesses.

"No, she's not dead."

"That would have been my guess, too," Johnny admits.

Mr. Huxley deadpans, "And that would make you both wrong. She has been taking time out of her schedule for the purposes of reflection. You have perfect timing. If you'd like to visit with her you can find her in church at this very moment."

Veronica looks to Johnny for an answer, as she knows he would be the one out of the two of them to have an issue with seeing her. Their history together, Veronica believes, might be too much for Johnny to deal with. She shrugs her shoulders in question at Johnny. He responds with a shrug back at her. "It's up to you," she admits.

"I'm fine if you are." For clarification he adds, "We can pay her a visit."

***

"Are you sure you're ready?" Veronica asks, hand on one of the door-pulls of the church.

"No, but I guess I'm about as ready as I'll ever be."

Veronica opens the door and a gust of cold air welcomes Veronica and Johnny, along with the scent of incense. "There's a smell I haven't missed," Veronica confesses. They enter the church and the door closes behind them.

Johnny peers left and right. "She's not here. We can go."

"Not so fast," Veronica reassures. She takes a tentative step in, followed by another one. She blesses herself with the holy water from the pool at her right. She flicks some water at Johnny. "Bless you." He wipes his face with the back of his hand in response. He follows Veronica into the aisle and stops when he walks into her because she, too, has stopped. She extends her right arm and points with her index finger. Johnny follows her finger. There it is, the familiar outline. The black habit trails down the back of her head. The massive arms fill the black uniform. The stoic stance as she kneels there in the pew, hands assuredly clasped in front.

"Let's go," Johnny whispers to Veronica. His whisper, a little too loud due to nerves, reaches it at its pew. It stiffens. The black habit begins to crease as the head underneath it rotates toward their direction. Veronica and Johnny remain frozen. The head and habit continue their rotation. The silver-grey tuft of hair peers out from the habit. Johnny grips Veronica's arm from behind her. The menacing blue eyes slice through the air and fix their stare on Johnny. The hands unclasp and push down on the ledge of the pew in front of them. Sister Petunia rises to her feet. She treads her way toward Johnny and Veronica and lands about one and a half feet away from them. Johnny mentally measures, *striking distance.*

"You brazen things," she addresses them.

"It's nice to see you, too, Sister Petunia," Veronica counters.

"Who are you?"

"Sister," Johnny begins, "it has only been four years. It's Veronica," he motions to Ronnie, "and Johnny," he motions to himself.

"How dare you set foot in the Lord's house dressed like streetwalkers."

Veronica agrees with the comment as per the lift in the corner of her mouth which forms a half smile. Johnny realizes he wears a cap in church and takes it off. He shakes his dark brown, shoulder-length hair and tucks the bill of his baseball cap into the back pocket of his jeans.

"Sorry, Sister," Johnny apologizes.

"Too little," Sister Petunia admonishes.

"We just came to say hello," Veronica offers.

"Hello and Goodbye," Sister Petunia responds.

"Johnny, we shouldn't have come. That much is clear. Some people don't change."

"Some people don't need to change," Sister Petunia counters.

"The people who think they don't need to change are merely the people who won't change. The people who do change are the people who usually don't need to. You obviously fall into the former category. I take that back. You're just a bitch, change be damned." Sister Petunia reaches for Veronica's throat but Veronica jumps back. Sister Petunia lurches forward. Veronica pushes her hand out and it lands flat against Sister Petunia's forehead. "Play nice," Veronica directs.

"Ronnie, please don't assault a nun," Johnny pleads.

"She reached for my throat. Don't blame me for

this," she states, as her hand keeps Sister Petunia at bay. Sister Petunia relents and stands ramrod straight. Veronica relaxes her arm at her side. "Maybe we should go now," Veronica offers.

"That would be the best idea. You don't belong here," agrees Sister Petunia.

Johnny notices the confessional behind and to the right of the altar. "Ronnie," Johnny begins, "I'd like to make use of the amenities while I'm here."

"There's a public restroom at the park down the road. I'm sure you're familiar with it," directs Sister Petunia.

"I meant the confessional."

"Oh," exclaims Veronica. "Sure thing. Well, I'd better go. I know when I'm not welcomed, and that's fine. It's not you, God," she directs upwards, "it's me. Rather, it's Sister Petunia. Sorry you have to deal with someone so awful on a daily basis. Must suck, but I'm sure you manage just fine. Okay, tootles," she directs upwards. "Johnny, I'll see you later. Sister Petunia, I'll see you later, too. In hell. Let's face it, I know I'll be there, and, well, there's no way you're not going to be there."

Sister Petunia huffs in response and grips her rosary beads in her hand. Veronica leaves through the church doors. Johnny silently makes his way to the confessional as Sister Petunia resumes her position in the pew from whence she came. She kneels and reflects as Johnny enters the screened confessional. He kneels in the dark and slides the screen in front of him open. A few seconds pass. He wonders if a priest mans the confessional at this time of day. No response or

movement from the other side yet, so maybe not. Johnny shifts his leg to rise when the screen opens from the other side. He remains on his knees. "Forgive me, Father, for I have sinned. It has been… it has been about four years since my last confession."

"Four years?" the Father repeats. "That's quite a long time to go without confession."

Johnny recognizes the voice in an instant. That gravelly voice, deep, rich, resonant. Johnny considers, *Thankfully, some people don't change; Father Mann certainly doesn't need to.*

"I know, Father. Life happens. I know what you're going to say, that it's not this life we should be concerned with, but the afterlife. I know. Believe me, I know."

"What brings you to confession today, then, after four years?"

"Well, I came back primarily to visit the school, to show them how I turned out. I used to go here."

"You did? I thought I recognized that voice. Might I inquire as to with whom I speak?"

"It's Johnny. Well, to you, it's…"

"Young Jonathan!" Father Mann exclaims.

"Yes," Johnny laughs and feels himself blush in the darkness, "it's Young Jonathan."

"Young Jonathan, come around, none of this screen business between the two of us," Father Mann directs. Johnny exits the screened confessional and barely turns to go toward the face-to-face entrance when he finds himself face-to-face with Father Mann who captures Johnny in a bear hug. Johnny breathes in Father Mann's scent. Father Mann releases Johnny from his hold. "It's been years, Young Jonathan. What has kept you away for so long?"

"Oh, you know," Johnny demures. "A little of this, a little of that."

"Well, I see you're not little any more. How old are you now?"

"Eighteen. Just turned eighteen."

"What a fine, strapping young lad you've turned into." He takes a moment to take in Johnny's form. "Come," he takes Johnny's hand, "let's get more comfortable," he states as he leads Johnny into the face-to-face confessional. He closes the door behind them. Sister Petunia glares over her rosary at the confessional. Father Mann and Johnny seat themselves on chairs that angle in at each other. "Eighteen, huh?" Father Mann extends a hand to Johnny's knee. "My how you've grown."

"Growing by the minute," Johnny responds.

"Sounds promising." Father Mann catches himself and removes his hand from Johnny. "Who did you see at the school?"

"Huxley. And Sister Petunia, but I just saw her outside. Neither of them remembered us at all."

"Us?"

"I was here with Ronnie and they didn't have a clue who we were, not even a glimmer of recognition."

"You have to keep in mind they have scores of students each year who pass through their doors. One is liable to forget some. How they could forget you, however, I can't explain."

"Thanks, Father, that's very kind."

"It's true, Young Jonathan. I couldn't forget you

if I tried."

"That's what they all say, then they never call."

"What's that? Oh, clever." An awkward silence follows an exchange of glances.

Johnny lowers his gaze from Father Mann's eyes down to Father Mann's chest. He wears just the white cotton t-shirt today. It's a v-neck and it forms to Father Mann's amply muscled chest. Johnny lusts after the dark, moderately hairy portion of chest he can see where the v-neck affords him a view. Johnny thinks, *Oh, to be the cross that dangles so perfectly against his chest. To feel his skin against mine. To feel his warmth. The movement. The bumping, the pounding... the releasing.* Johnny wipes the corner of his mouth with his index finger in fear that a drop of drool escapes.

"My eyes are up here," Father Mann directs Johnny's attention to his eyes.

"I wasn't, I mean..." Johnny stammers.

"Just messing with you. I take good care of it."

"I can tell."

"So I definitely appreciate when people notice. I have to admit, I occasionally check out other guys' as well."

This conversation is going places I didn't think of. "You do?"

"All the time," Father Mann admits. "It's kind of a prerequisite in this field."

"Really?" Johnny asks in disbelief.

"Assuredly. The feel of a good one against you at night, whether it's on top of you or underneath you, you feel it press against you and there's nothing else like it. Brings you closer to God. At least, I find it always works for me."

Beads of perspiration form along Johnny's forehead. He notices his hands have become clammy.

"Are you hot? It is a tad warm in here." Father Mann stands, his crotch at Johnny's eye level. The beads of sweat begin to roll down Johnny's face. Johnny swipes at them with his hands. Father Mann looks around and finds a box of tissues. He holds the box out to Johnny. "Sometimes we get criers in here." Johnny takes a few tissues from the box and dabs at his face. "Better?" Father Mann moves some of Johnny's hair that obstructs his face and places it behind his ear. He delicately traces Johnny's earlobe with his finger before he sits down again. Johnny nods he is better.

"So…" Johnny starts cautiously, "even though you're a priest…"

"Yes, Jonathan…"

"You can still have sex with men?"

Father Mann looks down and clasps his hands together between his knees. "What makes you think… Ohhh… you thought I was referring to…" he places his hands on his own chest. "I meant…" he pinches his cross with his fingers.

"I'm so sorry, Father Mann, I didn't mean to imply…" Johnny blurts as he stands.

"Jonathan," Father Mann jumps to his feet and grabs Johnny's wrists. "Jonathan, you did nothing wrong. You didn't imply anything wrong. A person loves who they love. That's all. Apologies are not necessary between us, I promise you."

"Are you sure?"

"Yes. Can you sit back down?"

"Umm, I guess so." They sit down and Father Mann moves his chair closer to Johnny's. He extends both hands to Johnny's knees. "Young Jonathan, so apologetic, so innocent, so young. You could never offend me in any way, and there's nothing offensive about two men being with each other. I want you to understand that."

"But the church…"

"But the church nothing. Love conquers all, Young Jonathan." He presses his hands into Johnny's knees. "Love conquers all."

Johnny lowers his head. His eyes rest on Father Mann's hands. He reaches down and places his hands on Father Mann's. "I want to believe you," he states.

"Then do." He gently squeezes.

"Sometimes, I don't know. Sometimes I want to act on it, and then sometimes, even though it's been years since I've been here, I hear the church's views on how bad," he whispers the next word, "homosexuality is. I haven't even told my own mother yet." Johnny releases his hands from Father Mann's and he sits back in his chair.

"Young Jonathan," Father Mann leans in, "trust me. Furthermore, trust yourself. If the feeling comes from within you, then it must be good. You're a good person, Young Jonathan." Johnny breaks eye contact with Father Mann. Father Mann notices and takes it as a sign that Johnny doesn't fully believe in what Father Mann says. Father Mann takes Johnny's face tenderly in his hands and tilts his head up so they can regain eye contact. "You, Young Jonathan, are a good person."

Johnny's face rushes with heat as his arms rush

with goosebumps. "When you say my name like that," he breathes.

"Young Jonathan," Father Mann breathes in return. He pulls Johnny forward without effort, as Johnny moves his head forward himself. Lips meet. Pillowy, supple lips press together. One, two, ten seconds pass. Father Mann releases a soft, yet assertive, groan. Johnny places a hand on Father Mann's chest. He feels his heart beat beneath the white t-shirt, beneath the muscle. He slowly presses away with his fingertips and moves his lips back from the pair they press against.

Johnny wants to say, *We can't,* but stops himself. He hears Father Mann in his ear, *If the feeling comes from within you, then it must be good.*

"Trust me," Father Mann urges. He takes the hand that recently pressed him away and places it on his chest. He holds it there. "Trust me," he repeats.

In her pew, a mere forty feet or so away, Sister Petunia fingers the rosary beads that drape over her hand. Her mouth moves along in silent prayer and her eyes split their time between the rosary beads and the door to the face-to-face confessional.

28 VACATION FROM VOCATION

"When was the last time you heard someone scream, 'F-
me, Father, F- me now!' in church?" David, formerly
known as Father Mann, asks Johnny.

"Haven't you ever seen *The Exorcist*?"

"That's a movie, Johnny, that's not real life."

"It was based on real events, don't discount it."

"It might have been *loosely* based on real events,
but that's neither here nor there. You can't scream things
like that and not expect other people to overhear."

"Are you saying I knew that busybody was
going to be listening? I resent the insinuation."

"I'm not saying you knew she was listening. I'm
saying this could have been avoided."

"Well, you could have put a hand over my
mouth or something. Gagged me, maybe?"

"It was our first time together, I wasn't very well
going to gag you."

"Waiting it out, were you? Not on your agenda
for the day?"

"I resent *that* insinuation. I did not have an 'agenda' that day nor any other day. I was there for you when you needed me. Remember that, *you* came to *me*."

"Yeah, well, you came *on* me. Remember that. You still owe me for the dry cleaning by the way. Don't think I forgot."

"Think of it as your little blue Gap dress. You can sell it on eBay one day for a pretty penny. Make sure the description includes, 'Shirt contains DNA of the one-time Father Mann who found himself excommunicated before the stain had time to set.'"

"You don't have to be so saucy."

"You're right. I'm so selfish. It was only my vocation!"

"Exactly," Johnny agrees.

"Exactly nothing. My savings are almost depleted. It's about time you got a job around here to help us."

"*Me* get a job? I have no skills. What do you expect me to do?"

"I know one thing you're good at," David offers.

"I'm not becoming a prostitute. They always show you good looking guys that go to prostitutes on television shows but I know that isn't the case. I'm sure they're all old, ugly, or both. Not for me."

"I wasn't going to suggest you become a prostitute. I'm concerned, now, hearing the reasons you have for not becoming one." He adds, "Glad to see your love for me wouldn't be an issue at all. That's always reassuring."

"Hey, extended scene, cut to the chase. One thing I'm good at?"

"I was going to say you could get some kind of job in the service industry."

"Still sounds like sex work."

David shakes his head. "Service industry like as in serving others."

"Yep, that's what I heard."

"Food, drinks, items… not sex. Bartenders, waiters, jobs like those where people serve others. You have a pleasant, for the most part, personality. You'd be a shoe-in for a job like that."

"Neat. And while I'm doing that you're going to…" Johnny searches the apartment with his eyes in mock search of an answer.

"I'm going to focus my energy. I need to realize who I am, who David is. David is no longer Father Mann, and David needs to discover who David is."

"David needs to stop speaking in the third person before David gets hurt."

"You'd never hurt me, Young Jonathan. It's not your style." David gets to his knees.

"David, unless you're about to beg my forgiveness and tell me you'll be the one to go and get a job, I'd get up. If Jonathan has to work, little Jonathan goes on strike."

Charlie Casso

29 FALLEN ANGELS

Johnny removes himself from the apartment for the day and pounds the proverbial pavement for work. As he walks down the street, he notices a *Help Wanted* sign in the *OfficeGear* window. *Hey,* Johnny thinks, *I'll bite.* He stands in front of the doors and they automatically open for him. *I can get used to this,* he thinks. Once inside the store, he peruses its wares. Lots of paper, first and foremost. Then there are the paper shredders to shred the paper, staples to staple the paper, envelopes to mail the paper, pens to write on the paper. The store should be called *PaperGear. But hey,* Johnny wonders, *what do I know?* He ambles about the store and remains on the lookout for a store manager. Shiny paper clips in the shape of angels distract him.

"Can I help you?" booms a voice behind Johnny. He whirls around, container of paper clip angels in hand, and smacks into the column next to him. He makes an exclamation in pain and the container pops open against the column and sends paper clip angels to the ground.

"I'm sorry, young man. I didn't mean to sneak up on you."

"I'm sorry, myself. I sent these poor little paper clip angels to the ground." Johnny picks one up by its little wing. "We'll have to call you Lucifer now, won't we?" he asks it. The store manager, as he must be a store manager since he wears the managerial red shirt, laughs at Johnny's remark.

"You've certainly got a good sense of humor, kid."

"Thank you, sir."

"And respectful, too. Your parents done well with you. So, how can I help you?"

"In terms of being in the store, I'm fine. I was just browsing. I came in, though, because I noticed you have a *Help Wanted* sign in the window."

"Looking for a job, are you?"

"Yes, sir." Johnny holds the paper clip angel out in front of the manager, moves it up and down and, in a squeaky voice, says, "Give the boy a job, give the boy a job."

"You realize that's the angel you referred to as Lucifer, right? Because if…"

Johnny picks up another paper clip angel from the ground, holds it out, and squeaks, "Listen to me, I'm the patron saint of paper. Give the boy a job."

"Patron saint of paper, huh? First I need to see the boy's credentials."

Johnny holds Lucifer out again and states in a deeper voice, "I knew I liked you."

The manager looks Johnny in the eye and tells him, "Kid, while I appreciate the show, I am going to have to check out your credentials, experience, and references. You do know that, right?"

Johnny puts both arms, and thus both angels, down by his side. "I know. It's just I never really had a job before. I'm fresh out of high school. I was a good student. I'm responsible, punctual. I won't give you a hard time, not at all. Why would I? I really need a job and something about this place drew me in. Maybe it was the call of the paper clip angels for all I know."

"I did give you quite a scare," the manager admits. "I'm Todd." Todd extends his hand to Johnny.

"Johnny. Nice to meet you, Todd."

"Likewise. Listen, how about we get some paperwork filled out and then we put you on the floor and see how you interact with customers? If it's a good fit you're welcome to stay. If not, well, you can't say we didn't try."

"Sounds more than fair to me. Thank you, Todd." ·

30 GET A ROOM

The door to the apartment creeks open. Johnny enters, drops his messenger bag on the floor, and plops himself down on the couch. "You were out an awful long time," David addresses Johnny.

"It's called a job."

"You found a job already? That's amazing! Congratulations! I'm so proud of you," David exudes.

"It's not a life changer, but it's something, at least for the time being."

"Don't keep me waiting. Tell me, what is it?"

"Isn't patience a virtue?"

David glares at Johnny.

"Too soon?" Johnny asks. "All right. I got a job at *OfficeGear*. Nothing glamorous, but it looks like it'll be about thirty-five hours a week and decent pay. Actually, any pay is more than what I have been earning, so it sounded good to me."

"That's terrific, Young Jonathan. I'm so proud of you."

"Thanks. What have you been up to today? Find yourself?"

"I have been searching the internet for ideas, looking for what I want to do with my life."

"And…?"

"It's a work in progress," David replies. He leans over the computer desk and clears the browsing history. Johnny notices but doesn't say anything.

"If you need a hand," Johnny offers, "let me know."

"That's kind of you to offer. I don't want to detract from your fine day though. Shall we celebrate?"

"I'm a little tired, David. I've been on my feet all day, and I'm not really used to it yet."

"How about you rest up for an hour or so while I make us something to eat. We can have dinner and then go out for a celebratory drink. What do you think?"

"But you don't drink, well, aside from the blood of Christ that is."

"I can get a soda, Jonathan. What do you say?"

"I guess it can't hurt. Might be nice, actually."

"Then we have a plan! Go lie down, I'll wake you up in a bit."

Johnny heads to bed, even if for a brief nap. Time off his feet will do him well. He pulls the sheet over his head and burrows himself into his pillow.

***

"Thanks again for making dinner, David. It was very thoughtful of you."

"No problem. You can be the bread-winner and I

can be the bread-maker."

"I think I'll have to veto that. You need a job, too."

"Jonathan, tonight is for celebrating your accomplishment. Can we not discuss my shortcomings at the moment? Tonight's for you, all about you."

Johnny reluctantly nods his approval. "All right, all right."

Johnny and David make their way to BarN, the only country-themed gay bar in the city. Upon their entrance, Dolly Parton blares at them from the speakers as three bartenders line dance atop the bar. *Please don't let me take a beer glass to the head when they do their kicks,* Johnny prays. He and David work their way through the crowd and over to the bar as the song ends. The bartenders jump down from their stage of sorts and resume their positions mixing cocktails.

David orders, "Can I get a Long Island and a diet coke, please?" He looks to Johnny for money. Johnny hands him a twenty dollar bill. David exchanges the money for the drinks, tips the bartender, and pockets the change. He gives the Long Island to Johnny. They clink their glasses together at David's toast, "To new beginnings." They sip their respective drinks and gaze at the diverse crowd.

"I'd expect more cowboy hats," Johnny shouts to David. David nods in response, but whether he heard Johnny or not remains uncertain. David points toward a group of four young men, each with a cowboy hat atop his head. He has, in fact, heard Johnny. Johnny nods. One of the group members notices David and Johnny looking their way. He elbows the group member next to him and nods toward David and Johnny. They exchange hushed words. The other two members turn smoothly around to check out the people in question. Eyebrows arch and heads turn as the group splits into two. Two work their way between David and Johnny to order drinks at the bar. They face Johnny's direction as their order is given to the bartender. The other two move toward David.

"Where's your cowboy hat?" one asks David. David looks behind him.

"I'm talking to you, handsome. Where's your cowboy hat?"

"Cowboy hats aren't really my thing," David responds.

"Oh," he takes his hat in his hand, "then I'd better take this one off. Anything you don't like on me, believe me, I'll gladly take off." His sidekick laughs.

Mere feet away, Johnny stands perturbed. He can't even see David since Frick and Frack stand in front of him and block his view. One of them smiles a somewhat good-natured, yet somewhat pity-ridden smile at Johnny. Johnny rolls his eyes in return. "You can smile, you know," the one Johnny considers as Frick says to him. Johnny smiles an obnoxious smile. "Or not," Frick replies. They take their drinks and walk away. In doing so, Johnny has a clear view of David, who is involved in a playful conversation with the friends of Frick and Frack. *Yep,* Johnny thinks, *this night is all about me.* Johnny moves to David's side and stands unnoticed. He clears his throat, but the loud music drowns it out. He coughs loud, louder, and ultimately reaches for a napkin from the bar and hocks a loogie into it to get their attention. *Yep, always classy.*

"Johnny," David finally notices. "Johnny, this is, hmm, I didn't quite catch your names."

"We haven't pitched yet, but we're glad to know your position on the field."

If looks could kill, Johnny would be on trial for double manslaughter.

"I'm Sebastian."

What a fake name, Johnny thinks. *That's his 'going out' name. Whore.*

"And this here is Christian."

All right, jury's out on that one. Slut.

"Nice to meet you Sebastian and Christian, I'm David and this here's Johnny."

Johnny? Not even Jonathan? Certainly not Young Jonathan. I'm onto you, David, just like crabs onto these two.

"Ooh, David. Strong name," Sebastian coos. "Reminds me of that statue in, like, France or somewhere. 'David Statue' or something like that. All buff and naked. And hard, so hard. Scrumptious." Sebastian gives David the once over. "You know you could totally have been the inspiration for that statue." Christian laughs softly at Sebastian's audacity. "Are you?" Sebastian cluelessly asks.

"Not that I know of," David responds, somewhat embarrassed.

Christian extends his hand to Johnny and claims, "Nice to meet you, Johnny." Johnny begrudgingly shakes hands with him.

"Yep, same here," he lies.

"What brings you out tonight?" Christian asks.

"Celebration of sorts."

"Oh, nice. What are you celebrating?"

"I didn't think it was a big deal, my boyfriend did. I got a job today and he wanted to take me out to celebrate."

"That's incredible! Who's your boyfriend?" Christian's hands hold up the air as if to say what's incredible is the fact Johnny has a boyfriend.

"David." Johnny indicates David with a splay of the hand.

"David, as in *our* David?" Christian asks incredulously.

"No, David as in *my* David." Johnny sees Sebastian, a mere two feet away, fawn all over David. He playfully strokes David's arm while he laughs, and with his other hand he covers his mouth as if he laughs too hard. *Anything to draw attention to the mouth,* Johnny notices. Johnny reaches out and grabs David's hand. "Hey, sweetie, how are you doing?"

"Sweetie?" Sebastian reproaches. "He doesn't seem like a 'sweetie' to me. He seems too rugged, too... too manly to be called 'sweetie.'"

"That's funny you say that," David chimes. "That's my name. Mann. My last name is Mann."

"Get out," Sebastian pushes his palm against David's chest to mirror his words. "Oh, you *are* manly." He squeezes David's chest. "How firm. Is everything about you this firm?"

David and Johnny both blush but for different reasons. No one has to wait long to discover Johnny's reason as he blurts, "His firmness is none of your business, whore!"

"Meow," Sebastian claws at the air. "Kitty has claws."

"Kitty's gonna scratch your eyes out," Johnny rebukes.

Sebastian laughs it off as if Johnny is not a threat in the least. "Okay, calm down there Hello Kitty. It was just a compliment. I have no interest in stealing your man. Borrowing maybe, but certainly not stealing."

Johnny clenches his jaw and looks toward the door.

"I'm kidding," Sebastian offers. "Calm down, I'm only messing with you."

"Tell us about this new job," Christian cuts in.

David squeezes Johnny's hand and gloats, "I'm so proud of him, he landed his first job today."

Johnny tries to prepare a lie in case they ask him what means of employment he found, as it's certainly none of their business what he does. His mind goes blank though right at the very moment Christian asks, "So, what is that you do?"

"I work at a laboratory," Johnny lies. He doesn't look at David for fear David's face will give away Johnny's lie.

"A laboratory?" Sebastian questions. "Like a *Frankenstein* kind of laboratory?"

He read a book? Johnny wonders, *No, he probably just saw the movie.*

"No, not a *Frankenstein* laboratory," Johnny responds. Descriptions from when Huxley made the class read *Flowers for Algernon* run through his mind. Johnny offers, "A medical testing and fieldwork laboratory." Since believable lies require a moderate amount of detail, but not too much detail, he adds, "We test on small animals mostly. Depending on the project we do get the occasional human."

"Sounds intriguing," Sebastian offers, although he looks bored out of his gourd. "Do you all know these two miscreants?" He directs everyone's attention to the two men who had separated Johnny from David at the bar. Their cowboy hats remain atop their heads.

"Allow me to make the introductions," Christian offers. "David, Johnny, meet Sal and Anthony." The two men shift their drinks to their left hands and extend their right hands, in turn, to David and Johnny. Anthony's tank top reveals his obsession with Keith Haring's art. His tall, solid physique affords a decent amount of workspace for a tattoo artist, but, at this point, little available space remains. Sal, on the other hand, shorter yet more muscular, appears to be tattoo-free. He wears his attention-getter around his neck. A thick, gold chain displays itself as much as it displays his hairless, or possibly waxed, chest. He has the *trying too hard to look Italian* thing going. Fortunately for him, it works.

"What's going on, guys?" Anthony asks to no one in particular.

"I'm bored," Sebastian offers. David and Johnny watch the interchange.

Christian replies, "You're only bored 'cause someone's tongue isn't down your throat." Sebastian glances at David.

"Whatever," Anthony offers, "night's young, relatively. And so are we."

"Relatively," Christian tacks on.

"Hey, we got a room," Sal speaks. He shrugs

and takes a sip of his drink. "What? We got a room."
Sebastian, with a bow of the head, urges Sal to explain.
Sal continues, "I told ya before but no one listens. We
got a room couple blocks up." Sebastian prods again.
"A'right, so, a friend a ours knows a guy, a manager
guy, and he got us a room, a suite, free. Not gonna turn
down free. So, yeah, like I said, we got a room."

"Shall we take the party there?" Christian
wonders aloud. Johnny grips David's hand in his and
Christian notices. "Oh, it's not going to be like that. Do
we look like sex party people to you?" Johnny casts a
discerning eye at Sebastian. "He's harmless. All bark, no
bite. Or, we could just stay here. Makes more sense to go
to the room. We can drink there, and be more
comfortable. You did say *suite*, right?"

"Yup," Sal responds.

"So?" Christian turns to David and Johnny since
everyone else is clearly game.

David requests, "Give us a minute." He and
Johnny confer with each other. Johnny shakes his head
no, his reluctance quite obvious to anyone with eyes and
a central nervous system. "They're nice people," David
whispers to Johnny. Johnny shakes his head in response.
"It's just a hotel, just a get-together." Johnny continues
to shake his head no. "I thought you wanted to celebrate.
We could make some new friends out of this." Johnny's
head-shaking continues.

"Hey guys," Anthony interrupts, "I can tell
you're on the fence about coming. They're all good
people, we're all good people. Nothing funny is going to
happen. We know each other for a while now and, well,
it's just good people and good conversation. If you're

not up for it I understand. But don't not have a nice night out doing something different just out of fear of the unknown. Sometimes I actually tell myself, the difference between a person with and without agoraphobia is fear. Blows my mind. Think about it."

Anthony and his tattoos move over to the other three. Johnny and David continue their, mostly one-sided, discussion. "See that?" David asks, "You don't want to be an agoraphobe, do you?"

"David, if it weren't for me you wouldn't even know what that meant. I'm the one who made you watch *Copycat* in the first place."

"I do love Sigourney Weaver."

"See, I make good decisions and I don't want to go to their den of iniquity."

"If that's how you feel, that's fine by me. I was only trying to go with the flow. This is your night. I just want to make you happy. I don't care where we go or what we do, I'm contented being next to you, especially with your new job and all, Mister Scientist," he jests.

"Did you like that?" Johnny smirks.

"It caught me off guard, that's for sure."

"Way to roll with the punches." Johnny smiles, authentically happy during the latter part of this exchange. A pang of guilt creeps through him. "Did you want to go to the suite?"

"Not necessarily. I thought it was an opportunity to do something different, something unexpected. Doesn't matter to me in the least." Some moments of silence pass. "Why? Are you reconsidering? We can do whatever you'd like. You let me know."

Johnny considers and sees the want in David's

eyes. He decides to give in. "All right, nothing funny though. Clothes come off and we are out." David nods his consent.

David turns to the group and shouts, "We're in!"

***

"This is a really big suite," Johnny offers to the group.

"Sal's got the hook up," Sebastian offers. The others exclaim kudos amongst which, "Way to go, Sally Boy!" dominates. David pats Sal on the back and briefly leaves his arm around his shoulder.

"Boys, make yourselves at home," Sal offers. The six members of their party fragment to explore different sections of the suite.

David tells Johnny, "I'm going to find the bathroom."

Johnny notices the oversized couch behind him. "I'll stay here." He pads over to the couch and reclines on his back, hands at his sides. "I feel like a corpse," he says aloud. He clasps his hands behind his head. "Much better." He gazes at the ceiling while distant sounds of laughter manage to barely lick his ears. *Could be worse,* he thinks.

"Hey buddy," Anthony and his tattoos stand in front of Johnny.

Thought too soon, Johnny thinks. "It's Johnny," he replies."

"I remember your name, how could I forget? How's it going?" He ushers Johnny closer to the back of the couch as he sits himself down on it. Johnny stays lying down, mostly because his legs are trapped between the couch's back and Anthony's side.

"It's going," Johnny offers.

"Why you over here all by your lonesome?"

"I'm not alone. David went to find the bathroom is all."

"That may be a while. Last I noticed, Sal was heading in there to take a bath or something."

"Oh."

"May just be you and me out here for a while then."

"What about the other two?" Johnny asks.

"Sebastian and Christian?" Anthony looks down at the carpet and then back at Johnny. "I think they are getting into their extracurricular activities right about now, if you know what I mean." He places a hand on Johnny's torso and tugs gently at his shirt. Johnny instinctively starts to remove a hand from behind his head, to move Anthony's hand away, but he realizes the feel of the hand against him is actually nice. He leaves his hand behind his head and Anthony rubs Johnny's torso with his fingers. Johnny thinks better of it and moves Anthony's hand off him. "Was just being friendly." He gets up from the couch and begins to pad away. He and David pass each other.

"Sorry I took so long," David offers. He sits on the floor in front of the couch.

Johnny pats him on the head. "No worries."

"Was Anthony entertaining you?"

"What's that smell?" Johnny asks.

"What smell?"

"I don't know, hence the question. Smells like

rotten meat." David cups his hand over his mouth to check his breath. Johnny gets another whiff and realizes it is, in fact, David. "Is there, like, a tray of meat to snack on or something? That smells bad, I hope you didn't eat a lot."

"Not really." David stammers for the right words. "Just had a taste."

Charlie Casso

31 SWEET DONUTS

"Don't eat the whole thing, I wanted to try it," Johnny
directs Veronica as she's about to finish her hot dog.
"Thanks for joining me on my lunch break. It's nice to
talk about something other than paper or paper products
during the day."

"I can see that. It must really burn you up.
How'd your little celebration go last night?"

"Interestingly. It went interestingly. We wound
up meeting a few guys at BarN and they took us back to
a suite they had for the night." Veronica's mouth gapes.
Sauerkraut dangles out of her mouth and plops onto the
table. "Gross," Johnny observes. "And close your
mouth, nothing sexual happened if that's what you're
thinking, and I know that's what you're thinking because
I know how your mind operates." Veronica's mouth still
gapes open. "Okay, something sexual could've happened
but it didn't. Some tattooed guy tried to, like, I don't
know, basically just touch my stomach, but that was
about it. It ended there."

"And David?"

"David? David nothing. David didn't see the guy try to make a move or anything. I'm not really sure what his response would've been if he had. He's been acting weird lately. And, for someone who used to be a priest, that's saying something."

"Acting weird how? Handcuffs and safe words weird?"

"No, more like *I need private time* weird. I'm not used to him wanting so much personal space. Yet last night he was all about going to the hotel and being with new people. Weird contrast. Personal time and time with others, time with strangers practically. How do those two go hand in hand?"

Veronica tilts her head to the side. "Well…" She extends the last bite of her hot dog over to Johnny.

"Well what?" Johnny takes the inch of hot dog in his hand and holds it by its bun.

"By personal time you mean time away… from you. But he was all about spending time with others… And you mentioned before that he is trying to find himself."

"Yeah…" Johnny places the hot dog on his plate.

"Well, my only concern is, well… make sure he doesn't find himself… inside someone else."

Johnny feels himself gag. A lump forms in his throat as his lunch desires to make an encore appearance. He tries to gulp down.

"Don't get too concerned," Veronica advises, "but get concerned. You know the saying, *where there's smoke there's fire.* Well, where there are flamers there

218

are long, thick water-hoses waiting to be whipped out."

"Excuse me," Johnny manages as he rushes toward the bathroom. He enters so abruptly he knocks the mop over and it careens head first to the ground. The long grey ropes of hair spread out against the tiled floor. Johnny's own head propels downward toward the open porcelain bowl. He retches into the bowl, and images of last night swirl before him as the chunks of his lunch swirl in the water below him. He sees Sebastian's hands on David in the bar, David's arm around Sal, the flush look of arousal on David's face. Johnny retches another time and heaves spittle into the bowl. He uses the back of his hand to wipe away any leftover remnants from his cheek and lips. "David wouldn't do that to me," he tells himself in the mirror. "David wouldn't cheat on me." Once more, this time with at least an iota of conviction, he tells himself, "David. Would not. Cheat on me. Damn it! I still don't believe it." He pounds the sink with the undersides of his fists. David saying, 'Just had a taste,' echoes through his mind. "You wanna play?" Johnny asks the mirror. One eyebrow shoots up. "Let's play."

***

"Hey, Peaches. Hey, Sugar Peach," calls the waitress who leans over her counter. "Peeeeee-ches." Veronica and Johnny turn. "Yeah, you." Veronica points to herself. "Not you, doll. Peaches." Johnny points to himself. "Yeah, you. C'mere." She curls her index finger to draw him in. Johnny checks with Veronica if she's for real, Veronica's face contorts in a show of *your guess is as good as mine,* and Johnny removes himself from the booth and moves toward the counter. "I don't wanna embarrass ya in front of your girl over there, but did you just ralph in my john?"

"You don't want to embarrass me? I guess that's why you called me Peaches, or Sugar Peach?"

"It's a term of endearment. Consider yourself lucky. Actually, consider yourself not lucky. Like I said, you just ralph in my john?"

"Umm, maybe."

"Maybe? Listen kid, I got no time for games. You ralph in my john you clean it up. We don't got the man power to be cleaning up after you. Now, I'm not kicking you out or anything, I'm just sayin' clean up after yourself."

"Understandable. My apologies." Johnny notices her nametag. *Rose.* "I'll take care of it right now." He politely adds, "Rose." Johnny quickly remedies the bathroom issue, washes his hands, and returns to Veronica.

"What was that about?" she asks.

"Oh, you know how it is, if you're gonna puke in my bathroom at least have the common decency to clean it up."

Veronica throws her arm up and exclaims, "Check, please."

***

Later that night, Veronica sits on her couch as Johnny paces her living room. "I don't know. I mean, what you said today made complete sense. Silly, yes, but it made sense. He definitely seemed intrigued, or at least interested in the guys, in some way. I don't want to believe he would ever cheat on me though. He's a former man of the cloth. That would be like adultery."

"You're not like man and wife, Johnny. You need to be man and wife in order for adultery to happen. And you have butt sex, let's not forget that."

"I'll try not to…" Johnny says. He wonders why she made mention of the butt sex.

"The church doesn't exactly advocate butt sex, Johnny. It's considered sodomy. According to the church, you're a sodomite." Confusion paints Johnny's face. "I have to spell it out for you, I guess. Okay, David used to be a priest, right? He's very familiar with the church's views and the church would consider cheating as adultery if it were between a man and a woman and they were married. Not only are you not man and woman, and not married, but the type of love, the type of sex you guys have together is, well, it's immoral, at least according to the church. I, personally, find it hot. Two men together? Count me in. David probably has no other choice but to go with what he knows. Cheating on you, if he is, and maybe he's not, but cheating on you, to him, wouldn't be adultery. It would be additional sodomy. That's all."

Johnny's pace slows to a halt. "So," he says more to himself than to Veronica, "he would find nothing wrong with cheating." Veronica goes to say something but Johnny cuts her off. "He'd see nothing wrong with it, nothing more wrong with it than it being sodomy. No guilt, no feelings of remorse or betrayal, just… just… nothing. His carnal desires could run rampant and he'd be fine, because he knows the only thing the church could find wrong with it is that it's sodomy. He could keep that in his back pocket and go to town with whomever he wants, whenever he wants, and wherever he wants. He could be plowing his way through everyone's fields for all I know."

"Johnny, you know you're the only hoe for him." Veronica's humor lands flat.

Johnny continues, "I made a promise to myself today. I'm not going to let him go without a fight."

"You're getting way ahead of yourself. He probably doesn't even want to leave you, and, if he does want to leave you, would you want to fight for him to stay?"

"That's not what I meant at all," Johnny laughs. "I meant if he wants to leave, if he even acts like he's unhappy, he's going to leave. But he's not going to leave without a fight first."

Veronica's eyes widen as she takes in the magnitude of his declaration. She thinks about the previous fights Johnny has been in and her mind drifts back to their elementary school as all of Johnny's fights have been there, and with adults, and all one-sided. "Johnny, no offense, but I don't think you'd be prepared for a fight. All you've ever fought have been Huxley and Petunia, and they were the clear winners in those matches.

"I didn't mean I was going to fight him like physically fight him."

"Oh, you meant a mental battle, like a battle of wits."

Johnny considers the statement. "I don't know exactly what I meant, but I meant it. And you're either with me or against me."

"With you, duh. Totally with you. Hey, we can start now if you want." She motions toward her computer. "Want to do a little reconnaissance?"

"Like what?"

"I don't know, it's the internet. Our options are unlimited. Actually, if he's cheating on you, and using the internet, his options are unlimited as well. He can be meeting people from next door all the way to Timbuktu, wherever that is."

"And how, pray-tell, do we do this?"

"Oh it's easy. I have all these accounts on different sites, don't judge me, that I use for meeting the gays. I should say e-meeting the gays, we never actually meet in person or anything. I don't think they'd appreciate it that they wasted their time talking to she-who-has-vagina. You know I find guy-on-guy action hot. Once in a while I chat up a gay and get him to send me some action shots. Don't be judgey. It's harmless. Anyway, we can use my accounts. I'll just change the names et cetera and make them more appealing to David. I know what you're thinking and it's not entrapment. Listen, if he is on here and he goes for us, that's on him. We aren't making him create an account or make a profile or anything."

Veronica starts opening different tabs on her computer and logging in to each respective site. Johnny eyes the muscle bound hunks that appear on each of Veronica's profiles. "Ronnie, where'd you get those photos?" She waves his question away and continues swiping away at her keyboard and running her poor mouse ragged. "My God, Ronnie, you're a whore. My little girl's a whore, a big, giant, beautiful whore!" He hugs Veronica from behind as she sits in her chair at work on the computer.

"I need the functional use of my arms in order to continue here. Your little girl's a better whore with two functional hands, you know."

"Yes, yes, sorry." Johnny releases Veronica briefly but then traps her in his embrace again and exclaims, "I love my little whore!"

"Arms, please!"

Johnny releases Veronica and stands at her side. He gawks as she works her rainbow magic and creates new gays to play with online.

"Voila!" Veronica exclaims as she throws her hands up. "I'm a-mah-zing, I know." She pats herself on the back, literally.

Johnny begins to ask, "So now what do we..." but finds himself cut off by a loud *bloop* sound. "What's that?"

"That's the sound of your future calling. Aren't you going to answer?" She points to a new message on the screen and moves the mouse toward Johnny. *Bloop.* "It's waiting."

Johnny clicks the message icon and reads aloud, "You're hot. I want to make you my angry dragon." Johnny looks perplexed. "Did I read that right? 'You're hot. I want to make you my angry dragon.'"

"It sounds sweet," Veronica offers. "Except for the 'angry' part. I'm not sure about that. You know what, just respond. You'll find out what he means."

"Sounds like a good idea." Johnny types and reads slowly as he does so. "Hi there. Thank you for your message. I hope you are having a good night…"

"Shakespeare, cut to the chase," Veronica interrupts.

"I was getting there." Johnny continues to type. "Just wondering, is 'angry dragon' a good thing?" Johnny and Veronica stare at the screen in wait. *Bloop.* "He wrote, 'I'll say. The best. You won't be able to complain at all.' That sounds reassuring."

Veronica prods Johnny from the chair. "Move over. A true friend's work is never done."

"What are you doing?" Johnny asks.

"Just give me a sec." Veronica types away and reads aloud. "Hot stuff, love to be your angry dragon. Just need to know what it is. Details, please, then let's make it happen." *Bloop.* She reads, "I'm gonna bust my nut in your mouth, then slap you on the back of your head so hard my jizz pumps out your nose."

"Ronnie!"

"Ronnie?" she repeats as she slaps her hand to her own chest, "I didn't write it! I kind of wish I did though, that's a very detailed description. I imagine you'd actually look like an angry dragon." She shakes the thought away.

"Close that screen now, please. What are we doing, anyway? This feels like we're cheating on David when we were just supposed to check to see if he's cheating on us, well, me." *Bloop.* "What now?"

"Don't worry, it's someone else. They're not all freaks. See? This one here is being very sweet, and he doesn't even know you yet. He asked you out. You have a date, well, a date proposal. He said, 'Hey, handsome. Gorgeous outside. Can I tempt you with a jelly donut?'

He wants to meet! He wants to meet! Guys don't offer to take me out for donuts."

"Ronnie, technically he did. These are your accounts."

"Oh. True. But not *me,* not the real me."

"We can't meet him anyway. I don't exactly look like that profile picture."

"Valid point. Okay, let me let him off easy. He was sweet after all." She types and reads her message aloud. "Thank you for the kind offer, but I have work to tend to. I at least hope you still have yourself a jelly donut." She looks it over again and nods in contentment with her response. *Bloop.* "It's him again. He wrote, 'Hey, asshole. You really expect me to cum on my own face then punch myself in the nose? Stop wasting my time on here if you're not going to meet!'"

"Oh my God," Johnny squawks.

"Oooh, *that's* a jelly donut! Johnny, that was going to be you! You were going to be a jelly donut. Gay sex is very educational. I feel like a rainbow should arc above us as *the more you know* chimes in the background."

"Thanks, Ronnie. I'll probably never look at a jelly donut the same way again. You've single-handedly ruined jelly donuts for me for life. I hope you're happy."

"Actually, I want a jelly donut. The regular kind, of course." She looks at Johnny's face and tilts her head.

Johnny covers his face with his hands. "Stop it, Ronnie, stop it right now. I know what you're picturing. Not cool!"

"Fine," she relents and turns back to the computer. "To return to the task at hand, we just have to look for David. If he's carousing, he's likely to be on one of these sites. They are for the more anonymity-conscious. And who's more anonymity-conscious than a former priest?"

"A priest?"

"Eww. Oh," Veronica raises her hand to her mouth. "I'm sorry, I forgot you were all hot and bothered when David was a... when he was Father Mann."

"Kettle, lest ye forget, your loins were once set ablaze by the very same man of the cloth. What was it you used to say? Oh yeah, 'I'd kneel for him anytime,' 'It's not the communion wafer I want him to put in my mouth,' and, wait, I'm sure there was another gem, oh, I still can't believe you did this, when you went up for communion and drank the blood of Christ you'd say 'I swallow every drop' when you were finished. Every time!" Veronica shrugs one shoulder. "So don't tell me *I'm* the one with the priest fetish."

"Regardless, priest or former priest, these sites are good places to meet people on the down-low. Speaking of which, Johnny, does this look familiar to you?" She enlarges a picture. It's a person from the neck down, fully clothed, at the botanical gardens. "Doesn't that look like..."

"David. That's David. That's the shirt I got him for Kwanzaa. Don't shake your head at me, I like holidays. Come to think of it, I took that picture! I take good pictures," Johnny says, impressed with his own work. He becomes infuriated, "And then he takes the picture *I* took of him, crops it, and uses it on a hook-up site? In the words of the indelible child-actor-cum-meth-head-cum-recovered-meth-head Jodie Sweetin, *How rude!*" Johnny stands, hands on hips, next to Veronica and faces the computer. "Send him a message. Threaten him. Tell him to get out of this city and go… go somewhere else, I don't care where."

"You want me to slap you, don't you? Slap some sense into you?" Veronica asks. "We can't message him and we certainly can't mandate he leave the city. Who does that? Besides, messaging him would only make him delete his account. You really want that?"

Johnny's response drips with sarcasm. "No, I want my boyfriend to have an online account where he can meet hot guys who'll turn him into an angry dragon or a jelly donut. That's exactly what I want." Johnny stands there. His eyes take their time as they peer left, right, up and finally left again. He repeats his last words slowly. "That's exactly what I want." He takes a breath in and a more exuberant breath out. "I want my boyfriend to meet a guy who'll make him an angry dragon or a jelly donut." He smiles a sinister smile, the kind which could easily be accessorized by the sprouting of devil's horns or a tail. Neither sprout, but the smile remains carved on his face. "Ronnie, dear…"

"Already working on it," Veronica responds as her hands navigate the keyboard and mouse rapaciously. Several minutes pass as Johnny paces the floor.

"Trust me, I know what I'm doing, Johnny." Veronica sums up what she's done so far in an effort to alleviate Johnny's concern. "I created new accounts: a fake David account and a fake Jelly Donut Guy account. I am using the fake account of each to talk with the real account of the other. It's amazing what 'copy' and 'paste' can do. Anyway, I'm almost all done. I'm setting up a meeting between the two of them. They know what each other looks like and all that factual stuff. I just kept David clear of knowing exactly what Jelly Donut Guy is going to do to him."

"Are we sure Jelly Donut Guy is going to make a jelly donut out of David?"

"Well, I also made sure to let Jelly Donut Guy know I, err, David, is all into it. I'm pretty sure it's a done deal. Unless, of course, David backs out of meeting this guy."

"You think he'll back out?"

"You're the one who lives with him, you know him better than I do."

"True. I don't know. Listen, no matter what happens, thank you for helping me with this. I would never have been able to do any of this, let alone even talk with this guy."

"You know what they say," Veronica starts, "the meek shall inherit the earth. The ones with balls, though," she continues and grabs herself, "they'll still be the ones to run it." She peers at the final messages of *see you soon* she sent to David and Jelly Donut Guy and, with one final click of her mouse, logs offline.

Charlie Casso

32 CAREFUL THERE

Johnny holds the handle of the pan on the right of his stove-top and jars it slightly as the soon-to-be fried chicken pieces slide across the pan. Johnny turns to his left and notices the steam rise from his waffle-maker. *Comfort food,* he thinks. He tries to distract himself from thoughts of David and what David might possibly be doing at this very moment, but wild thoughts consistently creep into his consciousness. He lets go of the frying pan, jogs to the television, and turns it on. He grabs the remote and pumps up the volume. He checks both the chicken and the waffles, readies a plate to deposit them on and turns off the sources of heat. "Almost there," he narrates as he deposits the food onto his plate.

With a bottle of maple syrup and an inch-thick's worth of napkins in hand, he pads toward the giant coffee table in the living room where he intends to have his meal. He makes an encore trip to the kitchen and retrieves his plate of chicken and waffles. As he nears the coffee table, the sound of the front door unlocking brings him to a halt. He stands, plate in hand, and watches as the front door opens and David enters. David closes the door behind him, looks up, and finds Johnny there, plate in hand. Johnny gasps at the sight of David's face. A big white bandage covers David's nose and the better part of his face. The plate descends from Johnny's hand to the surface of the table where it smashes. Chicken and waffles rain over the table and onto the floor where they seek shelter from the foreboding storm.

"What happened to your face?" Johnny asks, not realizing what a jelly donut would look like in real life.

"I, umm, you're never going to believe it," David stammers.

As David stumbles for words, Johnny realizes without a doubt that David has indeed met Jelly Donut Guy. In a delicate transition, Johnny's face changes from worry to sadness. He doesn't really hear what David says as the white noise of fury and disbelief cloud his ears. He notices David's lips move, enough to interpret what he says.

"You fell down a flight of subway steps? It's not even raining!"

"What do you want me to say, Jonathan? I don't like this any more than you do."

"I'll bet you did though, at least a little, at least at some point," Johnny protests.

"What does that even mean? You're making no sense. You'd think I could get a little sympathy, my nose is broken."

"Sympathy?" Johnny screams. His eyes dart around. He notices the pieces of chicken being stomped into the ground. "Sympathy? I'll give you sympathy. Here's your sympathy…" Johnny is about to tell David how he feels sorry for himself for spending so much time with the man he thought he loved and who he thought loved him in return. However, he lets his rage deflate. "Sorry. It's just, I didn't expect to see you like this."

"I didn't expect to see me like this either. It happens. I guess I have to be more careful in the future."

Johnny winces.

"What?" David asks.

"Nothing. I just thought you'd maybe think twice about taking the subway any more now, seeing what can happen and all."

"I wouldn't not take the subway because of one little trip up. What do you expect me to do?"

"Stay with what you have. You have feet, stick with them. Walk more, it's healthier."

"Johnny, I can't just walk everywhere. Besides, even if I could, I'd get tired of it. The routine of it all. Sometimes it's nice to change things up a bit."

"And sometimes it's better for everyone to stick with the road more travelled, to stick with the one you know and love."

"Sometimes, yes. But that's not for everyone. Some people need options. There's nothing wrong with having options. Would you really want to limit me in such a way?"

"Yes," Johnny answers honestly.

"No," David responds emphatically. "If I want to take the subway, I'll take the subway. If I want to take a bus, then a bus it is. And, you know what, some days

I'll take more than one subway. Maybe I'll ride two, even three in a day." Johnny's eyes widen at this. "There's no telling."

"Fine. If that's the way it's going to be, then fine. At least now we each have a part of us that's broken."

33 PRACTICALLY A VIRGIN

"Why the long face, kid?" Todd asks.

Johnny's nostrils flare. He responds, "Born this way? I don't know, I never really thought I had a… oh. I never understood that expression. Do sad people's faces really appear longer? I'd think that would make them even sadder. You know, if you're sad and you look in the mirror and see you look all horse-like, wouldn't it make you even sadder?" Johnny sighs.

"You're clearly a thinker, kid."

"Thanks."

"Care to share?"

"No, I'm all right. I have to finish this inventory."

"You have to have lunch, too, you know. Come on, my treat."

"No, no. I'll be fine."

"Wait right here, I know what you need." Todd runs off and leaves Johnny in the aisle by his lonesome. A customer off in the distance peruses the shelves of envelopes. Todd returns. "I brought you some friends." He pulls his hand from behind his back and produces the little tub of paper clip angels Johnny had played with not so long ago. "What's that?" Todd shakes the container. "They're saying, 'Go to lunch, go to lunch!' It's like they're cheering!" Johnny smiles in response to Todd's antics. "Is that a smile I see? I think it is," Todd says as if he speaks to a child. "C'mon, we can bring your little friends."

***

At the diner, Todd places the container of paper clip angels on the table between himself and Johnny. "Everyone needs someone to talk to, kid, whether it be a paper clip angel or a human. We all need someone. Now, you can tell me what's going on, or you can tell the paper clip angels." He opens up the container for effect. "So what's it gonna be?"

"What's it gonna be? I ain't got all day," Rose interrupts.

Johnny's head shifts back and forth between Todd and Rose, and, intermittently, down to the container of paper clip angels. "You're a special one, aren't ya?" Rose asks of Johnny.

"I'll have silver dollar pancakes, please. Something got me in the mood for pancakes. Maybe I'm craving the syrup I haven't been able to have in months."

"Months? Something happen with syrup I should know about?" Todd asks.

"Ahem," Rose regains their attention.

"I'll have, hmm, I'll have a banana split. That should spruce things up a bit." Rose writes it down. "And can I get a glass of pineapple juice?"

"Just water for me," Johnny directs Rose. She walks away. "A banana split for lunch? Impressive," Johnny nods to Todd.

Todd picks up where he left off, "Months? Incident? Syrup?"

"It's nothing. I was making chicken and waffles for dinner a couple of months ago."

"And you were out of syrup," Todd finishes for him. "Sometimes I find whipped cream is a nice substitute for maple syrup. The texture's different, yes, but there's something about the taste of it in your mouth. It's pure," he picks up a paper clip angel, "…heaven. I digress. Tell me about what happened. Is that what has you down?"

"Yes." Johnny re-thinks. "Well, no, at least not the syrup part. I wasn't out of syrup. I always have plenty of syrup."

"I'm sure you do."

"I do. It wasn't that. My boyfriend came home a couple of months ago with a broken nose."

Todd is taken aback by the new information. "I wasn't aware you had a boyfriend." He twists the paper clip angel in his hands. "Broken nose, huh? He's a fighter I guess? A real tough guy." He bobs his head as he mulls over the information. "Figures."

"Are you kidding me? He's not a fighter at all. For God's sake, the man used to be a priest."

"A priest?" Todd asks to confirm he heard correctly.

"A priest."

Todd tries to untwist the angel back to its original state. He presses it against the table with his thumb. "That's nice," he offers.

"It was… in the beginning. I think he's cheating on me."

Todd enlivens but checks it. "Well, if you think he's cheating on you then you know what you need to do."

Johnny says, "Speak with him," at the same moment Todd says, "Sleep with someone else."

"What?" Johnny asks.

"Huh?"

"What did you say? I couldn't hear you."

"I said… speak with someone else. That's what I said."

"Oh. For a second I thought you might have said 'sleep.'"

"Now what kinda guy do you think I am…"

"It wouldn't have been the worst idea."

"Now that *you* mention it though, maybe…"

"Oh, who am I kidding? When it comes to sex, I move slower than a paraplegic in a swimming pool. I just kind of drift to my position at the bottom and lie there, flat on my back."

Todd fans himself with a napkin. "Go on," he urges.

"Yeah, so I don't really see myself sleeping with someone else, even if he is charging his plug in someone else's outlet."

"I'm sure your outlet's better."

"I'd like to think so. Don't have anyone else to

tell me though. He's the only person I've ever been with."

"You've only ever been with one person? You're practically a virgin."

"I mean, we've done it a lot, don't get me wrong. He is the only person I've done it with though."

"I'm intrigued. He's the only person you've ever been with and you believe he's cheating on you. Why wouldn't you then sleep with someone else? You deserve to, not just to get even with him but also to see what it's like being with other people. The unexamined sex life is not worth living. It's a famous quote."

"I don't think that's a famous quote."

"Yes it is. Nietzsche or something."

"It was Socrates and that's not the quote."

"Tom-*ay*-to, Tom-*ah*-to, same difference. Do you really want to live with an unexamined sex life? Do you?" Todd presses for a response.

"Examine this," Rose intrudes. She slides the plates in front of her customers as the sharply sweet scent of maple syrup sweeps into Johnny.

"Wow," he mesmerizes, "these pancakes are something." He starts to slice his silver dollar pancakes into bite-sized pieces as Todd eyes his banana split.

"Get a load of the size of my banana," Todd directs. "It's huge." He picks up his spoon. "Hey, want a taste of my nuts? They'll go well with your pancakes," he offers. Johnny eyes the walnuts and then focuses on his pancakes again.

"That's okay," he responds. "This is going to keep me quite busy. Hey," he addresses Todd, "thanks for lunch by the way. And for the chat. It's nice to have someone to talk to once in a while."

"No problem, kid. You got me and you got your angels over here looking out for you. Eat up. And my offer still stands, you know. If you want some of what I've got… just let me know."

***

"I think your boss is a gay, Johnny," Veronica whispers behind a mountainous display made out of reams of paper. "And I think he wants to dip his *OfficeGear* pen in your *OfficeGear* ink."

"Hush, Ronnie," Johnny whispers.

She picks up a box of envelopes. "He wants to stuff his huge, white paper into your small, tight envelope."

"Not amused."

Veronica jumps to the mountainous display, puts her hands on it, grinds her pelvis against it, and says, "He wants to ream you!"

"*Rim*, Ronnie, he wants to *rim* me."

"This doesn't sound like *OfficeGear* conversation I hear." Todd's statement sends Johnny into a spin. Veronica leaps out of view, behind the display. "Sorry. I see I have a habit of doing that to you, sneaking up on you from behind."

"That's okay," Johnny offers as he clutches his chest. "No damage done. Certainly got my heart racing though."

"Mine, too," he smiles at Johnny. "Who were you talking to?"

"My friend…" Johnny trails off as he realizes

Veronica is gone. "My friend was here a moment ago." He shrugs it off. "Anyway, what's up?"

Todd looks down toward his belt and then shakes himself free from his thoughts. "Was passing through, doing a once-over, and heard you over here." He shuffles his feet. "Carry on. I'll be around." He plods away down the aisles.

"Ronnie?" Johnny whispers. "Ronnie?" She sneaks around the display and pinches his butt. Johnny shoos her hands away.

"Yeah, he wants to fill you like a loose leaf binder."

"Enough, I've heard enough," Johnny protests. "Do you really think he…?"

"Johnny, let me put it this way, if Helen Keller, Marlee Matlin, and you had, like, a conference… well, they wouldn't want you to be the one taking the notes."

"That was way harsh, Tai."

"Truth hurts, babe."

"Anyway, he suggested maybe I consider sleeping with someone else, you know, to even the score. Actually, he suggested I sleep with someone else just for the experience of it and I kind of see his point. When you spend your life swimming amongst the fish you never realize what life is like on land."

"Some people are made for the ocean, Ariel. Deal with it. Don't go carousing out on David just so you can say you peered in on the Rubyfruit Jungle." She pretends to look between the reams of paper for effect. "The grass always seems greener on the other side but it still comes out brown on the other end, you know, through your pooper."

"What do you suggest, then?"

Veronica sucks her cheeks in and places a hand to her heart to show how touched she is that Johnny asks her for advice. She slowly takes a step forward along the side of the display. She faces Johnny, her left hand pulls along on the side of the reams of paper. Her fingernails make a soft *shhh* sound along the reams. "I don't think it's me you need."

"I don't?"

"You don't." She reaches for Johnny, no, she reaches past Johnny. He doesn't turn to see what she reaches for. Instead, he keeps his focus on her face as it approaches his. She pulls an object from the shelf behind Johnny, this much he knows, but he doesn't know what it is. She takes the object between her hands and turns it around to face Johnny. It's a rectangular, metal lunchbox she now holds by its red handle. It dangles before him with a cartoon image emblazoned on its front. It's a fire-breathing, and quite angry-looking, dragon.

34 YOU'RE SO UNBELIEVABLE

"Jonathan," David calls when he enters their apartment. "Jonathan, you're never going to believe this." He closes the door and locks it behind him.

Johnny comes from the bathroom to greet David but stops in his tracks when he notices David has a fresh white bandage across his nose. "What happened?"

"You're never going to believe this. Don't worry, it's not broken again. I was just… this is so silly… I was just drinking some apple juice today when all of a sudden I sneezed, out of nowhere. So the juice spurts out of my nostrils and ruptures something. I had to go to the hospital and everything. They said it was a freak occurrence and it only happened because of the recent nose issue I had. It's really nothing to be concerned about, they just want me to be extra careful for the next couple of weeks and to go back for a check-up and all."

"You're right. Absolutely unbelievable," Johnny agrees.

***

"Mission accomplished," Johnny speaks into the phone.

Veronica comforts, "I'm sorry, babe. I wish we were wrong on this one. I thought there was a chance he'd change his ways after the jelly donut."

"What do we do now?"

Silence fills the air on the line until Veronica manages, "I'm kind of out of ideas here. You have definitive proof he's been cheating on you. I don't know what else to tell you. Wait. How do you know he met Angry Dragon Guy?"

"His story was lame, but he came home with his nose all bandaged up. Whatever fluids ran through his nose ruptured something."

"Sounds ugly."

"Looks worse. Thoughts?"

"I'm all out. The only other place I know you used to go for guidance was to the church, or to Father Mann. That's kind of weird referring to him as Father Mann come to think of it."

"Church. That's not a bad idea. Beggars can't be choosers, right?"

"Beggars can totally be choosers. You learn that when you get whaled in the back by the tuna sandwich you just gave a guy on Fifth Avenue. It's a little known fact but beggars are actually amongst the choosiest. That's how they wind up beggars. They're too picky and wind up with nothing. Almost nothing. Could have had my tuna sandwich."

"Let the tuna sandwich go, Ronnie. Let it go."

"I did until it came sailing back. It hurts, Johnny. A five-dollar foot-long hurts."

"All right, Ishmael. Let the tuna go, for real this time."

"But…"

"Let it go."

Charlie Casso

35 CONFESSION

Johnny approaches the church he used to frequent on pretty much a daily basis growing up. He registers a feeling of warmth and belonging, but, at the same time, a feeling of coldness and distance. The stairs to the church doors loom before him. He approaches and, with every step, piercing shouts reverberate through his mind. The voices of Huxley and Petunia, in turn, torment him.

Left foot, step one: *You brazen thing.*

Right foot, step two: *What is wrong with you?*

Left foot, third step: *Insipid.*

Right foot, fourth step: *Stupid, ignorant child.*

Left foot, step five: *Lump of humanity.*

Johnny stops, mid-stairs. He shouts, "I can't! I can't! I can't!" He presses his palms to his ears. "Make them stop."

Bzzz cuts through the air and slices through Johnny's thoughts. Tiny particles of brick sprinkle to the ground. Workers hang against the building, positioned on scaffolds, completely oblivious to Johnny and the memories that plague him. Johnny collects himself, bolts up the remaining stairs, through the doors, and into complete silence as the doors block the noise from outside. Johnny notices he is the only soul he's aware of in the church, but he hopes someone mans the confessional for him to speak with. He enters the private confessional, shuts the door, kneels, and opens the screen in hopes someone is on the other side. His hopes are answered when the other side of the screen grates open.

Johnny bows his head, clasps his hands in reverence, and begins, "Bless me, Father, for I have sinned. It has been... over ten years since my last confession."

The priest on the other side of the screen responds, "Tell me, child, what are your sins?"

"I'm actually here because I need somebody to speak with."

"It's been at least ten years since your last confession. Don't you have anything to confess?"

"Yes, of course. Not *of course*, I mean you probably never have any sins to confess since you're a priest and all. It's not like priests..." he trails off as he remembers David, as a priest, sinned mighty heavily. "Some priests sin, I guess, but my point..."

The priest interrupts, "Son, we are not here for me, we are here for you. Tell me what your sins are first and then we may proceed from there."

"Fair enough." Johnny's eyes go up and to the right to aid in the search of his memory bank for a list of sins he might have committed over the last ten years. *That's a long time,* he thinks.

"A lot of sodomy," he tells the priest. He then mouths the words *a lot of sodomy* again in puzzlement over how he just said that to a priest. He tries to recover some ground, "It was all with the same person though. A lot of sodomy," he hits himself in the head, flustered at his own stupidity, "but all with the same person. No, like, gang bangs or anything." *Gang bangs,* he dramatically mouths to himself in extreme shock. "I'm sorry, Father, I need to go."

Johnny reaches for the doorknob and is halfway to his feet when he hears, "Sit down, son, sit down. I can tell you're nervous and it's nothing to worry about. Trust me, I've heard far worse. You can tell me anything. Please, have no fear. Once we are through, if you'd like, we can have that talk you came in for. Maybe an introduction will help. You don't have to tell me who you are, of course. It's probably better that way." He continues, "I'm Father John. I've been in this parish for about the last ten years or so and will be here at least until the renovations are complete. They are working on the façade right now, as you might have noticed when you walked in."

An odd familiarity strikes Johnny as a déjà vu of sorts. He can't tell whether it's being in the church again or the confessional again, or if it's something about Father John's introduction, maybe even his voice, that seems familiar. He cocks his head to the side and confesses, "I feel like we've met before. I'd remember meeting you though. I don't know, something about you is so… familiar."

"I get that a lot. Occupational hazard. And now…?"

Johnny looks around his dark little space in the confessional for an answer. He doesn't find one.

The priest continues, "Your sins, son, tell me your sins."

"Right. You're aware of the first one, or the first sets. I said *sets* not *sex*," he clarifies. "It's not all sex with me."

Father John, hand on forehead, shakes his head on the other side of the confessional.

"Let's see," Johnny continues, "the only other sin I can really recall would be stealing, but not intentionally stealing. I might've taken someone else's drink at a coffee shop once or twice but it was purely by mistake. I paid and everything, I just took the wrong drink is all. No one was hurt."

"Is that all?"

"I'm sure I took the Lord's name in vain a few times over the years. No excuse."

"The Lord forgives you in the name of the Father, and of the Son, and of the Holy Spirit. In penance of your sins, say ten Hail Marys and ten Our Fathers. May you go in peace to love and serve the Lord."

"Thank you, Father."

"You wanted to speak with me," Father John reminds Johnny.

Johnny looks for a way to phrase his question delicately. "What do you do when you want to help someone who has lost their way, lost their path?"

"That's a question as old as time itself. The answer, my child, can be found right in front of you."

Johnny ponders, *The answer is right in front of*

me? How do I know the answer? "Father," he says aloud, "I really don't know the answer, that's why I need your help."

"And I am telling you, the answer is right in front of you. On the shelf. There should be a Holy Bible sitting there." Johnny notices the Bible and smirks at it. "Son, when a sheep loses its way we do not give up on it. Sheep are meant to stray, but as much as we are all sheep we are all shepherds. Find this sheep you speak of and bring him back to the herd."

"Back to the herd," Johnny repeats.

"Bring him back."

"I know you haven't said much, Father John, but you've certainly given me much to think about."

Father John imparts some final words of wisdom unto Johnny as he offers, "Every day is a winding road. Listen to your heart." He closes with a last reminder as Johnny, on the other side of the confessional, cocks his head. "That's the way love goes."

Johnny's face contorts in a mixture of confusion and revulsion. "You're rather peculiar," Johnny states.

"You wanted advice," Father John reminds, as the sense of odd familiarity continues to waft through the screen and around Johnny.

Charlie Casso

36 LICK IT LIKE AN ICE CREAM CONE

As Johnny restocks the *OfficeGear* shelves with boxes of pencils, he tries to assess his situation. His mind meanders between David's losing himself from Johnny and David's losing himself from his work. It's not a matter of the chicken and the egg at this point, because it's quite clear. David lost his job and then lost, or chose to lose, Johnny. He strayed from his job, or vocation as he would call it, and then he strayed from Johnny. *Bring him back,* Johnny thinks. Since David separated from his job first it would only make sense to reunite him with his job first. Then, maybe, Johnny and David could be like they once were. Johnny leans down, grabs more boxes of pencils, and continues to ponder. If there's a way for David to get his job back, Johnny doesn't know it. He doesn't even know if David *would* want his job back. He could find out though. Johnny contemplates whether he should discuss the matter with David as he realizes the large brown cardboard box he gets his supply from is empty.

He heads to the backroom, and the empty cardboard box leads the way as it is trapped between his hands. Johnny rounds a corner and knocks right into Todd who peruses the inventory. "Well, hello there yourself," Todd remarks in a jocular fashion. "That's quite a large package you're carrying around with you."

"It's empty. I emptied it onto the shelves in aisle three."

Todd's cheeks become more ample in response to the new information and an active imagination. "Wish I could've been there," Todd admits.

"You definitely could've helped. There was a lot. I almost thought it would never end."

"Really?" Todd breathes.

"Yeah. And then bam, all out. That's why I came back here. I need another load."

"Another load," Todd repeats in a breathy whisper. "My, it is warm in here." Todd fans his face with his hand. "So hot," he says, either in reference to himself, Johnny, or both. "You know what, I saw an ice cream truck outside earlier." He looks Johnny up and down and professes, "And I could really use some right now."

"Sounds great. I could go for some, too!" Johnny drops his box to the ground. Todd stands there and gawks at Johnny, so Johnny decides to take charge. "Shall we?" Johnny sweeps his arms from Todd toward the door. Todd, eager to please, leads the way from the backroom to the sales floor, past the cashiers, and onto the sidewalk.

They stroll to the side of the ice cream truck and gaze at the offerings on its fantastically colorful menu. A friendly face pops through the window, followed by another friendly face alongside it. A man and woman, husband and wife perhaps, purvey the ice cream on this beautiful day.

"What can I do you for?" the man asks down toward Johnny and Todd.

"You'll have to excuse him," the woman offers to her customers, "he only says it like that because he knows how it frustrates me." She turns to face John, "It's 'what can I do for you' not 'what can I do you for' and you know it."

"That's not true and *you* know it. You can say it either way."

"Yes, you're right. You can say it either way, it's just that one of those ways is wrong. Unless, of course, you mean you want to do him *for* something but, last I checked, prostitution was still illegal. Are you calling this young man a prostitute?"

John holds his hands up in honesty and declares to Johnny, "I promise you I don't think you're a prostitute."

"That's good," Johnny replies. "Unless you think I'm not good-looking enough to be a prostitute. I mean, I did get offered thirty bucks once at Port Authority. Actually they wanted to do everything for thirty bucks. I thought that was kind of low. Insulting, really. Not that I would have entertained it, even for more money. I'm just…"

"Irregardless, what he meant to say to you was 'What can I do for you?' and, so, what *can* I do for you?"

"I think we would like some ice cream."

"Well, you've certainly come to the right place," the woman remarks.

Johnny turns to Todd. Todd orders, "I would like a vanilla cone. Can you dip it in chocolate, please?"

"Surely," John offers as he turns to get it. "Barbara, if you'll be so kind as to take care of this other fine gentleman."

"I'll take an ice cream sandwich, please."

"You got it," she replies.

Mere seconds later, money and frosty goodness exchange hands and Todd and Johnny about-face to stroll back to their work environs. Todd stares at the ice cream cone in his hand as a droplet of ice cream pops out from beneath its hard chocolate shell and drips down. Todd catches it with the tip of his tongue. "How's tricks?"

"Good, no complaints here."

"Johnny, someone asks you how you're doing, how your day is, anything like that, answer honestly. If it's worth asking, it's worth answering. And if the person asks, but doesn't really care, then that'll learn 'em. Think about it. Someone asks you how you're doing, just for the hell of it, just to make conversation or whatnot, and you say your dear aunt just passed away, let 'em deal with it. That's what they get for asking."

Johnny nods his agreement because, truth be told, what Todd says makes sense.

"So when I ask you how's tricks, I expect an honest answer. Let's try again. So, how's tricks?"

Johnny takes a lick of the ice cream sandwich from between the two cookies. "Things are... things are interesting."

"Go on."

"I'm trying to help someone find himself, get himself back on track, and I'm just trying to figure out the best way to go about it."

"Is the person willing to get himself back on track?"

"I honestly don't know." Johnny tilts the ice cream sandwich in his hand in wonder.

"Because if you put a train back on its track, but it's not ready to be on that track yet, like it's not fixed, its just going to fall right off again."

"That's true, I guess. I didn't think of that."

"There are other trains," Todd adds. "Other trains that are fired up and ready to be on that track. You put them on that track and they'll follow that track wherever. In a tunnel, out of a tunnel, in a tunnel, out of a tunnel. It doesn't end. There's real stamina there. Maybe you should try another train. Maybe you *need* another train."

"My caboose can't take another train just yet. It's kind of hitched itself to this one."

"Oh." Todd takes a full on bite out of the ice cream atop his cone. He swallows and uses his free hand to rub the hollow under his Adam's apple, a sure sign the ice cream went down too fast. "Your caboose just might not realize what's best for it. People do get on the wrong track, you know."

"Exactly my point," Johnny concurs. He punctuates his words with his sandwich and takes a bite. He licks the chocolate cookie crumbs from the corners or his mouth before he continues his thought. "People do get on the wrong track. Like you said, does he want to get back on the right track? Is he ready to get back on it?"

"I'd be ready. I'm always ready," Todd offers.

"I know, but he's different. I'll bring it up tonight."

Todd looks down at the front of his pants. "Yep," he concurs as he holds the *OfficeGear* door open for Johnny.

37 FERRIS WHEEL OF FORTUNE

"What is that smell?" David asks Johnny, drawn as he is to the kitchen.

"I'm making dinner."

"Smells amazing."

"Don't get your hopes too high. It's just fried chicken and waffles. I know it's not the healthiest, but I figured it's been a while since I made them."

"You know what they say," David responds, "the higher the cholesterol the closer to God."

Johnny corrects, "It's the higher the hair, the closer to God, and that's mostly a New Jersey thing."

"They're both true. Higher hair makes one closer, in terms of geographical proximity if you hold the belief, as many do, that Heaven, and thus God, are above us. And, as for higher cholesterol, that's easy. The higher the cholesterol, the closer to death and the closer to death, the closer to God."

"So you actually believe in that trite expression, the Jersey one? I never heard the other one before."

"It's something to think about and it's something that puts a smile on people's faces."

"Speaking of something to think about, I was hoping we could have a talk."

"Sounds serious."

"Nothing a plate of chicken and waffles can't solve." Johnny deposits two heaping plates of food on the table and he and David sit. "I'm just going to come right out and say it. I was thinking maybe you should try to get your job back at the church."

"How surprising. And not surprising at all. I have been thinking the same thing lately. I cannot 'get my job back' easily, if at all, and certainly not at my former parish. I did a little research and while it's not easy to get in the good graces of the church again, it's not impossible. Once everything goes through, I'd have to find myself a position again and I fear that would prove quite difficult. It'd likely have to be in a parish that was going through some troubles, reparations, or what have you. I think I would do it though, should I decide to, of course."

"So that's something you want to do?"

"It's something I have been thinking about."

"You never told me…"

"I only started considering it after my… troubles. My nose incidents, they made me reevaluate my life and take a look to see where I was headed. I may seek to reclaim my place in the priesthood. I have to give the matter some serious thought."

"Where would that leave us?" Johnny pushes aside a hunk of chicken with his fork.

"Like I said, Johnny, I need to give the matter

some serious thought."

***

"'Like I said, Johnny, I need to give the matter some serious thought,' that's what he said to me. Can you believe it? Not *we* need to give the matter thought, *I* need to give the matter thought, well, *serious* thought. What is that? And don't think I didn't notice he called me Johnny. *Jonathan* I can handle, it means there's still something there. It's no *Young Jonathan*, but it's not that far removed. *Johnny* though? Really?"

"Easy, boy," Veronica urges. She presses a hand down on Johnny's lap. "I don't think being on a Ferris wheel and being angry go hand-in-hand. The operator is liable to kick us off when he sees that puss on your face."

"Oh, he'll never notice." He points down to the conductor who talks to a girl. "Especially if he gets that girl's puss on his face first."

"Johnny!"

"What can I say? You're finally rubbing off on me."

"Don't hate me for asking this, but, why are you even considering staying with him and letting him be the one to end things when you know, for a fact, that he's been stepping out on you?"

"He says he's been reevaluating his life. I think he realizes he has been on the wrong path. I think we made him realize that with the jelly donut and angry dragon set-ups. Maybe I didn't realize how I'd feel when it was all said and done but I think I can work with it, or work with him."

Veronica tries to manage her approach softly. "Johnny, he's not saying he'll stop and be with you. He's saying he'll stop and go back to the church. There's a difference." She looks at Johnny to see if he understands. He doesn't say anything, but she knows he listens. She continues, "He chose to be with the church, he chose to be with you, he chose to be with the donut maker and Angry Dragon Guy, and now he's choosing again. I just need to know you're prepared for what his next choice is going to be."

"I know. I appreciate it. I just need time to sit with things and think."

"You do. You need a little time to shake things off, you know, just be. That's kind of the reason I brought you here. Some time with your head in the clouds might do you good." Veronica delicately swirls her hand in the air above her shoulder to make as if she stirs the clouds around them.

Nearing the apex of the Ferris wheel, Johnny appears to literally have his head in the clouds next to Veronica. Johnny and Veronica's car reaches the apex as the wheel itself comes to a stop. The car rocks back and forth, swaying its occupants' heads in the clouds. Neither Johnny nor Veronica can see each other and, for what seems like a smaller version of eternity, Johnny lives with his eyes wide open and is happy with the fact that he sees nothing.

Johnny's head falls a smidge forward and he's hit by a strident smell. He can almost put his finger on the smell, but wouldn't expect any smell like it up where he is. He sniffs a couple times and comes close to a sneeze. He puts the back of his hand to his nose and tries to rub the smell from it. His head jars another smidge as the Ferris wheel moves. They are about to descend from the clouds.

The clouds clear from around them, or rather their car clears from the clouds. Johnny realizes the source of the smell is next to him and he could have put his finger on it, especially since Veronica puts the source of the smell on her fingernail.

He exclaims, "You're painting your nails… on a Ferris wheel?"

"You got all quiet, what was I supposed to do?"

"How could you even see to do that?"

"Are you kidding? Any girl my age worth her salt could apply polish to her nails with her eyes closed." She wiggles her fingers to show her pristine work. "See?"

"Lovely."

"How do you feel?" Veronica asks. "Is the ride helping or should we get off?"

"It's helping. I feel a little… lighter? It's nice to be taken off my feet like this. *Swept off my feet*, if you will. After thirty-two years, it's about time."

"You don't think you've been swept off your feet? Not even by David?"

"When you live life with your feet planted so firmly on the ground it's hard to get swept off them."

"Great line. Is that from something?"

"Yeah, a little thing called my life," Johnny confesses.

"So you don't even think David swept you off your feet?"

"Ronnie, as soon as anything happened between us he was instantly excommunicated. Everyone found out what happened between us, and my mom and dad kicked me out. There was no time for any semblance of a whirlwind romance. It was all, *now how are we going to handle this?* So, to answer your question, no, David didn't get to sweep me off my feet."

"Sorry to hear that. I mean it."

"I know. I do feel better though, even if it's just a little bit."

"Hey, that's what friends are for. That, and helping get rid of the body." She winks at Johnny. "I kid."

"You're kind of not kidding but, hey, I might take you up on that." Johnny's gaze drifts from Veronica to down below where children and adults take part in Coney Island's rides and games. "Sister Petunia and Mr. Huxley," Johnny observes.

"You got it, Johnny. I will help you get rid of their bodies once you kill them. You got it. You're not wired, bugged, or tapped, or whatever they call it, right? I'm in!" Veronica jokes.

"I'm serious, Ronnie."

"I'm serious, Ronnie," she mimics, "Yeah right. *You* kill people. You're afraid of mice."

"Not that, you nimrod. Sister Petunia and Mr. Huxley," he points below while he continues, "are right there. Look." Veronica follows his finger to where it points below. The black habit and silver-grey tuft of hair are unmistakable.

"Wow. I'd never imagine either of them here. It's too cheery for them. I would think she'd feel like a penguin out of water. Speaking of which, you think they'll play one of those games where you, like, knock the penguin over and win a prize? It'd be like penguin-on-penguin crime. It'd be fun to see her try, because those penguin things don't stay down."

"Yes, they are totally going to play games while they're here," he sarcastically intonates. "Huxley can play the old 'fill the clown's mouth until the balloon pops' game, only instead of filling it with water he'll fill it with insults. I'm sure he'll win, too."

"I don't know if it's the Ferris wheel or if it's the sight of those two, but I feel nauseous. Come on," she gestures to the Ferris wheel operator that they want to de-car. The operator breaks from the girl he chats with and jogs over to release the bars for their exit. Veronica and Johnny jump down in time for the next merry travelers to start their journey. "Do you want to get funnel cakes or something?" To illustrate her comment, a young woman passes in front of them, with a piece of funnel cake between her fingers that she feeds to her beau. Speckles of powered sugar float down and disappear before they make it to the ground.

"Sure, I can go for one. Strawberries on top. Wait, I thought you felt nauseous."

"I thought you were allergic to strawberries. Don't underestimate what a funnel cake can do. I'm better already just thinking about it."

"Good. I am allergic, but sometimes I can eat them without a problem."

"And the other times?"

"Then there's that," Johnny gives in. "All right, no strawberries."

"Two, please," Veronica places her order at the stand.

She receives the two plates and passes one to Johnny. They turn to saunter around and indulge in their fried, sugar covered treats. Johnny raises the edge of the funnel cake off the plate and rips a piece off with his mouth. He exhales a puffy cloud of powdered sugar when he body-checks a shorter person in front of him. The sugary cloud descends atop blackness. Johnny looks confusedly, and he wonders what's in front of him that the sugar landed on. The fallen sugar speckles rotate. A Rorschach test, made of sugar, turns and forms new images as Johnny stares. A piece of funnel cake dangles from his mouth.

"Animal," claws its way into his ears.

Jolted out of his stare, his eyes lower past the sugar, and past the black. Past the hair, past the glasses, past the nose, and to the lips, curled in disgust. Slowly, they ripple. The jaw lowers. The lips part. "An…" the lips press together, "im" they separate and press together, "al" the tongue lashes out. The tongue retreats and the mouth closes. Sister Petunia. Johnny stares. The process repeats. "Animal."

Veronica stares from two feet away. The funnel cake drops from Johnny's mouth, just misses his plate, and lands on Sister Petunia's shoe. Johnny's eyes follow the funnel cake down and then follow Sister Petunia's arm back up. Before he knows it, *whack,* the inside of Sister Petunia's palm strikes Johnny's face. Dumbfounded, he drops his plate from his hand. It, too, lands atop Sister Petunia's shoe with a *thud.* Her other arm lashes and she strikes the other side of Johnny's face with a *crack*.

Johnny brings his hands to his face, presses his cheeks against his teeth, and moves his jaw around to get the normal feeling back in his face.

Mr. Huxley walks forward. "Some *things*" he stresses as he looks at Johnny and then Veronica, "never change."

"He didn't do it on purpose," Veronica counters as she takes a step forward.

"That doesn't MATTER," Mr. Huxley screams. "That doesn't matter," he repeats lower, almost as if it's to someone else inside of him. "*You* don't matter. None of you ever matter."

"They are wastes of matter. Wastes of space. Useless bumps on logs," Sister Petunia adds.

"Always pleasant running into you two," Veronica lies. She grabs Johnny's hand and pulls him away from them.

He stops her and frees himself. "No, wait. I need to do this," he says, more to himself than her. "You know, you had me running scared for years but, you know what, I'm not a kid anymore." He bobs his head up, down, and around, splays his arms and states, "Yes, I realize I'm at an amusement park in Coney Island, but I'm not a kid. You can't scare me anymore."

"Vile," Sister Petunia seethes.

Johnny steps forward and points a finger in front of Sister Petunia's face. "I'm trying my hardest to restrain myself from slapping you right now. I'm not sure you're really a woman, so that's not going to save you, but... Let me tell you this: as sure as your pubic hairs are long, I want nothing more than to slap your face. I would but… you're lucky you're a nun."

Mr. Huxley grabs Johnny's finger in his hand, squeezes tightly, and throws Johnny's hand down. "Get your finger out of her face," he directs in a controlled screech.

Johnny peers at his hands. He looks, with determination on his face, up at Mr. Huxley. "You, however, are not a nun." Johnny's hand cuts through the air and lands on its target. *Smack.*

Mr. Huxley's face barely moves. His eyes widen and his jaw trembles with rage. "Help me," Mr. Huxley beseeches Sister Petunia. "I'm going to kill him."

She responds, "Don't waste your energy on either of them. Let the Lord deal with them, they will receive their comeuppance."

"What gall," Veronica exclaims.

"Unmitigated, that's the word people always use with gall. You two have unmitigated gall," Johnny adds.

"Yeah, out of everyone here it's you two who'll receive your comeuppance, not us. You hear that?" Veronica draws out the next word, "good," while she makes circular motions with her flattened palms around Johnny and herself. She then turns her palms outward and makes the same motions around Sister Petunia and Mr. Huxley and enunciates, "evil." She adds, "Get that in check and then talk about comeuppance."

"Clean her shoe." Mr. Huxley points a finger toward Sister Petunia's barely powdered sugar flecked shoe. "Get down on your knees and clean her shoe."

"If you think I'm getting my face anywhere near those shoes you're battier than a belfry," Johnny responds.

"Lick the shoe clean," Mr. Huxley demands.

Veronica and Johnny exchange looks that say, *Is he for real?*

"All right, let me make this clearer. I wouldn't voluntarily get near her shoes even if she were wearing ruby slippers and I needed to get home from somewhere far, far away."

"Palo Alto," Veronica adds.

Johnny shakes his head.

"What? It sounds far," she clarifies.

"Yeah," Johnny nods approval, "even if I were stuck in Palo Alto and she were wearing ruby slippers. Nope, not a chance."

Mr. Huxley snatches Johnny by the back of the neck and whips his head down. Johnny manages to resist about a third of the way down. He struggles to free himself as Mr. Huxley adds a second hand to help lower Johnny's face to the ground.

"Johnny?" Todd interrupts as he places a hand on top of the hands on Johnny's neck. Mr. Huxley releases Johnny. Todd curls his hand around Johnny's neck, to the front, and gently guides Johnny up. "I thought that was you. Is everything all right here?" Todd stares into Johnny's eyes as Sister Petunia and Mr. Huxley walk away unnoticed.

Johnny catches his breath. "Yeah, we were just…" he looks and notices the absence of Sister Petunia and Mr. Huxley. "Carny folk, you know how weird they can be," Johnny pretends.

"I noticed that," Todd agrees. "I said to myself, if anyone's going to manhandle Johnny…" he trails off and keeps the rest of that sentence to himself.

"This is Ronnie. I'm sure you have seen her around the store." Veronica and Todd formally introduce themselves to each other and shake hands. "What brings you to Coney Island tonight?"

"I like to come and see the fireworks." He takes in Johnny as he offers, "Beauty comes in many forms."

"Gross!" Veronica exclaims.

"Sorry. I take it you don't like fireworks?"

"Huh? Oh. No, I love fireworks as much as the next person. There's a lady over there letting someone lick her nipples."

Johnny and Todd turn to look. "She's breastfeeding her baby," Todd corrects. Johnny puts a hand to his forehead as a visor under which he hides.

"Same thing. And that's no baby. That kid has teeth."

"That's attachment parenting, I think. It's where the mother breastfeeds up until, well, up until the child decides it doesn't want to any longer."

Veronica remarks, "That's a big decision for someone who can't even dress themselves to make. It's also gross."

"I take it you're not a women's libber."

"I'm all for women's rights, human rights, you name it. It's just, well, I'd like to see how those women's libbers would react to nursing if it were the men who produced milk, and the milk came from their ding-dongs. If a man pulled his thing out to nurse you'd hear how loud the reactions would be from the very same people who are all 'breastfeeding is beautiful.' I don't care where the milk comes from, I'm not in the mood to see babies leech off the body parts of their parents."

"That's certainly an interesting take on the subject, I guess, and, like I said, beauty comes in many forms, should one choose to see it."

Veronica changes the subject and asks, "Do you want to go on the Ferris wheel? I don't think I can take another ride just now, but Johnny would sure love it."

Todd brightens as Johnny quickly casts a nasty glance at Veronica. "You know how much I love it, but I promised David, my boyfriend, I'd be home early," he lies.

Veronica realizes she shouldn't push Johnny's buttons, given his David situation and recent altercation with Sister Petunia and Mr. Huxley. She decides to let her shot at being Cupid between Johnny and Todd go by the wayside. "You're right, I forgot," she lies in turn.

"I guess we had better jet. See you at work tomorrow?"

"Wild horses couldn't stop me, Johnny."

"Nice meeting you, Todd," Veronica shakes his hand again.

"You as well. Make sure my fuzzy little worker bee gets home safely."

"I will."

Once out of earshot, Veronica cups a hand over her mouth and whispers to Johnny, "He wants you to put your stinger in him."

"I don't know if he wants to be the one doing the stinging or getting stung, Ronnie. I'm just glad he was there."

Charlie Casso

38 YOU HAVE A WHAT?

"Thanks for last night," Johnny offers to Todd as he checks the storage room for supplies.

Todd blushes. "Whatever do you mean?"

"You had perfect timing, coming when you did."

"Say what?" Todd pinches his own arm so quick it escapes Johnny's notice.

"So random, even going to Coney Island in the first place, and then to run into you there."

"Oh, that. Sure, my pleasure." He looks at Johnny. "Johnny, I have to ask you." He pauses before continuing. "What are you looking for?"

"Staplers, the chrome ones." Johnny searches the shelves.

Todd rolls his eyes and bites the inside of his bottom lip. "I meant in life."

Johnny stops what he is doing for a second to consider what Todd has just said. He exhales and then continues his search. "Well, for now I'd be contented with finding the staplers."

"All right, I'm going to come right out and ask you. Would you be... willing... to consider going out with me?"

"Like to lunch?" Johnny asks. He stretches on his tip-toes to get his arm further onto a high shelf. He wiggles his fingers in hopes he finds the desired staplers.

"A date."

"Yes!" he exclaims.

"Of course, if you don't want to I'd completely under... did you say 'yes' just now?"

"Whew! This is exactly what I've been looking for," Johnny says as he pulls down a box with a picture of a chrome stapler on it.

Todd's eyes go to the stapler as reality sets in. He deflates. "Oh, the stapler, yes. It figures."

"Now, what were you saying? You want to go to lunch?"

"Lunch would be great," he says quietly. He rubs his eye with the back of his hand and looks away.

"Are you all right?"

"I think a piece of dust just flew right into my eye. Don't mind me." In a lower voice he offers, "Don't ever mind me."

"Want to go at noon?" Johnny tosses the question at Todd. Johnny retrieves additional staplers from the shelf for the sales floor.

"Sure," Todd replies solemnly. He remedies his teary situation, brushes himself off, and stands straight. "Lunch at noon sounds fantastic." Todd retreats to the sales floor with lunch at noon in his sights, as well as a thought. He has until noon to devise a way to get David out of the picture. Forever.

***

Todd and Johnny situate themselves in a booth at the Poisoned Ivy. Before anyone even plops menus down on their table, Todd starts the conversation.

"Tell me about David, your partner, your boyfriend, your man, if you will."

"Funny you should say that," Johnny says, "His last name is Mann."

"Is it? Well if that isn't a barrel of laughs," he slaps his thigh in mock jest.

"What do you want to know? Hey, wait. You at least know some stuff about me already, but I really don't know anything about you. Why don't you tell me a little about yourself and then you can dig into me."

"I like the sound of that. Fair enough." Two glasses of water slide onto their table, followed by menus. "What would you like to know?"

"Longest relationship."

"Longest relationship. Okay, that's easy. Let me see." Todd does some mental calculations. His left index finger pops around in the air as it leaps over invisible obstacles. His face contorts in such deep thoughts one would think he was doing long division. He nods one big nod with his head, and then two smaller nods. He appears to have found the correct answer. "Eleven months."

"Hey, Beautiful Mind," Rose cuts in, "what'll it be?"

Todd pushes his menu to the side and states, "Monte Cristo, fries, iced tea."

275

"Sugar Peach?"

"Surprise me," Johnny directs. He turns to Todd. "Eleven months?" Johnny asks in shock. Todd can't tell whether it's shock because it was a long amount of time or a short amount of time. Todd is still getting used to relationships wherein each party carries the y chromosome.

"Is that bad?"

"Well, it's not bad, it's just the way you were doing your calculations I was thinking you were going to say six years, eleven years… I don't know. I wasn't expecting under a year."

"You think I'm old."

"Not at all. I know people in ridiculously long relationships who met each other when they were in high school, I'm talking like they met when they were fourteen and are still together in their thirties. I thought you were one of them. Didn't think you were old at all."

"That's good to hear." Todd appears a little relieved.

"Eleven months, huh? So what happened?" Johnny inquires.

"The honeymoon period ended and the masks came off."

"But that's bound to happen in any relationship. You get to know someone for who they really are. Was it bad? Did they, like, lie to you a lot? Had kids but didn't say it in the beginning? Smoked but tried to hide it? Drug problem?"

Todd's winces and shakes his head in disapproval. "Nothing like that at all. He didn't smoke, and didn't do any drugs. He certainly never had any kids, I don't think he was ever even with a woman, one of those gold star gays you hear about."

"Then what was the problem?"

"I told you, the masks came off. All of a sudden he's not into it anymore. I tried to make it work. Thought maybe just the gag, maybe just one toy or two, but he was just done with all of it."

"Just the gag, or some toys," Johnny repeats for clarification. "Do you have a dungeon or something?"

"Yes. Yes to the dungeon. As for the something, I'd prefer we say *many* things. I like to keep things lively, colorful… entertaining. Vanilla's for ice cream."

"And after a while his affinity for it waned," Johnny puts together.

"Yep. So, I finally said, you know what, this is not what was advertised in the brochure, buddy."

"You have a brochure?" Johnny asks incredulously.

"No." Todd answers in disgust. "What kind of a sicko would make a brochure? Anyway, so that was that. Eleven months."

"You learn something new every day."

"That's what my ex used to say. Then, one day, apparently, he learned too much. Ah, well, all the better for his next suitor I suppose. Now let's get on to you."

"I'd rather we didn't."

"Tell me about David."

"Oh, yes. What's there to tell? We met, wow," Johnny says as he thinks about it, "we met over twenty years ago."

"Twenty years? You must have been a baby."

"Hardly. I was in junior high."

"Childhood sweethearts, that's too sweet."

"Not exactly. He was the priest at the Catholic school I attended. And he presided over the masses at the church attached to it."

"My goodness, I wasn't expecting that at all. Are you all right? Did he rape you?"

"You boys and your sex talk, that's all I ever hear about," Rose snarks. She drops the plates on the table while the food manages not to bounce off. Johnny's surprise, a spinach and feta cheese omelette, emits steam at him. Rose saunters away.

"Well, did he rape you?"

"No, God no. I totally wanted it." Johnny shakes his head at his own words. "Not like that. I mean I wanted it, but not the way it sounded. We didn't do anything until I was of age. Nothing illegal happened."

"That's reassuring."

"I take that back. He was excommunicated because of it. Maybe it was *illegal* in the eyes of the church."

"How very lurid of you, Johnny. I suspected you had a dark side."

"Eh, it's not that dark. I fell in love with a man who happened to be a priest when I was thirteen years old." Johnny furrows his brows. "I see your point."

"And now, after all these years, everything's still on the up and up?"

"Not exactly," Johnny confesses. "He's sort of trying to *find himself*, whatever that means. I'm torn between helping him and helping myself."

"This wouldn't be that train you were talking about the other day when we got ice cream, now would it?"

"That's the train. Good memory."

"I'm good when it comes to trains." Todd smirks. "What are you up to now, regarding you and David?" Todd pries, in hopes he will hear something he can use.

"I'm waiting it out. If David wants to reclaim his position in the church I'm all for it. The one caveat is there might not be room for me in it. If he gets his position back he might want to cut ties with me for good, so as not to be tempted. I never could really understand how or why lust is considered a deadly sin. It's like a thought crime. Big whoop, you lust after someone. Murder I can see, but lust?"

"I don't think there's anything wrong with lust. Even the word, how it rolls right off the tongue without any effort at all. Lust. One little pedal of the tongue and the word blossoms to life. Lust. Do you feel it? Say it. Lust." He watches Johnny's mouth.

"Lust?" Johnny says. He turns it into a question. "It does. It comes right out, you're right."

"I know. Stick with me, Johnny, I tend to be right about a lot of things. I'm sure I could teach you a thing or two. I'd definitely like to try."

"Thanks. That means a lot to me," Johnny replies. He doesn't catch Todd's innuendo. "Yeah, so that's that. I just lie in wait for David to see what he's going to do with himself."

"What's the big holdup?"

"It seems a person can get un-excommunicated, and it's actually not the worst process in the world from what he tells me. The biggest glitch is finding a parish that'll let you serve at it. Most of them, obviously, aren't big fans of those who have been excommunicated."

"Obviously. What happens then? Because I assume no church will welcome him in such a way."

"He needs to turn over every stone, look for the churches that have recently lost a priest for whichever reason, or are getting renovated. You know, basically the churches that aren't on other priests' top ten lists."

"And are you ready for that? You're ready for him to leave you for the church, just like that?"

"If that's what he really wants, if that's what will make him truly happy, then yes, I'm ready."

"And what about you? What will make you truly happy?"

Johnny thinks for a few moments. "As soon as I figure that out I'll let you know."

Johnny and Todd begin to devour their meals. Johnny delicately forks his omelette while he ponders what will make him truly happy, and Todd sinks his teeth into his Monte Cristo as he postulates a way to get David out of the picture for good.

"You guys got awful quiet. I'll have to tell the cooks to make it less good," Rose interrupts them from their thoughts. "Ya want anything else?" Todd shakes his head no while both he and Johnny chew. Rose saunters away again.

"I kind of just want David to be happy. Everything else will fall into place."

"That's what you want? That's what will make you truly happy, to see someone else happy?"

"He's not just someone else. He had a life, he had a chance. I mean, so did I, but I ruined his, at least for a while. I was Lolita to his Humbert Humbert, the kryptonite to his Superman, the Ben Affleck or Marc Anthony to his Jennifer Lopez."

"Nothing ruins Jennifer Lopez."

"It's true. She's like bionic. She should play the Bionic Woman if they ever make a movie about her."

"That would be awesome."

"What were we talking about? Lopez, Superman, oh, Lolita, yes. I ruined him. I drew him in, with that word *lust*, and damaged him forever. I deserve to be punished."

Todd perks up. "Punished?" he asks.

"Punished. What I did was wrong on so many levels. His happiness, at this point, would make me happy. That would be all I could ask for."

"And then you'd be free to do what you want, date who you want…"

"Date? No, no. Not for a long time. Not for a very, very, very long time. I'm not one to jump back in the saddle so fast."

Todd squashes the french fry he was about to eat between his fingers. The top part of it falls off. "Why the delay? You're young and virile, take advantage of it while you can."

"It's not my way."

Todd grinds his teeth yet tries, as best he can, to appear undisturbed. "Well," he offers, "if ever I can be of any assistance, in any way, don't hesitate to let me know. I'm here for you."

"Thank you, Todd, I really appreciate it. Can't undervalue a man with a dungeon. I just might need you yet."

Charlie Casso

39 KEEP IT VANILLA

"Penny for your thoughts," the woman hanging out of the ice cream truck tells David.

"Huh?"

"I said a penny for your thoughts. It's an old expression, I guess. With inflation, I should probably say ten dollars for your thoughts." She cackles at her own joke. "Whooo," she exclaims as she tosses rainbow sprinkles down at David. He laughs and smiles at the absurdity.

"You're certainly jovial today."

"What's not to be joyous about? It's a gorgeous day, the sun is shining in the sky, the birds, oh, look at the birds. So spectacular." She leads David's eyes with her hand to follow a sweet little bird as it flies through the air. She extends her arm and hand outside of the truck window as a perch. A bird glides over toward the truck. "Come little one, come. Oh, so beautiful." David watches in amazement. The bird flies gracefully and delicately toward the side of the truck. The bird's wings span out as it glides close to its perch. Yet not close enough. *Splat!* The bird hits the side of the truck and the feathered ball lumps down to the ground. A brief burst of feathers softly fall after and finally rest atop and around it. The woman's hand remains outstretched as a perch. She falls into shock and she brings her other hand over her gaping mouth. She leans down to get a closer look. "Little one?" She whistles softly. "Little one?" She eyes David and then looks to the side and sees her arm still outstretched. She pulls it back to her.

"I think it's dead," David offers.

She looks down at the scene. Her little bird is lifeless, its feathers tossed on the ground around it, surrounded by the scattering of rainbow sprinkles she had tossed so gleefully.

"Tragic."

"I can offer it last rites if it'll make you feel better," he lies.

"You can?"

"Sort of."

She computes his response in her head. "What does 'sort of' mean?"

"It means I know what they are and I know how to administer them. I'm not what you'd call a fully functioning priest right now, but I was a priest before and I will likely be a priest again."

"So, you've fallen just like this little one over here I take it?"

"I guess you could say that. Probably fell just about as hard, too."

She thinks. "Last rites are given to those who are about to die. And you are not a priest, at least not at the moment. So, while I thank you for your offer, I think I will have to pass. I truly do appreciate it, though. It is terribly kind of you."

"It's no worry. We all have to look out for each other. Hey," he realizes, "how do you know so much about last rites?"

"Don't underestimate someone just because they work in an ice cream truck."

"I wasn't. I'm sorry, is that how I came off?"

"A little. I'm used to it, to be honest. You can basically be not of this earth but, once you're inside this ice cream truck, people won't even give you a second look."

David gives a half smile that shows he understands her plight.

"So," she continues, "you're on your way to becoming a priest once again? Why the delay? There's not trepidation I hope. When you commit to God, you commit forever. Nowadays, people think eternity and they think Calvin Klein. So gauche. The big G, that's who they need to think of."

"I hear you completely. Hmm…"

"Another penny for your thoughts?"

"I was thinking I wanted ice cream. That's why I came over here in the first place. That song your truck plays, it's somewhat hypnotic. It drew me right in."

"That's what it's there for. So, what can I do for you?"

"Can I get a cone?"

"Surely! We've got strawberry, pistachio,…"

"Vanilla, please."

"Just vanilla?"

"Just plain old, run-of-the-mill vanilla for me."

"With sprinkles?" she asks with glee. "We've got chocolate and rainb… oh." She leans out of the window and looks down at the little one, still there, dead amongst the sprinkles.

David bites his lip at the thought of sprinkles and the dead bird. "No, thank you. Just the plain vanilla cone."

She draws herself back inside the truck. "You got it," she says mindlessly as she goes to work on his cone. She returns to the window and offers David his cone. David goes to take money out of his pocket. "Consider it a gift," she tells David. "Keep it vanilla. Go with God and keep it vanilla."

"You know what? I think I'm going to take your advice. I think this was just what I needed." David knows he refers to the advice as what he needed but, upon tasting the ice cream, he briefly thinks the ice cream was just what he needed, too.

40 COMEUPPANCE

"He's going back to that cult and I just want to kill," Johnny admits. "I know I should feel good for him, but I don't. Instead, I feel bad for myself." He slams the box of manila folders on top of the other box on the shelf.

Veronica grimaces. She pats the box gently.

"He's leaving. He's up and leaving the apartment and me and everything, just like it was nothing, just like *I* was nothing. Who does that?"

"On the bright side, it's not like he's leaving you for someone else."

"But he is, Ronnie, he is leaving me for someone else. That's the kicker. He's leaving me for someone who he can't even sleep with. Jelly Donut Guy, Angry Dragon Guy... I could understand. Even that tweaked-out, pseudonym-using, human gloryhole Sebastian from BarN. But God? That really burns my britches." He slams another box of manila folders down.

"At least you still have your job," Veronica consoles. Johnny continues slamming the boxes onto the shelves. "That is, unless you keep Ike Turner-ing those manila folders there."

"And I tried, I mean, I really tried with him. He disappointed each time. Don't get me wrong, I tried. And to just up and leave? Leave? It makes me so mad I could just..."

Johnny's focus shifts as Todd passes by the aisle. Luckily for Johnny, it's at a time when no boxes are being harmed in the restocking of the shelves. Todd smiles at Veronica and Johnny as he passes.

Johnny continues in a very even tone, "I could just lock him in a dungeon and dole out my punishment."

"What?" Veronica asks, completely confused at how this idea has come out of nowhere.

"You are right. What am I thinking?" Johnny speaks slowly. He clearly gives a good weight to each thought here. "Why would I lock David in a dungeon to dole out his punishment? It's not just *him* who caused this... this..." he searches for the right word, "downward spiral that is my life. Sister Petunia. Busybody. Her time for comeuppance, as she'd call it, has come... up."

"So, you'd like to lock David and Sister Petunia in a dungeon while you 'dole out' some sort of medieval punishment atop their heads? I'm not being judgey, I'm just asking to make sure I got it right."

"Sounds right."

"Well, it's a beautiful fantasy you've got there, that's for sure."

"Ronnie," Johnny waves her further down the aisle with him. They move more toward the middle of the aisle. Johnny checks both directions to see if anyone is within earshot. Contented with the amount of privacy they have, he whispers, "Ronnie, it's not a fantasy. I have access to a dungeon." Veronica rolls her eyes. "Don't roll your eyes at me. I do. I do have access to a dungeon."

"Yeah, yeah, and I'm Cleopatra. The Liz Taylor version of Cleopatra, of course. I bet her jewelry had to be way better."

"I'm serious. I could probably serve both David and Sister Petunia their just desserts, nah, I like *comeuppance* better, in one fell swoop. All it would take is a little planning… and a lot of rope."

Veronica asks incredulously, "Where is said dungeon of which you speak?"

"Todd has a dungeon."

"That's fine, let the whole world know while you're at it," Todd bursts into their conversation.

"I didn't realize you were right behind me."

Todd grins in response. He hushes, "So why exactly are we telling our little friend here about my little friend at home?"

"I'm sorry," Johnny offers, "it was just a silly daydream."

"You can't stop at that. Tell me. What did this dream of yours entail? Leave *in* all the specifics, please."

Veronica leans back, crosses her arms, and watches the exchange.

"I feel embarrassed repeating it."

"Don't be," Todd directs. He reaches out and touches Johnny's arm. "Go on."

"To be honest, it involves a couple of people.

Basically, myself, a man, and a woman. Well, sort of a woman. She's not really all that…"

"I get it." Todd nods and wrinkles his nose. "I get exactly what you mean."

"And I think that's about it." Johnny shrugs as if that's the end of it.

"There's got to be more involved. Props, perhaps?"

"Oh, yeah. Rope. A lot of rope for sure."

"What about," Todd gasps as he says it, "chains?"

"I actually didn't think that would be possible. I didn't think for my purposes…"

"Johnny," Todd mirrors a parent schooling his child on the lessons of life, "what kind of dungeon scene is complete without chains?"

"Is that really an option?"

"I'd say it's more than an option. It's essential. Now, how about ball-gags?"

"What's a ball-gag?" Johnny asks. Veronica puts her hand a bit over her eyes, shakes her head, and lowers it a little.

"My, my, you are new at this." Todd checks to ensure customers aren't around. "It's a rubber ball, usually red, that fits perfectly in your mouth. It gags you. There's a strap attached so you can make sure the person who's gagged can't just spit it out."

"I see. Hey, was that that thing they used in *Pulp Fiction*?"

"You know what, I believe they did use one. Good eye. It must have piqued your interest for you to recall it."

"I guess it must have."

"So? Ball-gag?"

"Seems necessary to me."

Veronica can't help but interrupt. "You can't be serious."

"About the ball-gag?" Johnny asks.

"About everything. About this whole scenario. You can't go through with this."

Todd counters, "The only way to stop an itch is to scratch it, my dear."

"Yeah," Johnny adds, "and this kitty has claws." He claws the air between him and Veronica with his hand.

"You guys don't even see eye to eye on this. Johnny," she points a finger toward Todd, "he thinks you want a sex scene. Todd," she points to Johnny, "Johnny just wants to get even with a couple of people and to use the dungeon for, probably, what dungeons were originally intended to be used for."

"I'd be happy just to watch," Todd admits. "That's not a lot to ask for, is it? Use my dungeon for whatever you like. Just let me watch," he urges.

"See that? Todd's on board. Come on, Ronnie. You know an idea like this could be totally awesome."

"Yep. It's all fun and games until David fills his life with God and you get filled by some big guy who thinks you've got a," she grumbles, " real purdy mouth." She continues, "As for Sister Petunia, she's such a bull I can't imagine chains strong enough to contain her. She'd be the one to break free and land you in jail. You know I'm telling the truth. Todd, just say no to him. Even if he gets on his knees and begs for it."

"That'll be difficult." He eyes Johnny up and down. He leans his weight on the balls of his feet, as he wants to step closer and be nearer to Johnny.

"And, Johnny, you really need to think matters through before you continue with this nonsensical idea. It's borderline idiotic."

Johnny's eyebrows bounce and his eyes alight at this.

Veronica clarifies, "And by borderline idiotic I mean extremely idiotic."

His face depresses upon her words. "I like this idea. Revenge at its most carnal. I'm not giving up on it. I will, however, consider alternate… angles. But, we will have to wait and see. Ronnie, I have a lot of work to do."

"I know you do, it's just a dungeon is a terrible idea."

"No, I mean I literally have a lot of work to do." Johnny waves his hand around the aisle before him. Boxes of inventory litter the floor and wait to find their places on the shelves.

"It's not like he's going to fire you." Veronica looks at Todd. "Right?"

Todd responds, "Well, of course not. I'm just honored he remembered about my dungeon, about me," he emphasizes, "in the first place."

"You guys have a weird work relationship here." She darts her eyes between the two of them. "All right, I'll let you get back to work. Hey, Todd, what's Johnny got right there in his pants? I'll give you a hint. It's long, it's hard, and it's got a nice fat pink tip."

Todd's mouth falls open. He blinks a few times in rapid succession then stops. His eyes go wide. He blinks twice more. He sputters an unintelligible syllable.

Veronica casts a satisfied glance at Todd, turns the glance toward Johnny, then turns around to make her departure. She tosses the answer over her shoulder. "A pencil."

Charlie Casso

41 DUNGEON

Johnny pulls the door open as the sing-songy bells of the ice cream truck resound. He enters and the door closes behind him. The glorious signature sound of the ice cream truck isn't just hushed, it's obliterated. As is Johnny's sense of sight. *No sight? No sounds? How did Helen Keller manage? She really did deserve that book deal after all.* "Hello," he yells to check if he is more than a functional mute. *Ahh, okay, I didn't lose everything.* He takes a tentative step inside. He shuffles a foot in front of him and hears the friction and brush of his foot against what sounds like concrete. The coolness of the environs chills his skin. He puts his fingers to his nipples and confirms his suspicions. They are erect. He shrugs it off and moves a step further. He hears someone breathing. "Hello?" No response. He waits.

"Jahhhhn-a-thaaaaaan."

Johnny's whole body responds as fear ripples through him. "Who is that?" he asks. Every muscle in his body tenses. His stomach tightens and he can feel his abs contract. He would projectile vomit if he had taken the time to eat anything of substance today.

"It's Todd, silly." Todd makes his voice sonorous, "What brings a guy like you to a place like this?"

"I could ask you the same question," Johnny responds in the dark.

"I see. You want to play with me, do you?"

"Yes, can we play *turn on the light?*"

"I don't know that one. But I'm game."

"It's simple. Turn on the light, Todd," he directs.

"Oh. You're a tricky one. Hold on, I have one of those battery operated press-on lights here somewhere."

Todd moves his hands in the darkness around the walls until they find the desired plastic orb. "Got it," he says as he depresses the orb. Light projects forth and affords a view of about six square feet to Johnny.

"That doesn't help much."

"There are a few more scattered throughout. You know, in case you want some sections blacked out but light in others. You can turn all of them on and have a decent view of most of it. I wouldn't recommend it though, as it kills the mystery."

"Oh my God!" Johnny jumps to the wall and grabs a silver latch secured from it. "You really do have chains."

"Does that make you happy?"

"Does it ever," Johnny gushes.

"I like to make you happy. I was born to make you happy."

"Aww, that's so sweet," Johnny gushes. Realization creeps in. "Are you quoting Britney

Spears… in your dungeon?"

Todd blushes with embarrassment. "I'm just glad you're into chains."

"Totally. These'll work great."

"Care to try them out?" Todd asks. He grabs one of the cuffs that dangle from the wall behind Johnny.

"I guess. I mean, why not, right?"

"I did not see this coming," Todd admits. He takes the cuff with one hand and takes Johnny's arm in the other. He holds the arm out and, stealthily, as if he's done it many times before, clamps the cuff around Johnny's wrist and secures it with a click of a padlock.

"Whoa." Johnny walks two steps away from the wall and is yanked back by the wrist that's cuffed and chained to the wall. He pulls away from the wall but the chain does not give in the least. He widens his stance on the floor, bends his knees, grips the chain with both of his hands, and pulls. Still no give. The chain, to his satisfaction, is securely anchored to the wall. If he can't free himself using both hands there's no way anyone is going to do it using one. "Intense. Lock my other hand in, I want to see what it's like."

"My pleasure." Todd eagerly clamps and locks a cuff around Johnny's other wrist.

Johnny gives his newly restrained appendage a tug and smiles in satisfaction. He tugs with both arms. He stands, back to the wall, arms angled away from him at the sides, and leans forward until his body makes a sixty-degree angle against the floor. With the chain taut, he moves his arms up and down at his sides and, suspended in his angle, he makes what look like snow angels in the dungeon. "This is amazing and weird at the same time. I feel like, very… alive. Like I can feel every hair on my arm has a sensation to it. But, at the same time, I can't really do anything chained here. It's… wild." He pulls at the chains a few more times in awe. "All right, this seems perfect." He looks at Todd and nods toward the cuffs.

Todd smiles.

"Thanks, Todd. I appreciate it. You can unlock me. I think this will work perfectly."

"You didn't even get the full effect yet."

"Huh?"

Todd stares down at the bottom of the wall. Johnny follows his eyes and notices another set of cuffs chained there.

"There's more?" Johnny asks excitedly.

"Wait till you see what I have planned for you." Todd dives to the ground by Johnny and has both feet locked in record time.

Johnny tries to kick with his left foot but his kick is retarded by the restraint. He repeats with his other foot to the same effect. "This is unreal. I feel so alive but also so, like, helpless. You know what though, the *alive* part is because it's by choice. You know, because I choose to be in these restraints. But should someone who deserves it be locked up like this, they'd only feel helpless. And that's exactly what I want. Wow," he says, giving another pull against the chains. "Okay, *now* you can unlock me."

Todd paces in the span of light in front of Johnny. He paces from one edge of darkness, through the light, to the other edge of darkness, and back. "You think that's it?"

Johnny's heart pounds.

"You think that's all I have in store for you? Never underestimate a man with a dungeon, Johnny." He stops mid-pace, directly in front of Johnny, and wraps a ball-gag around Johnny's head. Red ball firmly in Johnny's mouth, the black leather straps follow around the ears to the back of his head.

Johnny's face flashes a myriad of emotions. Shock, relief, amazement, pleasure... and fear.

"My Pet," Todd declares as he stalks into the darkness. "We're just getting started."

And, with a *click,* the darkness takes over.

42 THE PARTY'S ALL HERE

Rose drops a menu on the table in front of Veronica and questions, "Hey, no Sugar Peach today?"

Veronica shrugs. "Guess not. I called him this morning but he didn't answer. Figured it's his day off, maybe he's sleeping in or something. But I'm here," she conveys in a chipper tone.

"Well, you tell Sugar Peach Mama Rose sends her regards."

"I will," Veronica responds. She opens her mouth because she knows what she wants to order, but Mama Rose has already made up her mind to walk away. "Oh, that's okay," Veronica mutters to herself, "I'll just sit here hungry until you come back."

Bell clinks against bell when the door to the Poisoned Ivy opens. Veronica notices the two patrons enter and wonders where she knows them from. She cocks her head at them, not sure whether she really knows them and should say hello or if they just look familiar and she should just mind her own business.

The man notices her look and greets her from only a table away. "Hi there," he says as he and his female companion take their seats. "Yes, you do sort of know us. We own the ice cream truck. Hopefully you see us at least every few days."

"We do hope so," his female counterpart adds. "It may not register with you who we are, but hopefully you at least recognize our existence."

"Truer words were never spoken," the man adds.

"Well," the woman laughs, "maybe not *truer words*, no, but surely equally as truthful."

"Hi there," Veronica finally greets. "And yes, that's probably where I recognize you from." She scans the diner and, since it's mostly empty, decides she can continue without interrupting anyone's meal. "I hate it when people go to a restaurant, a diner, an ice cream truck, or what have you, and they pay absolutely no attention whatsoever to the person helping them. You know the type of person I'm talking about. Their server's face could change like twenty times while they are giving their order and they would never even notice. Ugh, how I hate that."

"You, my dear, are preaching to the choir," the woman offers.

"True," the man adds, "and believe me, we are usually the preachers and not the choir." He, now, scans the diner with his eyes. "Are you here eating all by yourself?" He doesn't wait for a response. "Would you mind it horribly if we joined you?"

"Are you sure you want to? You know the saying, *two's company, three's a crowd*."

The woman guffaws. "Sweetie, where on earth

302

have you ever seen three people make a crowd? Give me Times Square on New Year's Eve, now that's a crowd. But three people? My, oh, my, no." The man and woman shuffle into Veronica's booth as they offer their names and hands in greeting, and receive Veronica's in return. "So," she continues, "why are you here by yourself? Look at you all alone like a latchkey kid all grown up yet still unaccompanied."

Veronica looks for anyone else who might have heard how socially awkward Barbara's statement was. She finds no one within range, so she looks to the salt and pepper shakers and shakes her head.

"Oh, dear," Barbara adds, "I think I've hit the nail on its big flat head."

"I'm not a latchkey kid, rather I *wasn't* a latchkey kid. And I'm not alone."

"No one is ever alone, dear," John reveals.

"I don't mean existentially I'm not alone."

"Sweetie," Barbara asks, "do you see anyone else here?"

"Obviously there's no one else here, but I'm not alone in a sad, oh, woe is me, alone way."

"Do you have cats?" John asks. "Lots of cats?"

Barbara exclaims, "Oh, how I love cats. Especially kittens."

"Not the hairless ones though, they look like snakes."

"Snakes are bad news," Barbara agrees.

"No, I don't have cats, or kittens for that matter. I don't have a wedding dress either that I never got to wear and just prance around the house in."

"Someone's defensive," John notices in a very

concerned tone.

"Did we say something wrong?"

Veronica tries to discern whether or not any offense was intended by their remarks and questions.

"Are you guys for real?" she asks.

"We are certainly sitting here," Barbara offers.

"Well, alone or not, a party of one is a party nonetheless, especially since now it's a party of three!" says John.

"Oh great, a party," Rose interjects with disdain in her voice. "What does the party want?"

"My, my," Barbara jumps in, "I'll have pan...cetta."

"Are you for real?" Rose asks.

"I'm getting that question a lot today, aren't I? Why, yes, I'm for real. Are you for real?"

"No, I'm a friggin' hologram. This is a diner, we don't have pancetta."

"What's pancetta?" Barbara asks.

"That's what you ordered."

"Oh, I know. I'm not mental. I want to know what pancetta is."

"You ordered it and you don't know what it is?"

"Right. That's why I'm asking."

"Why would you do that?"

"I'm asking because I don't know what it is."

"Are you for real?"

"You asked me that already," Barbara responds.

"Anyone else here want to order?" Rose asks the table.

John raises a hand, "I'll take a pancetta."

"Find out what it is," Barbara whispers to him.

Rose doesn't skip a beat. "We don't have pancetta. Next."

The diner's entrance bells jingle in the background.

Veronica immediately orders in fear Rose will up and walk away. "I'd like two hot dogs please, with extra sauerkraut."

Rose looks at John and Barbara as they sit next to each other in the booth. They both angle their heads up and lean toward her. They breathe one word, "Pancetta."

Rose glares at them. She smiles a tight, forced smile and, in a voice suitable to assuage children, says, "How about I bring you some pan... cakes? Would you like that?"

"Oh, we would love pancakes," John beams.

"Yes, we would," Barbara agrees.

Relieved, Rose takes the one menu that was at the table and turns around to depart. In doing so, she smacks into...

"Todd!" Veronica exclaims.

Todd looks annoyed, yet he stops where he stands. He pops a smile onto his face. "Well, hello there, Ronnie. So nice to see you."

"You joining them?" Rose asks.

Veronica, eager to have company with her to spread out the unusualness of Barbara and John, nods yes to Rose and invites Todd to sit with them.

Annoyance briefly makes a reappearance on Todd's face, but it flees just as quickly and he joins them.

"You know what you want?" Rose asks.

"Sure, banana split with the works and a pineapple juice." Rose takes the order and walks away.

Veronica makes the introductions all around and then politely focuses the conversation on her new acquaintances.

"How's the ice cream business?" Veronica inquires.

"Dreamy creamy," John answers.

Barbara shifts focus over to Veronica, "We own and operate an ice cream truck, but what is it you do, Ronnie?"

"I'm an IT girl." She pauses. "Saying it out loud, I really should have been more specific when I was a little girl. I always wanted to be an *it girl* and wound up an IT girl. Life can be funny. Or cruel. Depends on how you look at it." She fiddles with her fork and knife. "Todd over here runs *OfficeGear*."

"You do? How impressive," Barbara notes as the diner's bells jingle in harmony with her words.

"No work today?" John asks.

"I took the day off. Needed to take care of some things," he adds.

"How's Johnny been?" Veronica asks. "He hasn't returned my phone calls."

"Why are you asking me? How would I know?" Todd responds defensively.

"You do work with him."

"Work with whom?" Barbara asks.

John responds to Barbara. "Work with Johnny. Aren't you listening?"

"Who's Johnny?" Barbara asks John.

"That I don't know," he admits. "Who's

Johnny?"

"Johnny must be the boyfriend," Barbara surmises.

Veronica and Johnny respond in unison, "We're not together like that." The four at the table turn to find Johnny there.

"There you are. I was just asking Todd if you were okay."

"Why wouldn't I be?"

"Just hadn't heard from you is all."

"Come on, John," Barbara prods, "let's make some room." They move down in the booth so Johnny can sit on their side.

"You guys know each other?" Veronica asks.

"I think everyone knows... let me see if I got your names right, Barbara and John?"

"Yes, sir," John confirms.

"They run the ice cream truck. They're kind of local celebrities. Who doesn't like ice cream? It's a bit of heaven on a daily basis."

Rose notices the new addition to the table from her spot at the counter where she places a hamburger and fries in front of a man who merely grunts at her. She rolls her eyes at the recollection that, although the new addition is Sugar Peach, he's still the one who Jackson Pollacked the bathroom. "I swear that table's trying to make me quit," she says aloud. The man grunts as he bites his burger. Burger bits tinkle to the countertop. "I have to clean that, you know. It's not like we have someone else to do it." More grunts. She plods to the table. "What'll you have?" Johnny appears hesitant. "I know you don't need a menu, it's a diner. We have diner food." Barbara starts to open her mouth. "Don't you dare say pancetta." Barbara closes her mouth.

"I'll have pancakes," Johnny says.

"I like you, Sugar Peach. Pancakes it is." Rose departs.

"I guess I'll drink the syrup then. Does she just dislike taking drink orders or something?" Johnny asks the table.

"You can have some of my pineapple juice when it comes," Todd offers.

"That's nice of you to offer, Todd. I'll be fine."

"No, no, I insist. Really."

Johnny shrugs his acceptance. An awkward silence follows as each member of the party of five searches the environs for something in common they can all discuss.

"That food's probably going to take a while," Veronica observes. The rest of the party nods agreement.

"Todd has a dungeon," Veronica blurts out.

"Ronnie!" Johnny exclaims.

"Huh?"

"Who makes that declaration in public?"

"We're not in public. Oh, let it go. We're amongst friends." She gives Barbara and John a glance. "Well, new friends. And, you know what, we'll see if they last to be old friends once we continue with this conversation. Face it, if you can't take a little conversation about a dungeon, well, it pretty much ends here. Hey guys, anyone care for a jelly donut?" She smiles and quickly nods in Johnny's direction. No one responds in the affirmative. "Just checking," Veronica says. "Anyway, like I said, Todd has a dungeon. Johnny was supposed to get to see it recently. Details, please."

Johnny checks to make sure Barbara and John seem all right, and they do, seeing as how they haven't backed away from the table or anything. "Well," he starts with trepidation, "it was pretty great. The walls are concrete, it has that cold and hard feel to it. It's very dark, as expected, but I mean pitch-black dark, not a slant of light at all. Unreal." He stops his description there. While the rest of the party seems satisfied with the amount Johnny has offered, Veronica waits for more. She leans in and motions with her hand to keep the description coming. "What more do you want?" Johnny asks.

"That's it? Concrete and cold? That's the best description you can give?"

Johnny uses his eyes to indicate the presence of Barbara and John. They notice and shrug. John offers, "There's nothing you can say or do that will shock us. We've been around quite a while. We've seen it all."

Barbara adds, "And then some."

Johnny looks at Todd. He asks him, "Do you mind if I share?"

Todd stares Johnny straight in the eyes and responds, "Be my guest."

"All right, here we go guys," Johnny begins with gusto. "There are these cuffs that lock around your wrists and ankles so you can be chained to the wall."

Rose arrives with the food, distributes the plates and offers, "I hear nothing." She quickly retreats.

Veronica asks, "How did you know that if it was pitch-black?"

Todd clears his throat and shakes his head no.

Johnny omits the description of the lights and instead offers, "Well, you can just feel around and use your sense of touch and sound to understand what's there. It's incredibly invigorating."

"But why a dungeon?" John asks.

"Yes, why? It sounds so very medieval," Barbara seconds John's question.

"Why not?" Todd replies.

"And why are you so excited about it?" John indicates Johnny with his finger.

"Oh, that's easy," Veronica considers her next words carefully. "What's black... and white... and red all over?" She slowly scans the others at her booth for a response but no one offers any. "He's going to lock up a nun and a priest."

Barbara and John gasp.

"Lock. Them. Up." Veronica drawls. Neither Johnny nor Todd reply in any way. They sit there, frozen in time and space.

Barbara and John alternate between inspecting Johnny's face and Todd's face for a rebuttal of Veronica's claim. Finding none, John provides, "Surely she's not serious."

Veronica picks up a hot dog and uses it to punctuate her point. She bops it in the air with her hand three quick times. "Lock 'em up."

Barbara decides a short, to the point, lecture is in order. "Locking up people is bad. All around, it's simply bad manners."

Errrp, Veronica burps. "Excuse me."

Barbara continues, "I'm not even going to say how bad it is to lock up a priest and a nun. But it's bad.

Very bad!" She reaches out a hand and swats the tip of Johnny's nose with two fingers.

"Ow." Johnny places his hand to his nose and rubs it.

Todd notices the maraschino cherry as it slides down from the top of the whipped cream, so he digs into his banana split as John asks, "Why exactly do you want to lock people up? Let's forget, for a moment, who exactly. Let's just focus on the why."

Johnny searches his pancakes for an answer. He looks under one. Nope, he just finds butter. He searches under the next. Nope, same thing. He cuts himself a bite and chews to buy himself more time.

John reveals, "You can take all the time you need, but you're going to finish sooner or later."

"It's a tough one." Veronica reveals. "I'm waiting for him to say he's just fooling around, which I'm sure he is, but I can see why he wants to do it. We, Johnny and I, went to a grammar school, or an elementary or middle school, people always have their own way of naming it, that was very... strict. It was a Catholic school, and well, not to perpetuate a stereotype but it was what people usually think of when they think of Catholic schools. There were a couple of people who were more strict than the others. Kind of crossed a line, if you will."

"Oh," Barbara thinks she understands, "that would be the priest and the nun." John nods.

"Half right," Veronica corrects. "The nun, yes. The priest, no. Johnny only slept with the priest. The priest wasn't strict at all, he was actually rather nice."

This information takes John and Barbara back.

"Slept with the priest? Oh, I can see why you'd be angry. Molestation, rape, and sodomy are nothing to laugh at." Barbara shakes her head in disheartened disbelief.

Veronica looks to Johnny to check for resistance. She sees none. "It wasn't molestation or rape. Johnny wanted it. Hell, I wanted it too. I didn't get it though. The priest's dinghy didn't float that way. Sodomy, sure, you got him on that one." She directs to Johnny, "She got you on that one, you little Sodomite."

In search of an explanation, John asks, "So, if you 'wanted it' then why do you want to lock him up now?" He whispers, "Is this a sex thing?"

Veronica answers for Johnny. "The long story made short is: boy likes man, man likes boy, boy waits till boy becomes man, man gets it on with man, man leaves boy-cum-man for other man who likes to come on man and yet another man who likes to come *in* man, man returns to boy-cum-man, man takes man back, man decides man wants church back, boy-cum-man decides to get revenge on man for leaving. See? Like I said, long story short."

"Oddly, we follow," John says. Barbara nods, as does Todd. "But, dare I ask…"

"The nun?" Veronica anticipates. Barbara and John nod yes. "She was the super-strict Catholic school type. Beyond super-strict. The things she did were unwarranted. She wasn't molding young individuals into fine adults or anything, that was not her modus operandi, believe me. She slammed people left and right, and I don't mean figuratively. She literally would pick students up and slam them into walls. There isn't a word to describe her. *Intense* doesn't cut it. For a nun, actually for anyone," she pauses, "she was evil incarnate."

"Scary," John offers.

"It's difficult to imagine someone like that exists in the very same world as sweet, dear pancakes." Barbara bows her head to her plate. She picks up her fork and pushes the edge of a pancake with it. "I'm so sorry, little pancake, that such evilness exists out there."

Lines appear across Todd's forehead as he takes a deep breath in shock, not so much at the depiction of the nun as much as at Barbara's reaction to it and her pandering to the pancakes. "Okay, then." Todd shovels more of the banana split in his mouth so he himself may split soon. "By the way," Todd offers, between spoon-fulls, "he's not really going to do anything so don't you worry about it. I'm just putting that out there because, should something actually happen to a nun and a priest, I don't want anyone's eyes on me." Todd licks the hot fudge from his spoon. "Believe you me, my services are only available to a select number of people. And a priest and a nun certainly aren't among them."

"You mean I can't use the dungeon?"

"You can have access to it anytime you want. Trust me. You say you need it and I will be glad to give it to you. Over and over again. All night. Every night. You name it." Todd moans.

"That banana does look scrumptious," Barbara notices.

"I'll say." Todd's gaze lingers at Johnny.

"But I do need it, and you know what for," Johnny protests.

Veronica slams her last hot dog down and a few

shreds of sauerkraut somersault toward John. "Johnny, get a hold of yourself."

"I'll get a hold of him," Todd offers.

"Let me try," John suggests. "I think you are trying to show that actions speak louder than words, am I right?" He doesn't wait for a response but, instead, continues. "You have to remember that until you speak you have nothing to gain from your actions." He lets his advice sit with Johnny for a minute. "I can tell you haven't tried speaking with anyone yet, and that's not fair. It's not fair to the nun, it's not fair to the priest, and it's certainly not fair to you. Instead of barraging yourself with imprisonment, or worse, guilt, you need to speak with them and see if that clears the air. If not, well, you can take it from there. But, until then, there's no reason to take matters into your own hands."

"That sounds like sound advice," Veronica acknowledges.

Johnny concedes that John has a point. "I'll have to sit on it."

Todd enlivens at Johnny's choice of words.

"There's no sitting on it to be done, Johnny. You are going to go back to the church once and for all and get closure. Good Lord, you're like thirty-three years old. You have to close the book on what happened in the past and get on with the future, even if that means a life without David." Veronica opens her hands to Barbara and John and explains, "David is the priest."

"Ahhh," they reply.

Johnny begins, "And when do you suppose…"

"Right after you finish your pancakes," Veronica answers. "So get your strength now, because you're going to need it."

"We'll come!" Barbara exclaims.

"Yes," John adds, "We will be there for moral support and for encouragement. We can do that. Team Johnny all the way."

"That's a great idea," Todd acknowledges, "I'll come as well. I'll be right behind you, Johnny, don't you worry."

"And if I say…"

"No," Veronica, Todd, Barbara, and John all say in unison, as they know what Johnny is about to say. They confirm with smiles, nods, and raised eyebrows, that they are on the same page. They will be there with Johnny, whether he likes it or not.

Charlie Casso

43 ANOTHER DOOR OPENS

"Guys," Johnny pauses at the stairs in front of him, "you really don't have to come in. I can do this on my own."

"I said I'd be right behind you, and I meant it." The noise from the contractors working on the façade of the church prevents Johnny from hearing what Todd just said. Johnny cups a hand to his ear so Todd repeats himself. Louder, he yells, "I said I'd be behind you."

Johnny begins his ascent up the stairs. Half of him feels nervous to see David and, who knows if she's here or not, possibly Sister Petunia as well. The other half of him feels comfort that, at the very least, he has a small army at his side to make sure he's all right. He opens the door and his troop follows him inside. The door closes and quiet is restored.

Barbara coughs. "I can never get used to that smell, no matter how old I get."

Johnny holds his index finger up and the troop understands he wants them to remain where they are and let him proceed on his own. He uses the basin of holy

317

water to bless himself and he proceeds up the aisle to the altar. Aside from his companions, he finds the church blessedly empty. Johnny passes the altar and heads toward the confessional to check for David when he hears *snip, snip, snip.* He casts a glance over in the direction of the sound and finds it comes from the far wall of the church. A heavy-duty yellow and white yard glove props the side-door to the church open. As he approaches, the sound becomes negligibly louder. He looks back at his companions and holds his hand out flat to them, a signal to wait while he proceeds. He tentatively pushes the door open and steps out. He finds Sister Petunia, clad in her black and white penguin gear, kneeling in the dirt, tending to the garden. She doesn't seem to notice him and he begins to retreat. Her voice stops him. "You curious thing," she bellows.

Johnny shrugs it off. "Is that the best you can come up with? Old age isn't treating you well I guess."

"Be gone," she mandates to Johnny. She does not look up from her gardening.

"I'm not leaving. We need to talk."

Sister Petunia ignores his last comment. She digs her trowel into the earth and works the soil with it.

"I said we need to talk."

Sister Petunia stops working the soil, takes a deep breath, lifts the trowel, and stabs it down into the ground. She turns her head toward Johnny and states, "You don't tell me what I need."

"Sister, I…"

She cuts him off. "You don't dare to tell me what I need." She stares him up and down. "You brazen thing." Still on her knees, she directs, "Get out of my sight."

"But, Sister…"

She cuts him off again. "Did I ask you for an explanation? Did I *suggest* you leave?" She follows the question with her nose as it travels through the air to Johnny. "Any answer other than 'no' is unacceptable." Johnny stands stock still and Sister Petunia becomes more agitated by the second. "Do I confuse you? You deficient thing, I said leave."

As if slapped out of a daze, Johnny shakes his head and blinks rapidly. He stands up straighter. "No."

"If I have to get up..." she does not finish her sentence but, instead, lets the implied threat land on Johnny.

He receives it and returns, "I'm trying to take the high road here. Why do you have to make it so difficult?"

Sister Petunia gets to one knee. She pushes off it with both hands and gets to her feet. She brushes the dirt off her hands onto her sides. "The only road you will travel on is the road to Hell. Get out."

"Why's it always fire and brimstone with you? Why can't you be like the Flying Nun or something?"

Sister Petunia waddles toward Johnny. She gets to him and does not stop moving forward. She makes a plank with the four fingers of each hand and extends them at collar-bone height. She jabs Johnny and forces him to take a step back. She continues to move forward and jabs him again. He moves back another step. She goes to do it a third time but Johnny stops and crosses his arms to shield himself. He uncrosses his arms and breaks through her jab. Sister Petunia looks at her hands as if they have just betrayed her.

"I'm going to count to three," she says.

"I'm going to count to two," Johnny counters.

Sister Petunia curls a lip in disgust. "One," she counts. She shakes a finger at Johnny to punctuate her count.

"Two," Johnny continues. He steps forward and, with his hands the same way Sister Petunia's had been, he jabs her in the shoulders. The top part of her body moves back but her lower half remains firmly rooted to the ground.

She laughs. She looks down. "You silly…" her head starts to come up as it follows her right arm. The back of her right hand strikes Johnny square across the side of his face. His head spins. "…thing," she completes. Johnny spins and nearly topples over.

"You know what, I don't need this. I came to make amends with you, but clearly you're unamend-able." Johnny shrugs off the last word. "You're just a nasty thing who gets pleasure out of abusing people and yet, for some reason, you think you're doing God's work. You're like the upside-down version of Lucifer. Instead of falling from heaven, somehow you've managed to claw your way up from the bowels of Hell."

Sister Petunia stares in silence.

"Forget you." Johnny turns and walks back through the door and into the church. He sees his motley crew of friends exactly where he left them. Johnny holds up an index finger to them as he needs a minute to make his peace with David. He moves toward the door of the face-to-face confessional. He knocks but receives no response. He waits and still no response. A slow, deep exhale and Johnny about-faces and plods toward the aisle.

"Young Jonathan?"

Johnny freezes. His friends watch in the background.

"Young Jonathan, is that you?"

"Yes, David. I mean, Father Mann." Johnny turns around to face David.

"What brings you here today? It's so nice to see you."

Johnny feels the urge to puke. He swallows the distaste. "How can you be like that? So nonchalant. Don't treat me like I'm just anyone off the street."

"What did you expect?"

"I wanted... I... I don't know, actually."

"Johnny, we are at a weird place right now. I'm trying to handle things as best I can." He looks back toward the confessional. The door is ajar and a beam of light emanates from it. "I'm always here for you and you know it."

"I'm sorry I bothered you. I just... I don't know why I came." He stares into Father Mann's eyes.

The slam of a door startles them both. "You don't learn, do you?" Sister Petunia asks. Father Mann fears he's the target of her question. Johnny, on the other hand, assumes he's the target.

"I'm done," Johnny says and he makes his way to the aisle. Sister Petunia follows him as Father Mann watches and takes in the first hand account of their interaction.

"You will leave."

Johnny takes controlled steps down the aisle.

"You vile, putrid lump of humanity."

He shakes his head and tells himself it's almost over for good. He never has to come back. He tried and that's all he could do.

"Waste of organs. Waste of life."

He feels his heart beat faster the closer he gets to the door. He sees the concerned looks on the faces of his friends. His hands and eyes cue his friends to leave, as he will be right behind them. His friends quickly exit and move down the stairs with Johnny and Sister Petunia mere steps behind, yet still within the confines of the church. The doors are about to close when Johnny pushes through them with all his might. They open wide. Johnny exits, as does Sister Petunia right on his heels. The doors slam the sides of the church, propelled as they are by Johnny's push.

"I never want to see you again," Johnny directs at Sister Petunia. He stops in his tracks as he realizes Sister Petunia has just said, "I never want to see you again," at the same time. He turns to face her and, at the moment of eye contact, hears, "Look…" Sister Petunia flattens, crushed by an anvil. Johnny's friends below look on in terror.

"…out!" The workers overhead complete their exclamation as a second anvil flattens Johnny.

Johnny watches from above, with Saint Barbara and Saint John beside him. Todd turns away from the scene. Veronica's mouth gapes even though her two hands try to cover it. Saint Barbara's and Saint John's doppelgangers look up toward Johnny. David Mann comes out through the church doors and gasps in fright at his discovery.

Johnny turns to Saint Barbara and Saint John and asks them the very question that brought him here. "Am I dead?"

ABOUT THE AUTHOR

Charlie Casso was born, raised, and resides in Brooklyn, New York. Charlie Casso is the author of *Going Down and Moving On*, a true, but not *too* true, story of New York resilience. He received the first twelve years of his education in Catholic school where getting on his knees, daily, was required. To pray, of course, you dirty bird.